PRAISE FOR CASEY AND KYLE

"THEY MADE ME LAUGH OUT LOUD. THESE COMICS HIT THE NAIL ON THE HEAD OF EVERYDAY LIFE..."
LORI H, AT HOME: WHERE LIFE HAPPENS

"A FAMILY FRIENDLY COMIC THAT WILL MAKE YOU LAUGH..."
RENEE K, LITTLE HOMESCHOOL ON THE PRAIRIE

"...FUN AND ENJOYABLE FOR ALL..."
MELANIE REYNOLDS
THE OLD SCHOOLHOUSE® MAGAZINE

"I WAS LAUGHING AND GIGGLING RIGHT ALONG WITH MY SON... THESE ARE GREAT BOOKS!"
DESIREE WINZ
(MOTHER OF TWO BOYS AGES 10-12)

"THE *CASEY AND KYLE* COMIC BOOK SERIES REMINDS US OF WHY A SENSE OF HUMOR IS ESSENTIAL WHEN IT COMES TO RAISING CHILDREN."
LINDA S, APRON STRINGS AND OTHER THINGS

"ALWAYS WHOLESOME, FUN, AND OFTEN DOWNRIGHT HILARIOUS... GET THE *CASEY AND KYLE* BOOKS FOR YOUR FAMILY..."
WREN, FINCH 'N WREN

"THE *CASEY AND KYLE* CARTOONS ARE SO CUTE AND FUN TO READ! THESE ANTICS WILL TICKLE THE FUNNY BONE OF ALL AGES."
KEMI Q, HOMEMAKING ORGANIZED

for Patty and Ansel

ISBN: 978-1-7360044-3-2 (paperback)

Author photo by RJ Studio
Casey and Kyle is hand lettered by Wendy Robertson
Thanks to Dad (D), Sharla (S), Wendy (W), and Aidan (A) for bringing the funny.

For more information, Will Robertson can be reached online at caseyandkyle.com

Printed in China.

This book was previously published as
Casey and Kyle: I Think We're Gonna Need More Towels!!! © 2016, 2021 Will Robertson.

Casey and Kyle logo is a trademark of Casey and Kyle Inc.

Casey and Kyle Need More Towels © 2016, 2021 Will Robertson.
All rights reserved. No part of this publication may be reproduced, or stored in a retrieval system, or transmitted by any form or by any means, electronic, mechanical, photocopying, recording, or otherwise, without written permission, except in the context of reviews. *Casey and Kyle* is a work of fiction. Names, characters, places and incidents either are products of the author's imagination or are used fictitiously. Any resemblance to actual events or locales or persons, living or dead, is entirely coincidental.

ATTENTION SCHOOLS AND BUSINESSES
Our books are available at quantity discounts for bulk purchases for educational, business, or sales promotional use. For information, please contact us at caseyandkyle.com.

CASEY AND KYLE™

NEED MORE TOWELS

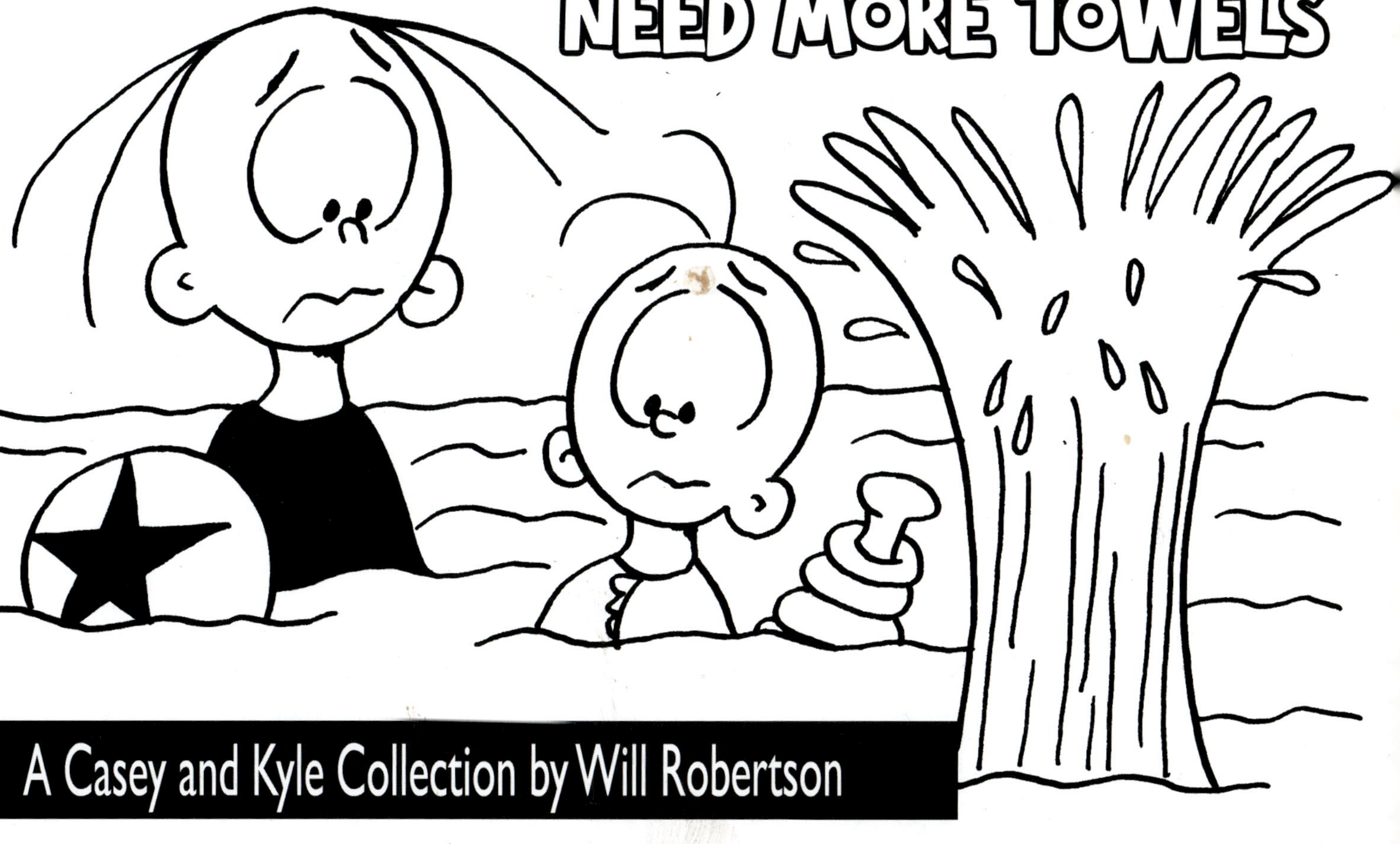

A Casey and Kyle Collection by Will Robertson

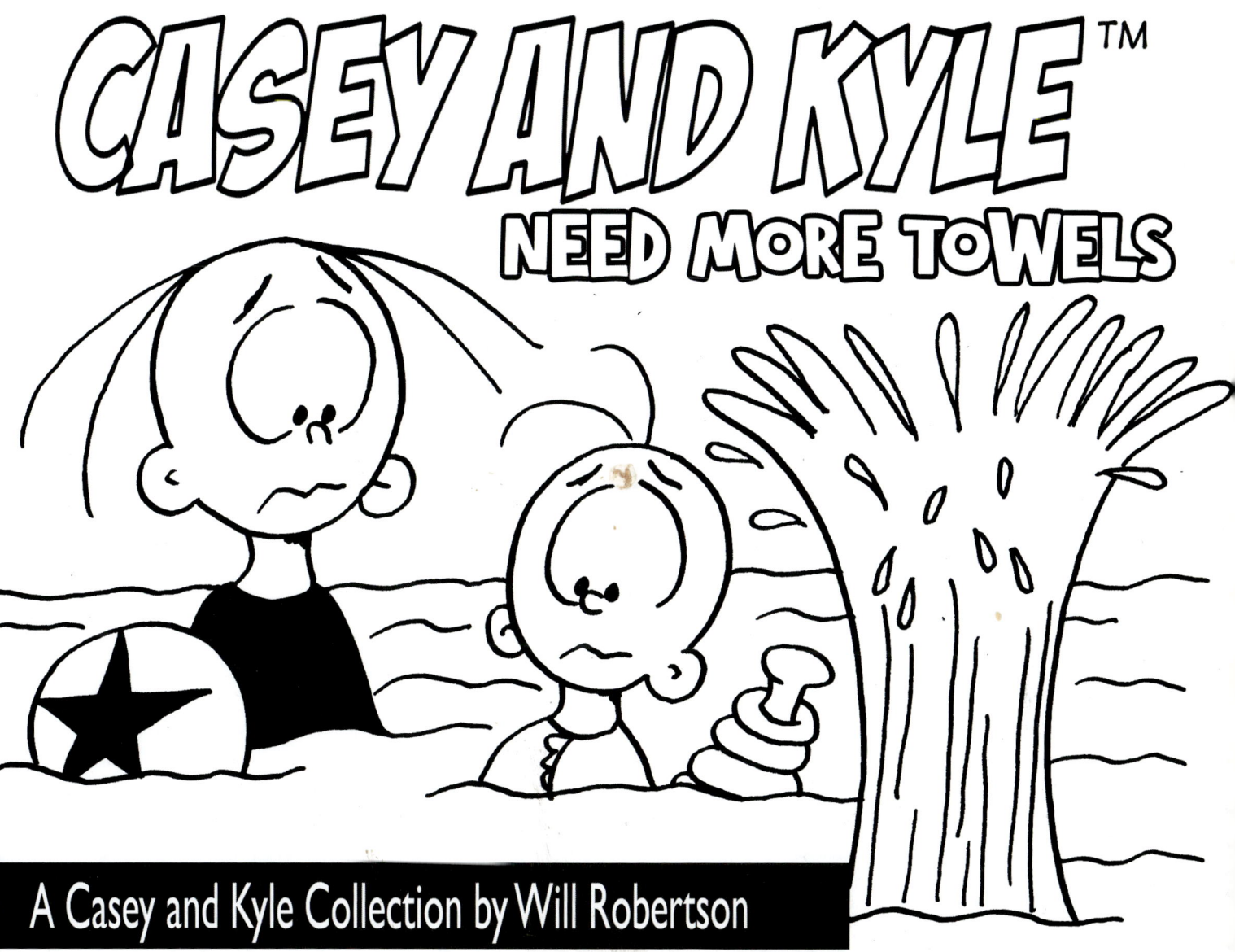

Don't miss a single adventure!

CASEY AND KYLE™

The fun never stops on our website and social media!

Visit us online at caseyandkyle.com
or simply scan the QR code to stop by!

On INSTAGRAM
@ caseyandkyleinc

On TWITTER @ caseyandkyleinc

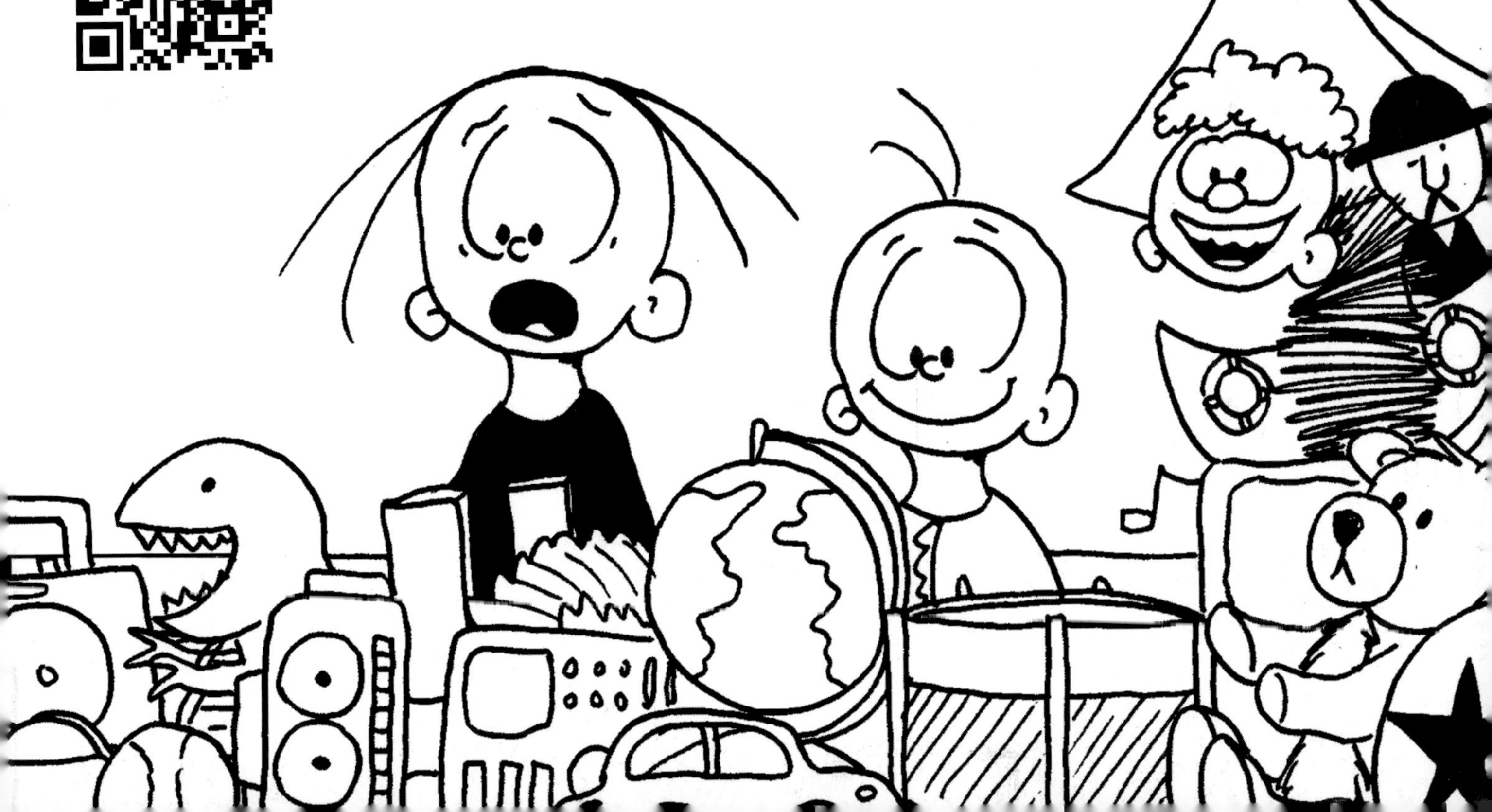

The Cast

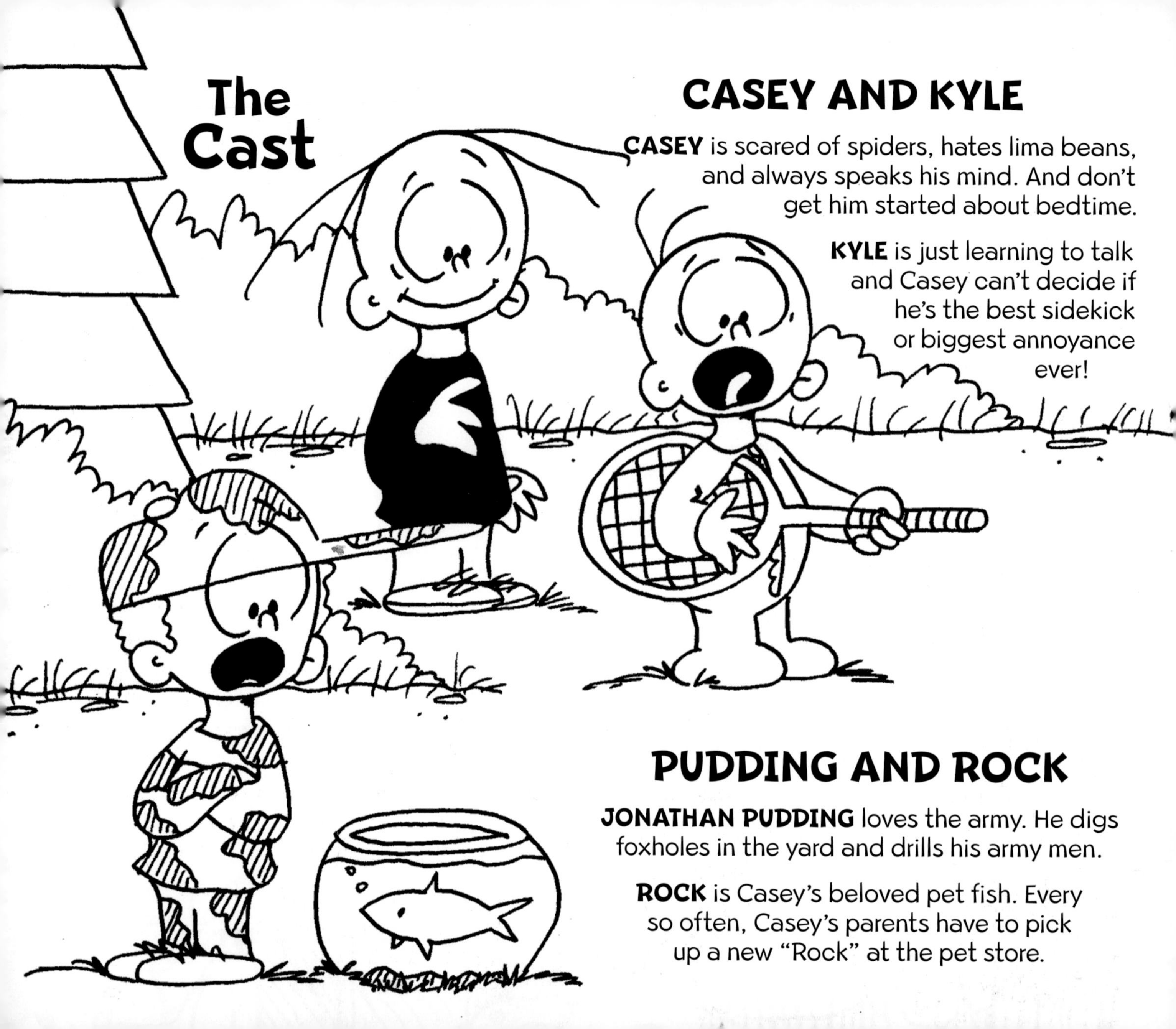

CASEY AND KYLE

CASEY is scared of spiders, hates lima beans, and always speaks his mind. And don't get him started about bedtime.

KYLE is just learning to talk and Casey can't decide if he's the best sidekick or biggest annoyance ever!

PUDDING AND ROCK

JONATHAN PUDDING loves the army. He digs foxholes in the yard and drills his army men.

ROCK is Casey's beloved pet fish. Every so often, Casey's parents have to pick up a new "Rock" at the pet store.

CARTER AND ZACHARY

CARTER is Casey's best friend. If there's going to be an adventure, he'll be the first one there.

ZACHARY is a punk. He's a bit older than the other kids, and he takes advantage of it.

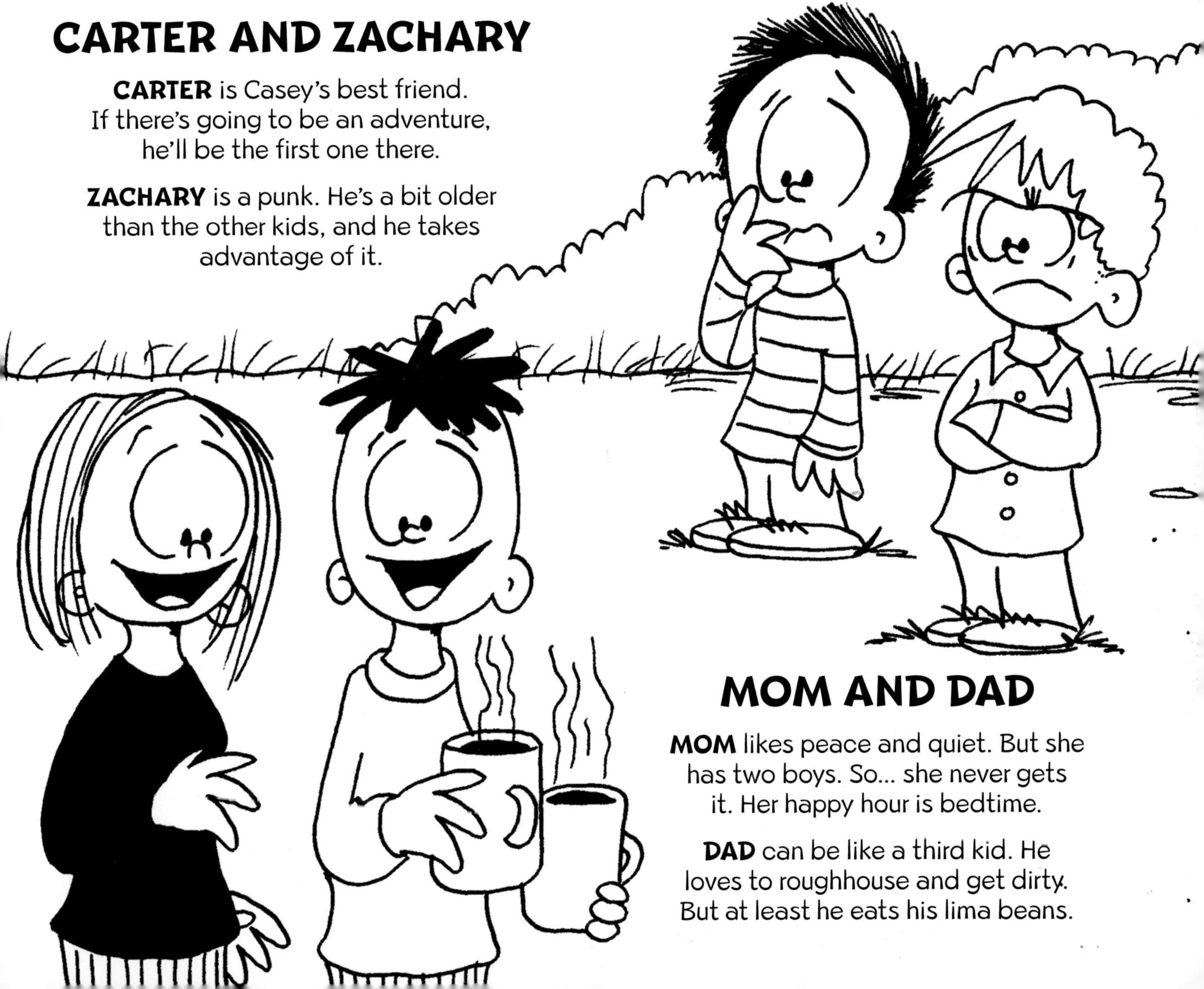

MOM AND DAD

MOM likes peace and quiet. But she has two boys. So... she never gets it. Her happy hour is bedtime.

DAD can be like a third kid. He loves to roughhouse and get dirty. But at least he eats his lima beans.

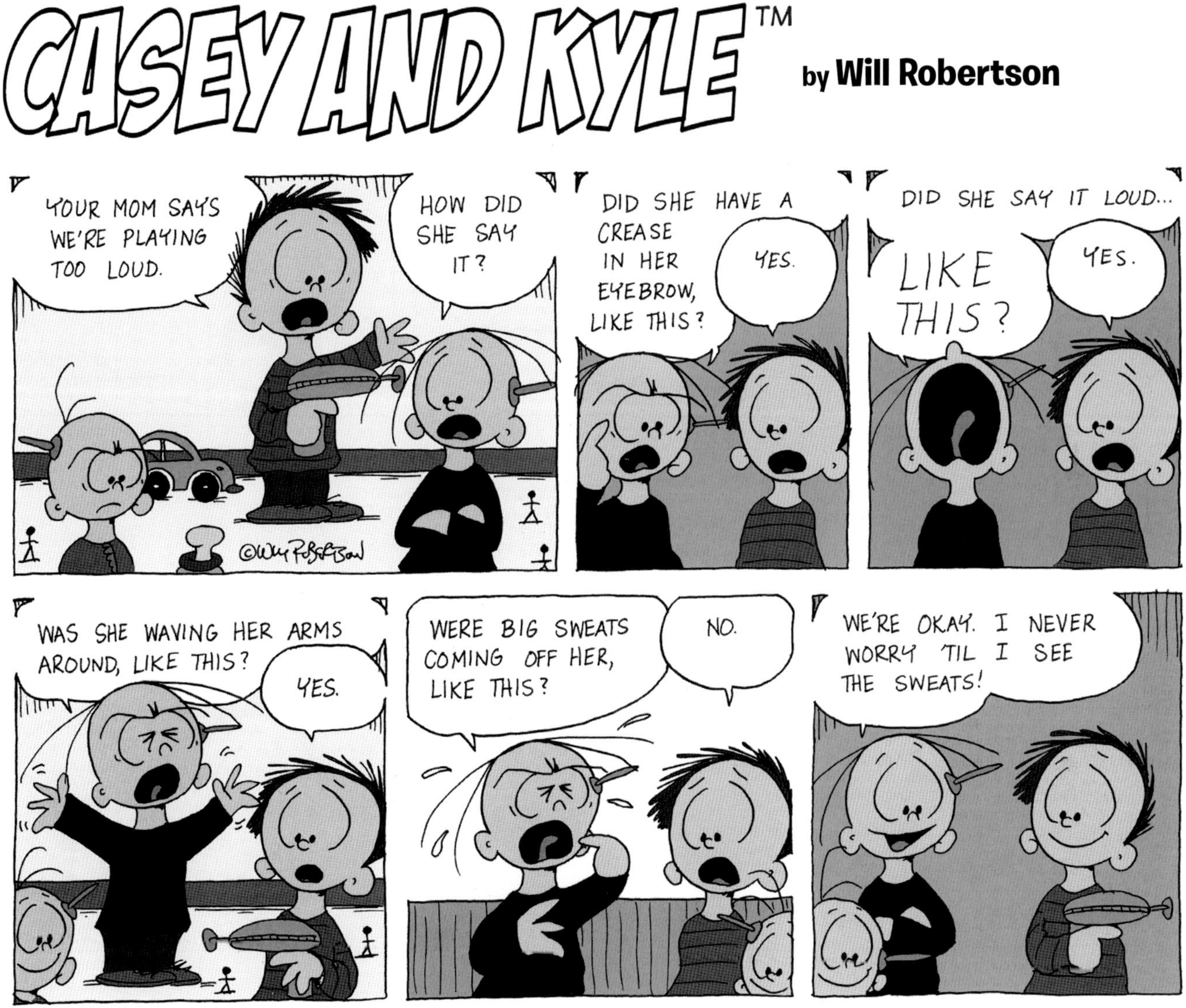
CASEY AND KYLE™
by Will Robertson
YOUR MOM SAYS WE'RE PLAYING TOO LOUD.
HOW DID SHE SAY IT?
DID SHE HAVE A CREASE IN HER EYEBROW, LIKE THIS?
YES.
DID SHE SAY IT LOUD...
LIKE THIS?
YES.
WAS SHE WAVING HER ARMS AROUND, LIKE THIS?
YES.
WERE BIG SWEATS COMING OFF HER, LIKE THIS?
NO.
WE'RE OKAY. I NEVER WORRY 'TIL I SEE THE SWEATS!

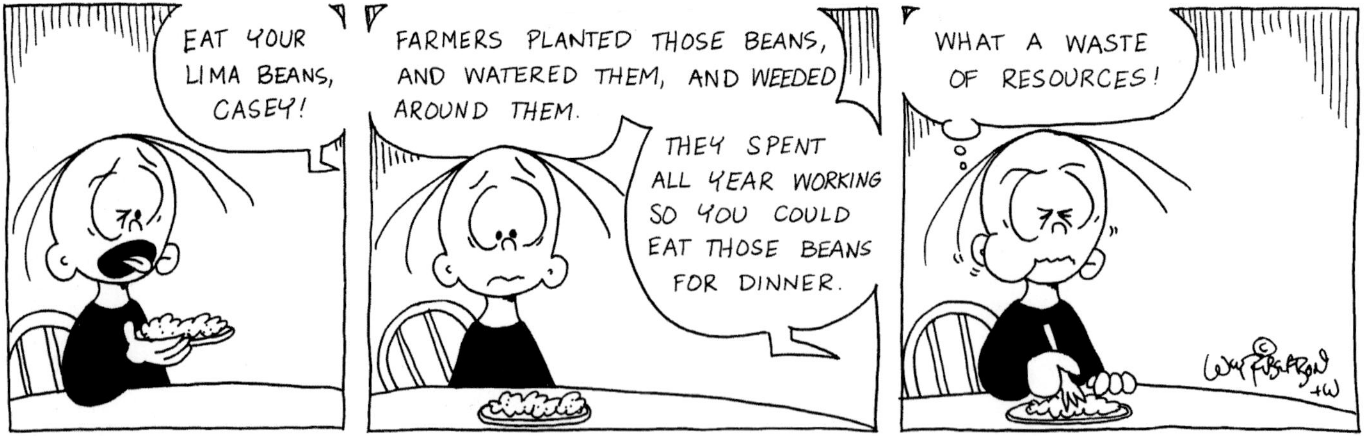
EAT YOUR LIMA BEANS, CASEY!
FARMERS PLANTED THOSE BEANS, AND WATERED THEM, AND WEEDED AROUND THEM.
THEY SPENT ALL YEAR WORKING SO YOU COULD EAT THOSE BEANS FOR DINNER.
WHAT A WASTE OF RESOURCES!

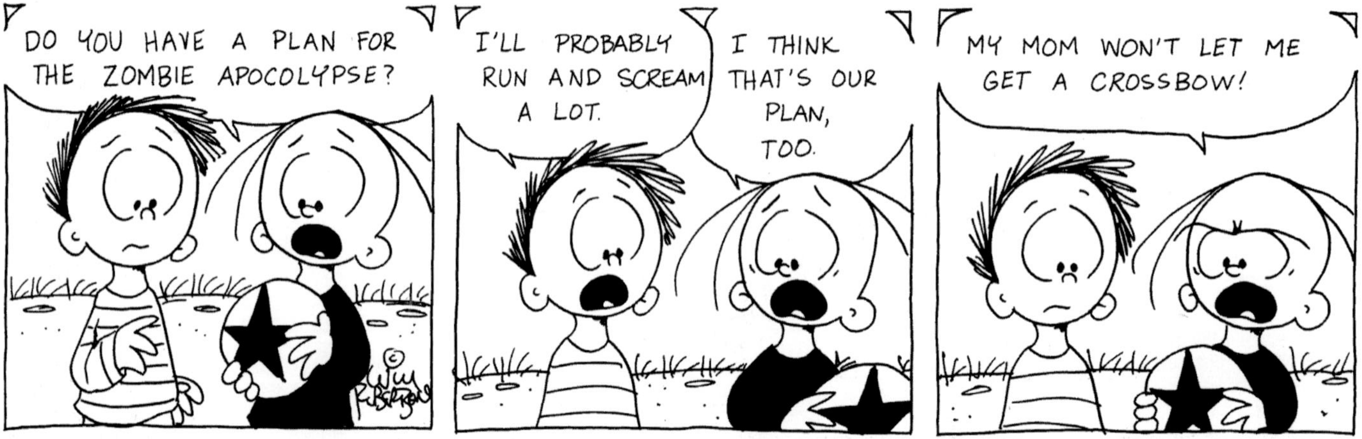
DO YOU HAVE A PLAN FOR THE ZOMBIE APOCOLYPSE?
I'LL PROBABLY RUN AND SCREAM A LOT.
I THINK THAT'S OUR PLAN, TOO.
MY MOM WON'T LET ME GET A CROSSBOW!

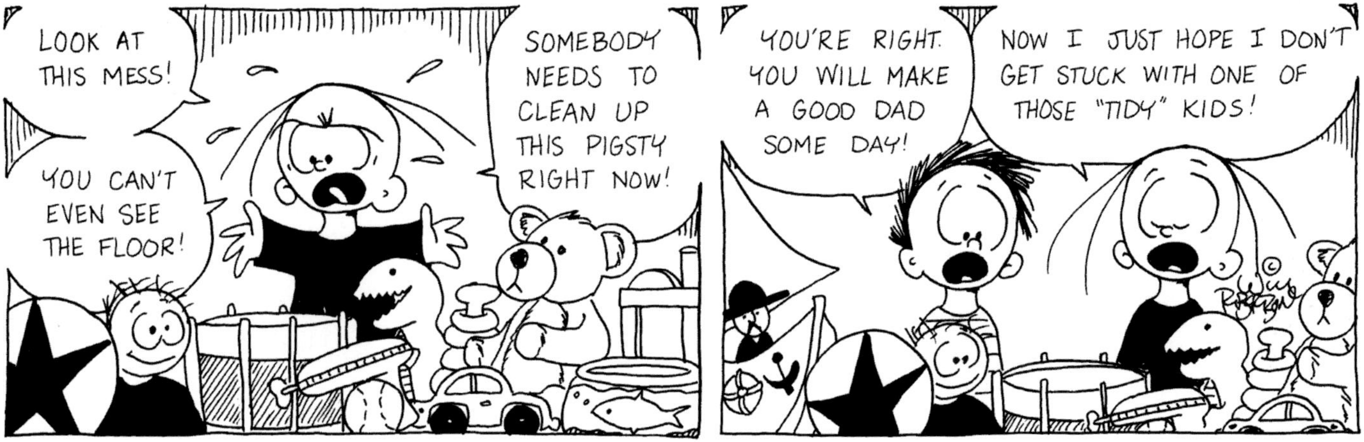
LOOK AT THIS MESS!
YOU CAN'T EVEN SEE THE FLOOR!
SOMEBODY NEEDS TO CLEAN UP THIS PIGSTY RIGHT NOW!
YOU'RE RIGHT. YOU WILL MAKE A GOOD DAD SOME DAY!
NOW I JUST HOPE I DON'T GET STUCK WITH ONE OF THOSE "TIDY" KIDS!

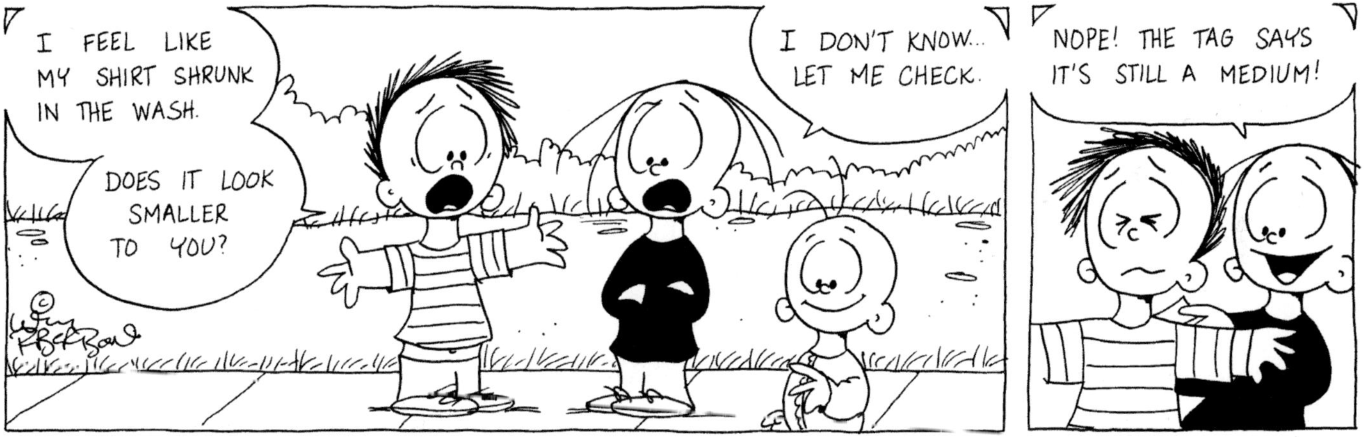
I FEEL LIKE MY SHIRT SHRUNK IN THE WASH.
DOES IT LOOK SMALLER TO YOU?
I DON'T KNOW... LET ME CHECK.
NOPE! THE TAG SAYS IT'S STILL A MEDIUM!

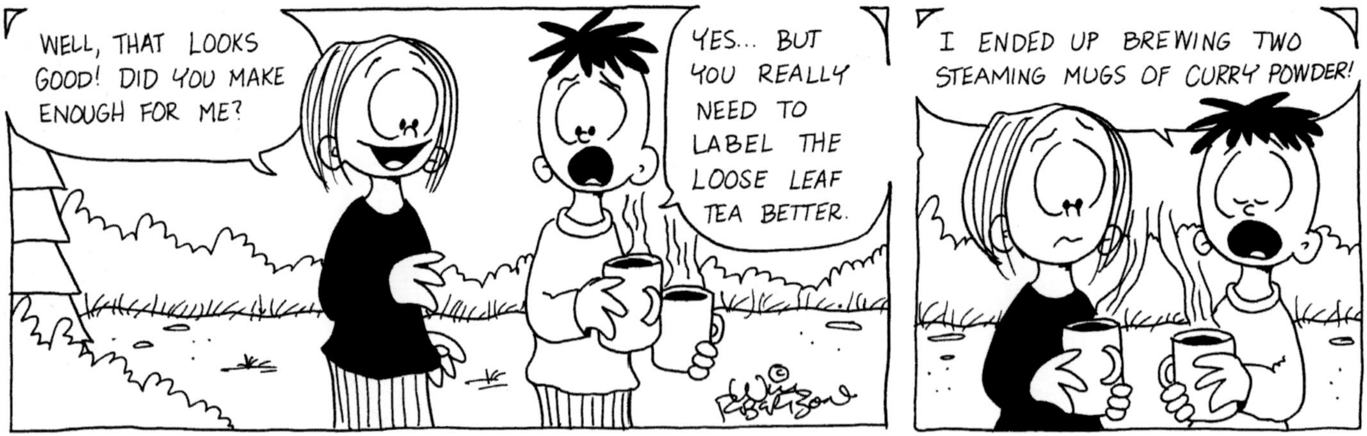
WELL, THAT LOOKS GOOD! DID YOU MAKE ENOUGH FOR ME?
YES... BUT YOU REALLY NEED TO LABEL THE LOOSE LEAF TEA BETTER.
I ENDED UP BREWING TWO STEAMING MUGS OF CURRY POWDER!

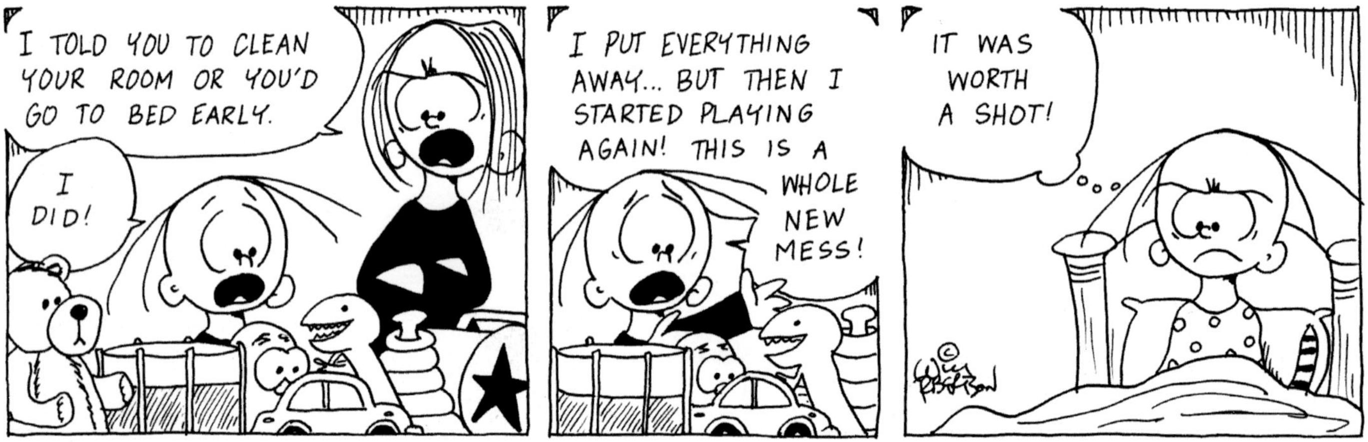
I TOLD YOU TO CLEAN YOUR ROOM OR YOU'D GO TO BED EARLY.
I DID!
I PUT EVERYTHING AWAY... BUT THEN I STARTED PLAYING AGAIN! THIS IS A WHOLE NEW MESS!
IT WAS WORTH A SHOT!

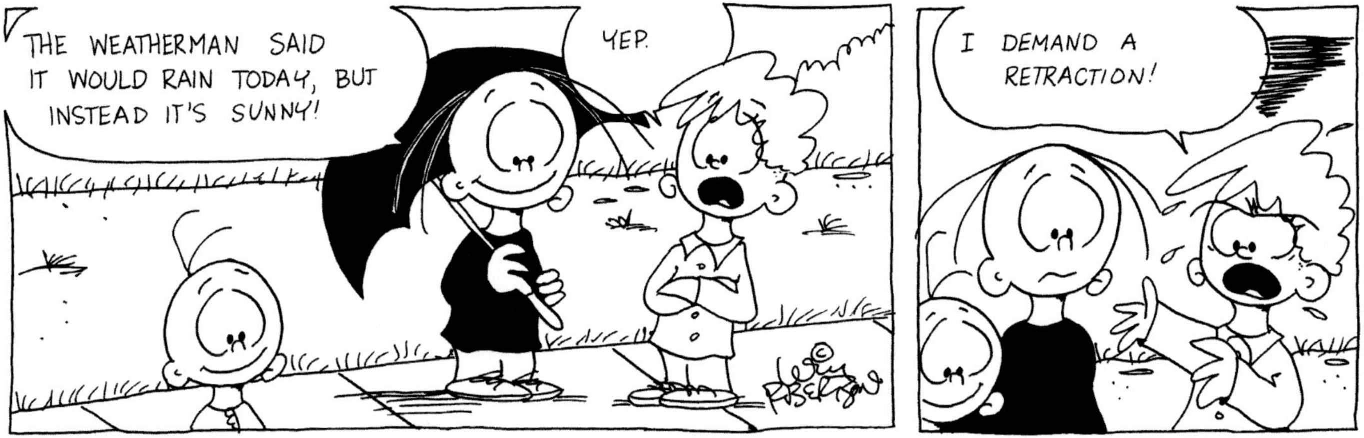
THE WEATHERMAN SAID IT WOULD RAIN TODAY, BUT INSTEAD IT'S SUNNY!
YEP.
I DEMAND A RETRACTION!

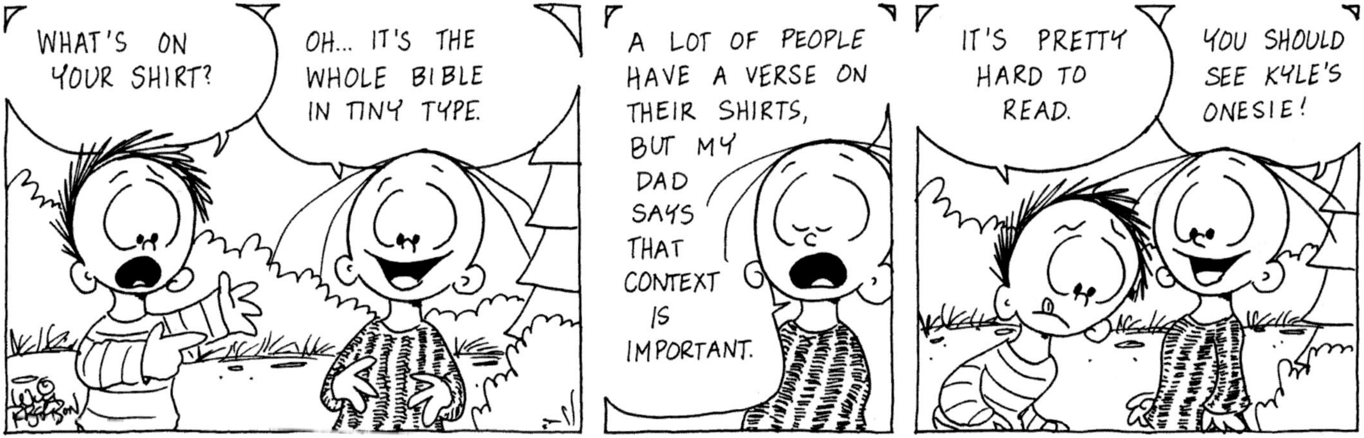
WHAT'S ON YOUR SHIRT?
OH... IT'S THE WHOLE BIBLE IN TINY TYPE.
A LOT OF PEOPLE HAVE A VERSE ON THEIR SHIRTS, BUT MY DAD SAYS THAT CONTEXT IS IMPORTANT.
IT'S PRETTY HARD TO READ.
YOU SHOULD SEE KYLE'S ONESIE!

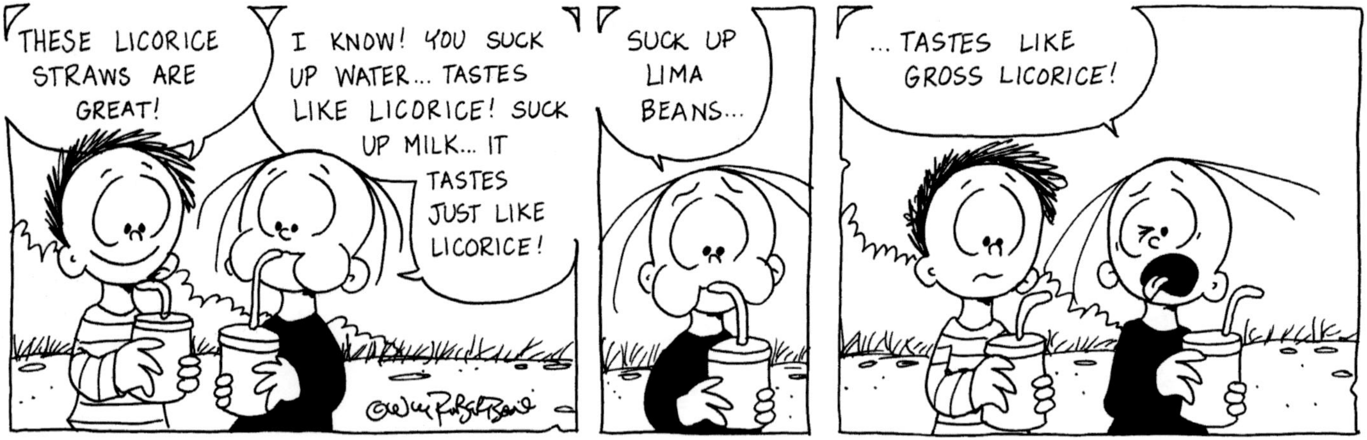
THESE LICORICE STRAWS ARE GREAT!
I KNOW! YOU SUCK UP WATER... TASTES LIKE LICORICE! SUCK UP MILK... IT TASTES JUST LIKE LICORICE!
SUCK UP LIMA BEANS...
... TASTES LIKE GROSS LICORICE!

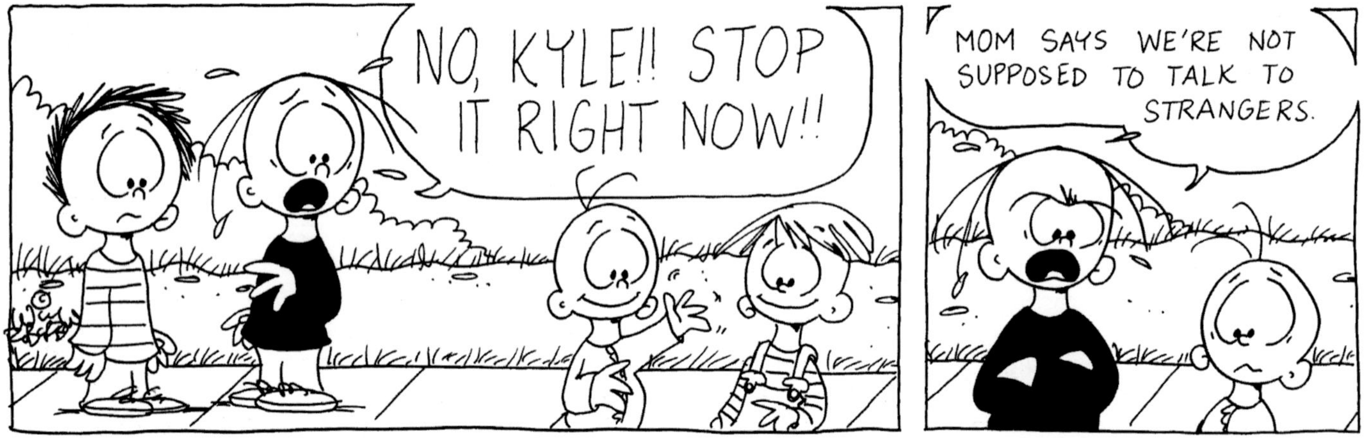
NO, KYLE!! STOP IT RIGHT NOW!!
MOM SAYS WE'RE NOT SUPPOSED TO TALK TO STRANGERS.

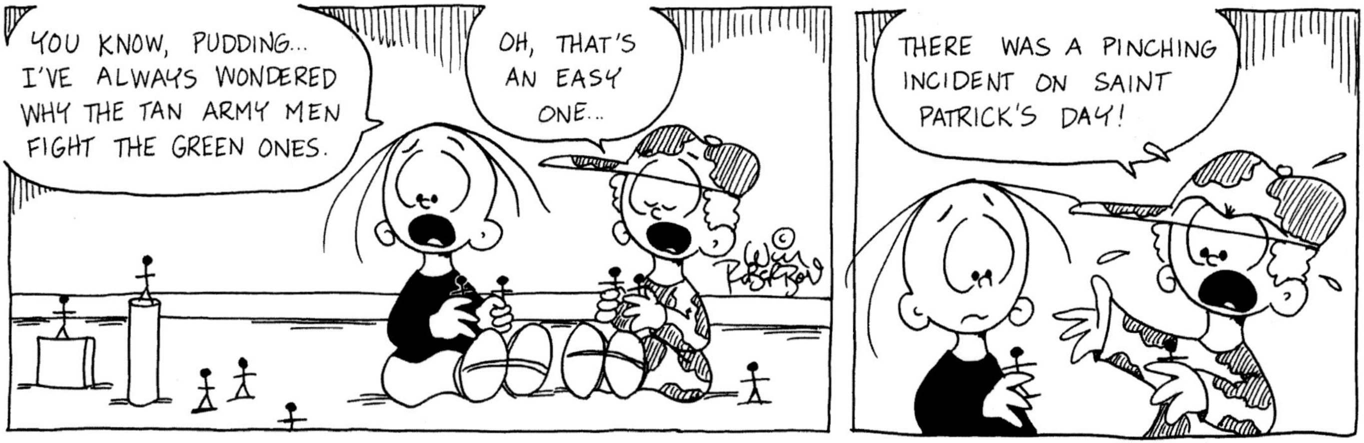
YOU KNOW, PUDDING... I'VE ALWAYS WONDERED WHY THE TAN ARMY MEN FIGHT THE GREEN ONES.
OH, THAT'S AN EASY ONE...
THERE WAS A PINCHING INCIDENT ON SAINT PATRICK'S DAY!

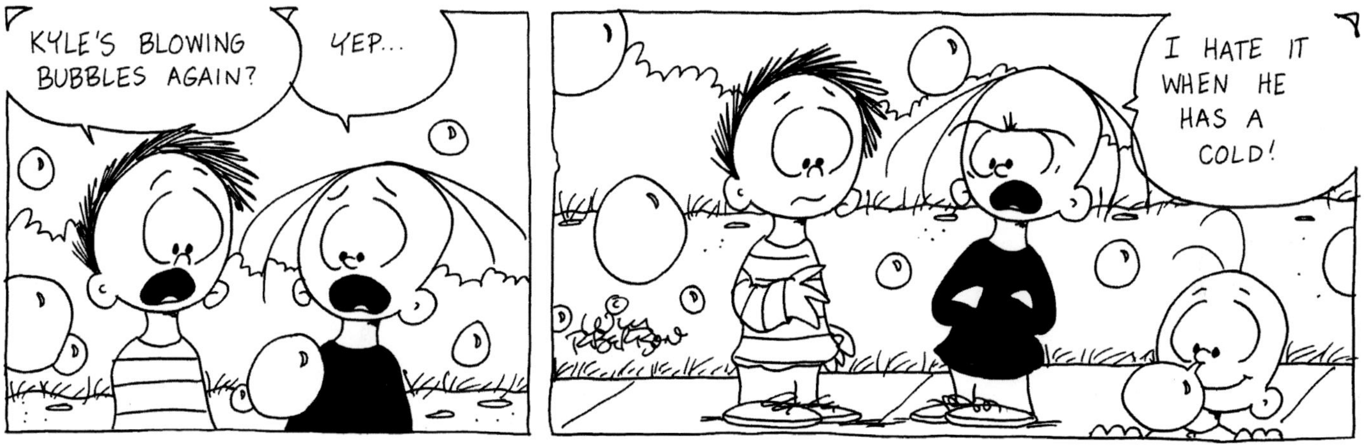
KYLE'S BLOWING BUBBLES AGAIN?
YEP...
I HATE IT WHEN HE HAS A COLD!

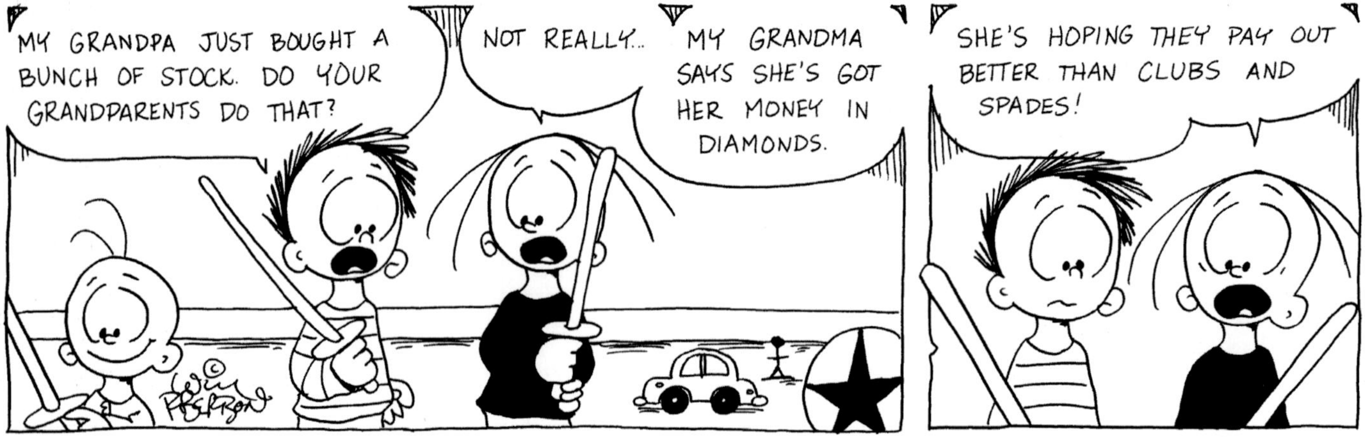
MY GRANDPA JUST BOUGHT A BUNCH OF STOCK. DO YOUR GRANDPARENTS DO THAT?
NOT REALLY...
MY GRANDMA SAYS SHE'S GOT HER MONEY IN DIAMONDS.
SHE'S HOPING THEY PAY OUT BETTER THAN CLUBS AND SPADES!

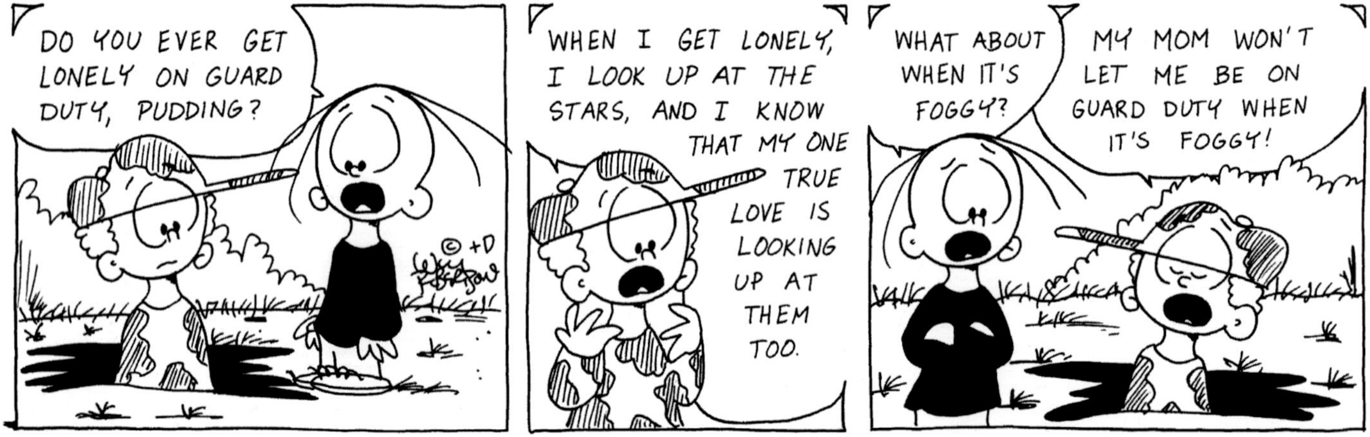
DO YOU EVER GET LONELY ON GUARD DUTY, PUDDING?
WHEN I GET LONELY, I LOOK UP AT THE STARS, AND I KNOW THAT MY ONE TRUE LOVE IS LOOKING UP AT THEM TOO.
WHAT ABOUT WHEN IT'S FOGGY?
MY MOM WON'T LET ME BE ON GUARD DUTY WHEN IT'S FOGGY!

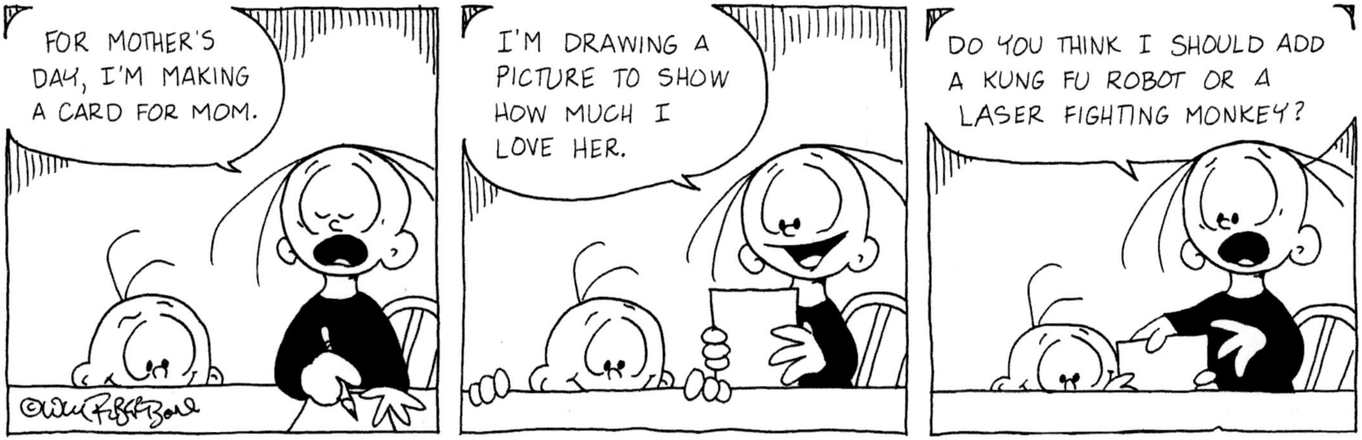
FOR MOTHER'S DAY, I'M MAKING A CARD FOR MOM.
I'M DRAWING A PICTURE TO SHOW HOW MUCH I LOVE HER.
DO YOU THINK I SHOULD ADD A KUNG FU ROBOT OR A LASER FIGHTING MONKEY?

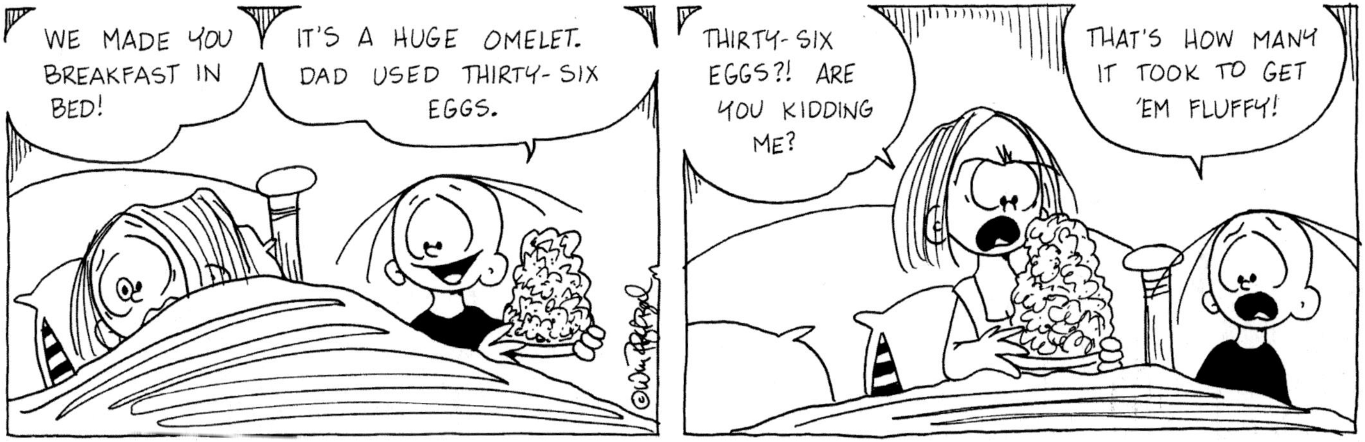
WE MADE YOU BREAKFAST IN BED!
IT'S A HUGE OMELET. DAD USED THIRTY-SIX EGGS.
THIRTY-SIX EGGS?! ARE YOU KIDDING ME?
THAT'S HOW MANY IT TOOK TO GET 'EM FLUFFY!

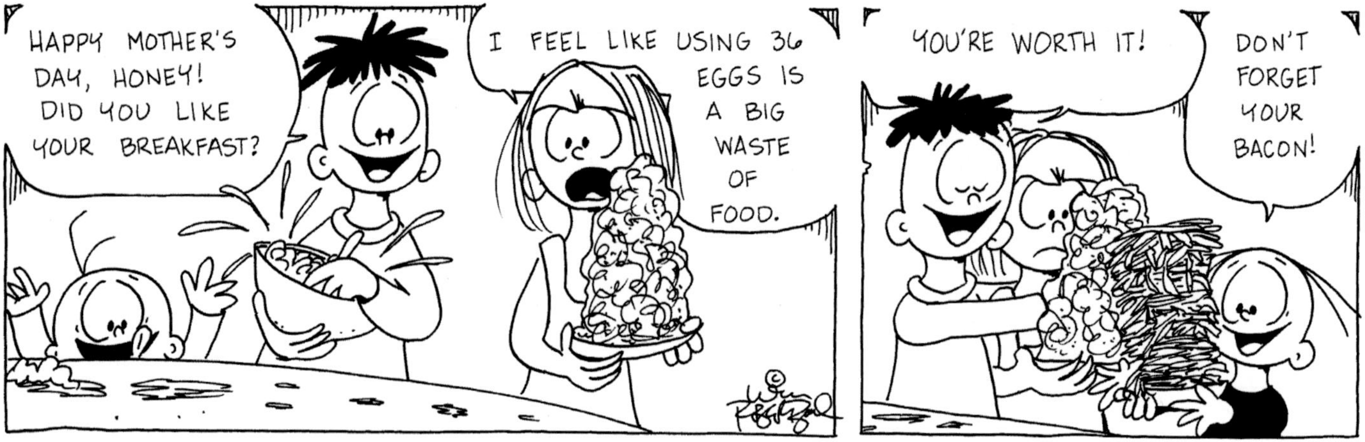
HAPPY MOTHER'S DAY, HONEY! DID YOU LIKE YOUR BREAKFAST?
I FEEL LIKE USING 36 EGGS IS A BIG WASTE OF FOOD.
YOU'RE WORTH IT!
DON'T FORGET YOUR BACON!

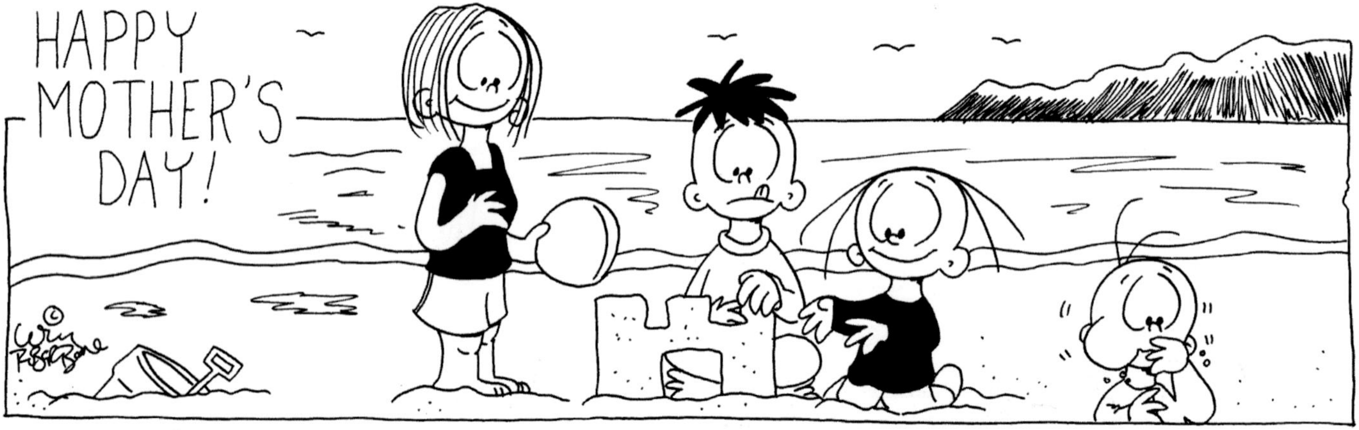
HAPPY MOTHER'S DAY!

CASEY AND KYLE™

by Will Robertson

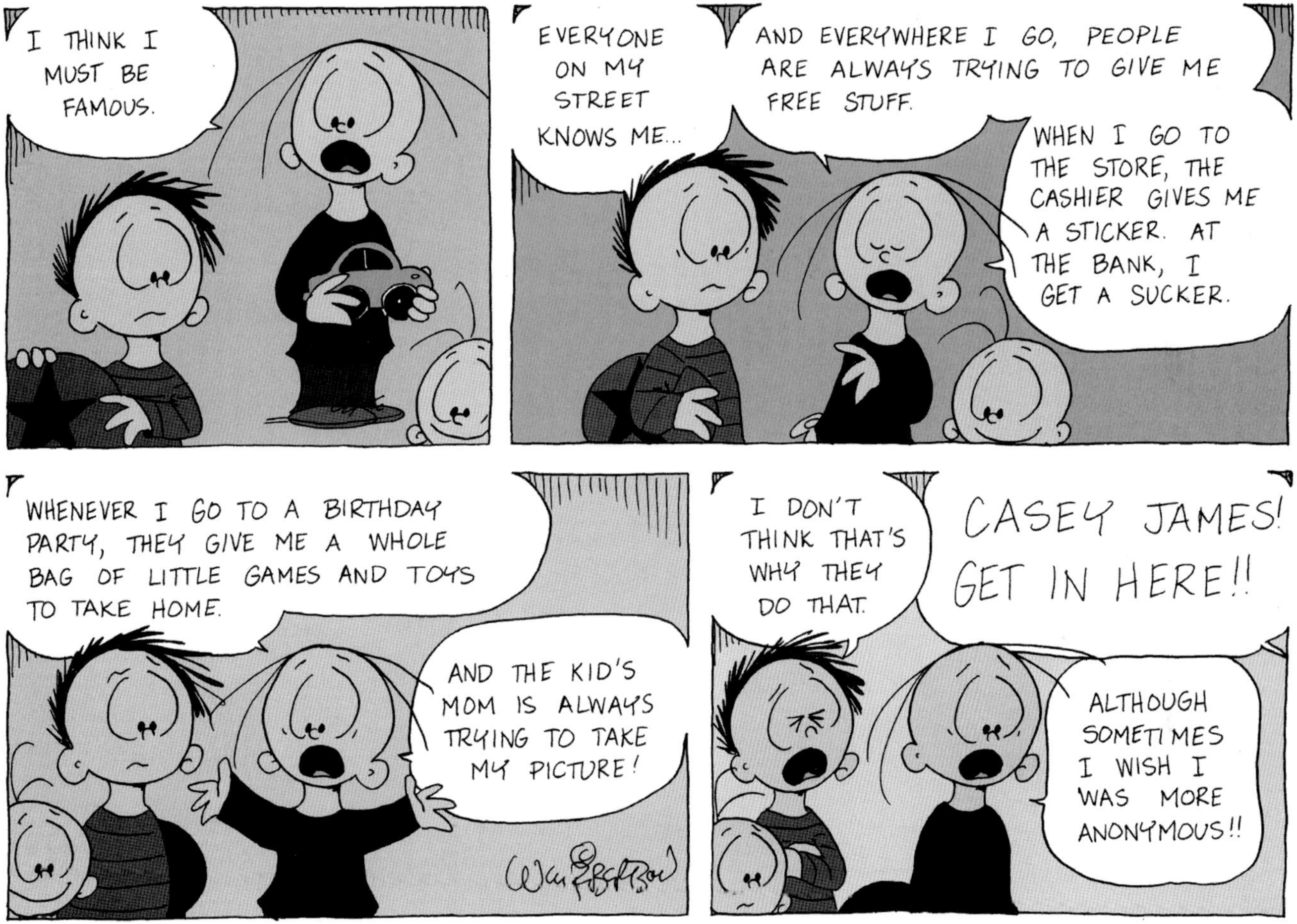

I THINK I MUST BE FAMOUS.
EVERYONE ON MY STREET KNOWS ME...
AND EVERYWHERE I GO, PEOPLE ARE ALWAYS TRYING TO GIVE ME FREE STUFF.
WHEN I GO TO THE STORE, THE CASHIER GIVES ME A STICKER. AT THE BANK, I GET A SUCKER.
WHENEVER I GO TO A BIRTHDAY PARTY, THEY GIVE ME A WHOLE BAG OF LITTLE GAMES AND TOYS TO TAKE HOME.
AND THE KID'S MOM IS ALWAYS TRYING TO TAKE MY PICTURE!
I DON'T THINK THAT'S WHY THEY DO THAT.
CASEY JAMES! GET IN HERE!!
ALTHOUGH SOMETIMES I WISH I WAS MORE ANONYMOUS!!

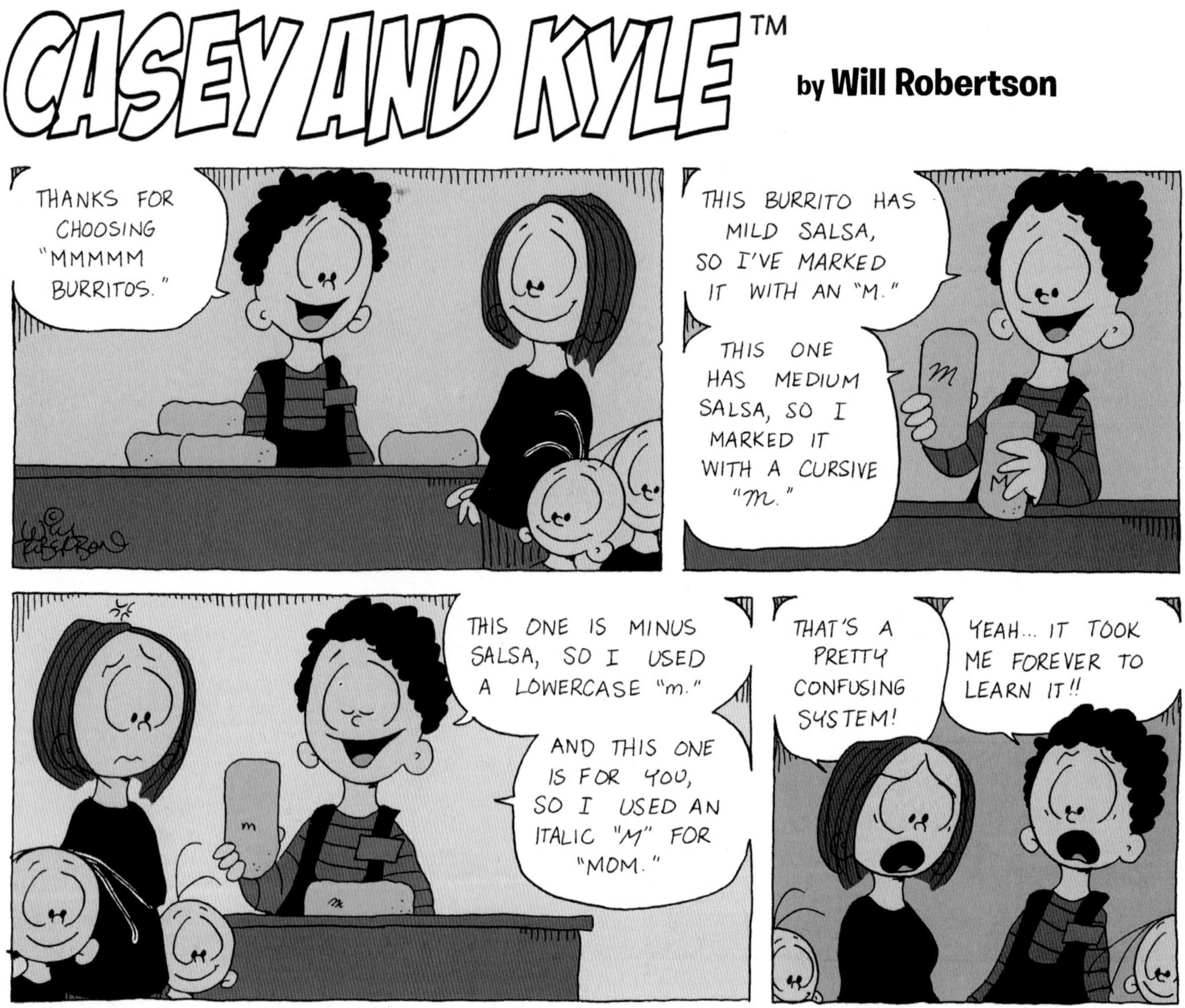
CASEY AND KYLE™
by Will Robertson
THANKS FOR CHOOSING "MMMMM BURRITOS."
THIS BURRITO HAS MILD SALSA, SO I'VE MARKED IT WITH AN "M."
THIS ONE HAS MEDIUM SALSA, SO I MARKED IT WITH A CURSIVE "m."
THIS ONE IS MINUS SALSA, SO I USED A LOWERCASE "m."
AND THIS ONE IS FOR YOU, SO I USED AN ITALIC "M" FOR "MOM."
THAT'S A PRETTY CONFUSING SYSTEM!
YEAH... IT TOOK ME FOREVER TO LEARN IT!!

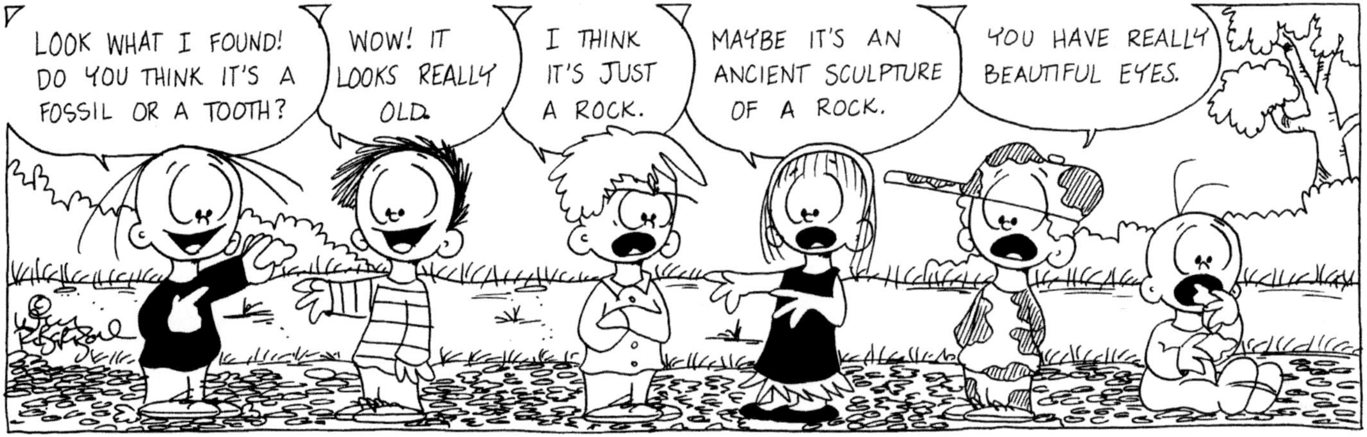
LOOK WHAT I FOUND! DO YOU THINK IT'S A FOSSIL OR A TOOTH?
WOW! IT LOOKS REALLY OLD.
I THINK IT'S JUST A ROCK.
MAYBE IT'S AN ANCIENT SCULPTURE OF A ROCK.
YOU HAVE REALLY BEAUTIFUL EYES.

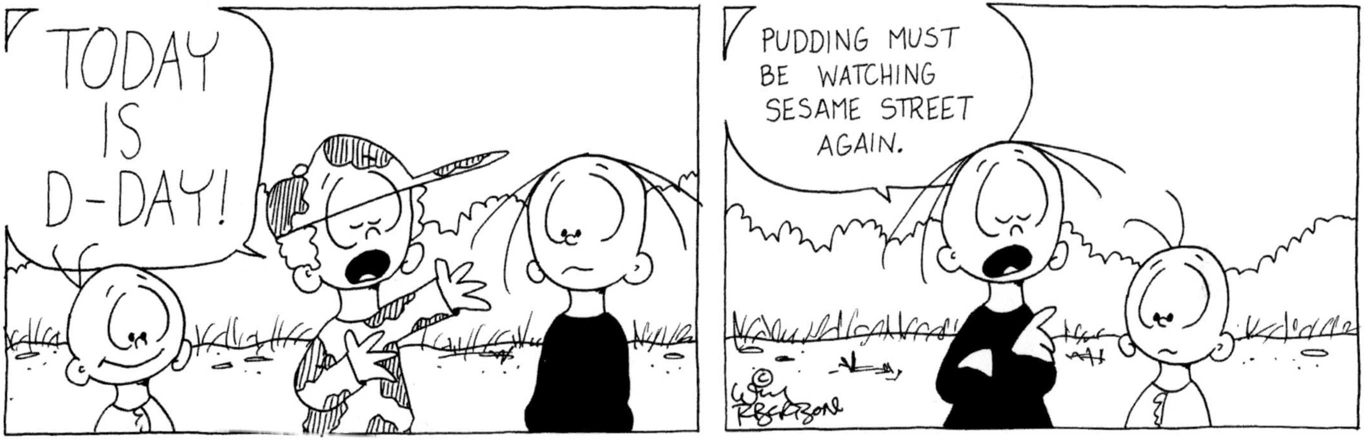
TODAY IS D-DAY!
PUDDING MUST BE WATCHING SESAME STREET AGAIN.

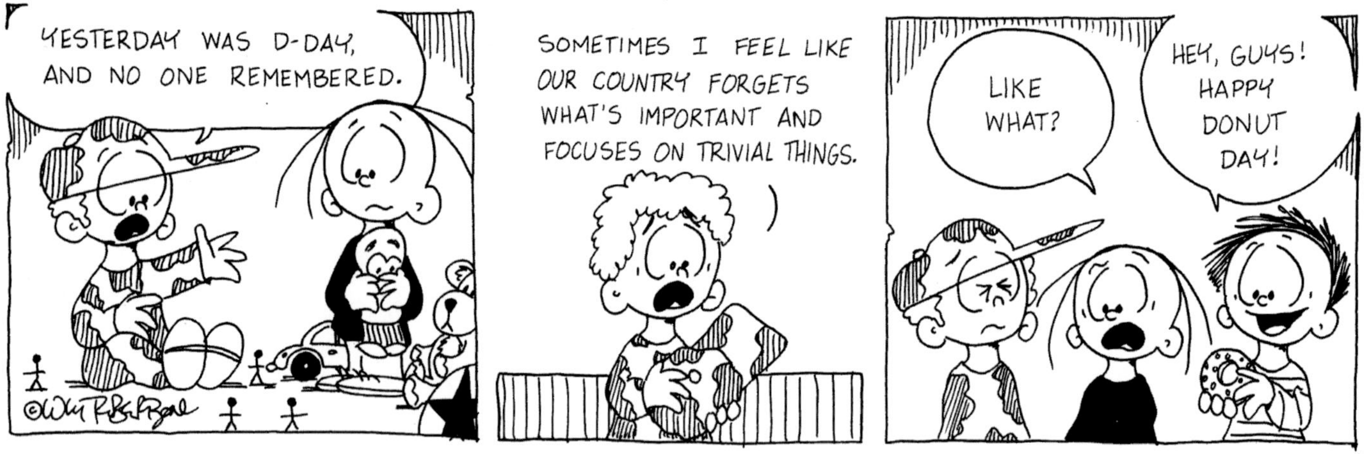
YESTERDAY WAS D-DAY, AND NO ONE REMEMBERED.
SOMETIMES I FEEL LIKE OUR COUNTRY FORGETS WHAT'S IMPORTANT AND FOCUSES ON TRIVIAL THINGS.
LIKE WHAT?
HEY, GUYS! HAPPY DONUT DAY!

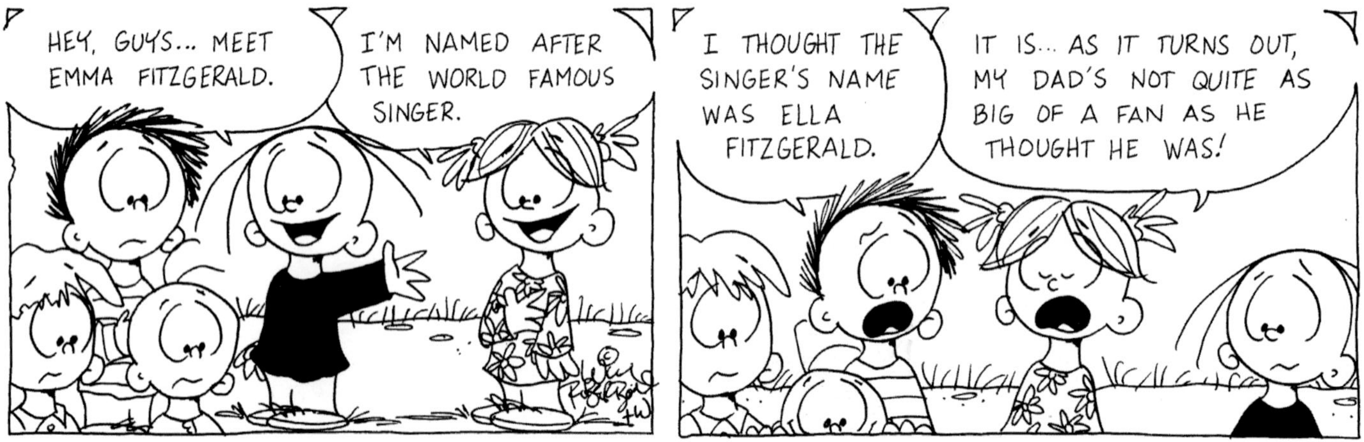
HEY, GUYS... MEET EMMA FITZGERALD.
I'M NAMED AFTER THE WORLD FAMOUS SINGER.
I THOUGHT THE SINGER'S NAME WAS ELLA FITZGERALD.
IT IS... AS IT TURNS OUT, MY DAD'S NOT QUITE AS BIG OF A FAN AS HE THOUGHT HE WAS!

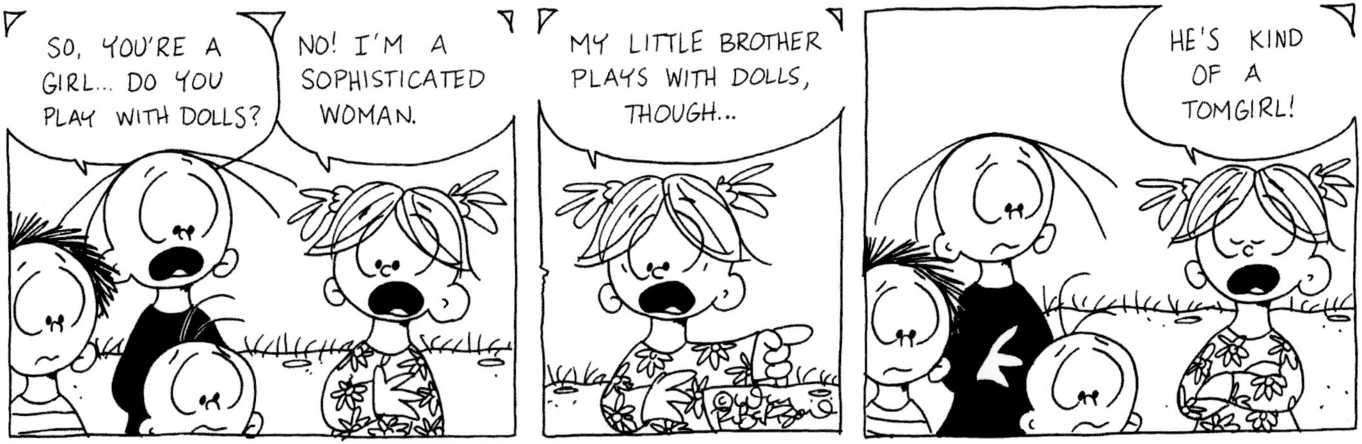
SO, YOU'RE A GIRL... DO YOU PLAY WITH DOLLS?
NO! I'M A SOPHISTICATED WOMAN.
MY LITTLE BROTHER PLAYS WITH DOLLS, THOUGH...
HE'S KIND OF A TOMGIRL!

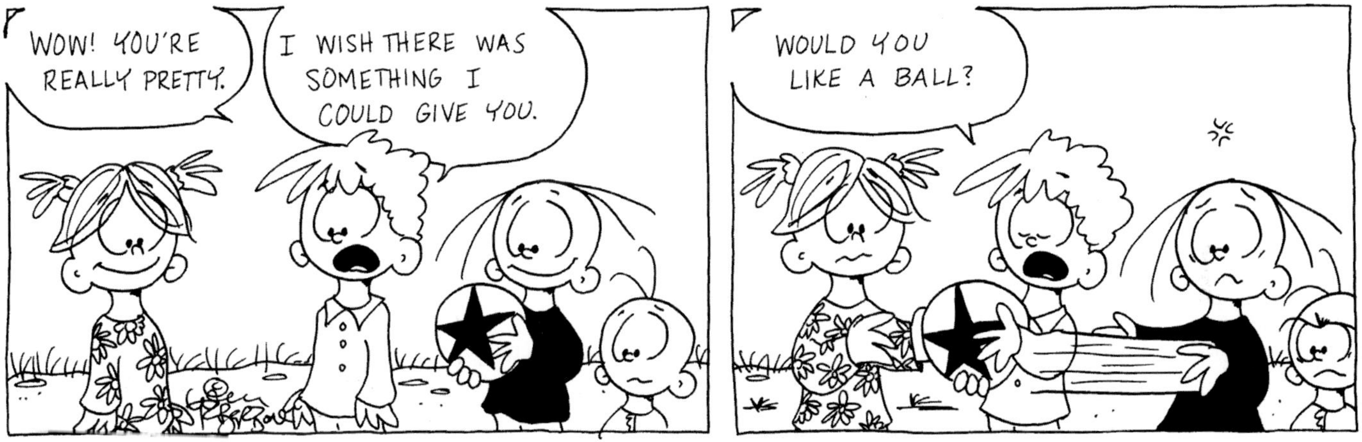
WOW! YOU'RE REALLY PRETTY.
I WISH THERE WAS SOMETHING I COULD GIVE YOU.
WOULD YOU LIKE A BALL?

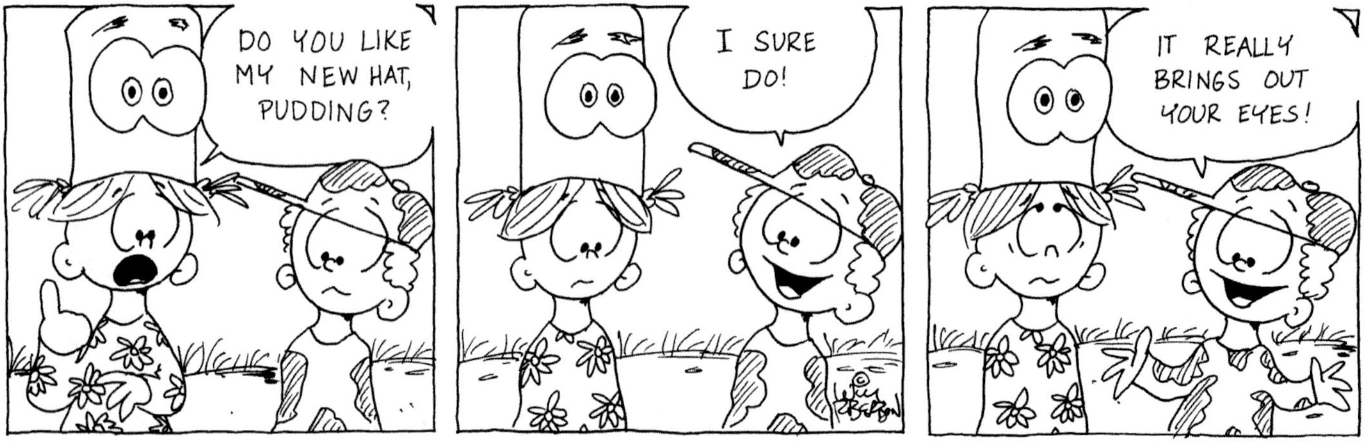
DO YOU LIKE MY NEW HAT, PUDDING?
I SURE DO!
IT REALLY BRINGS OUT YOUR EYES!

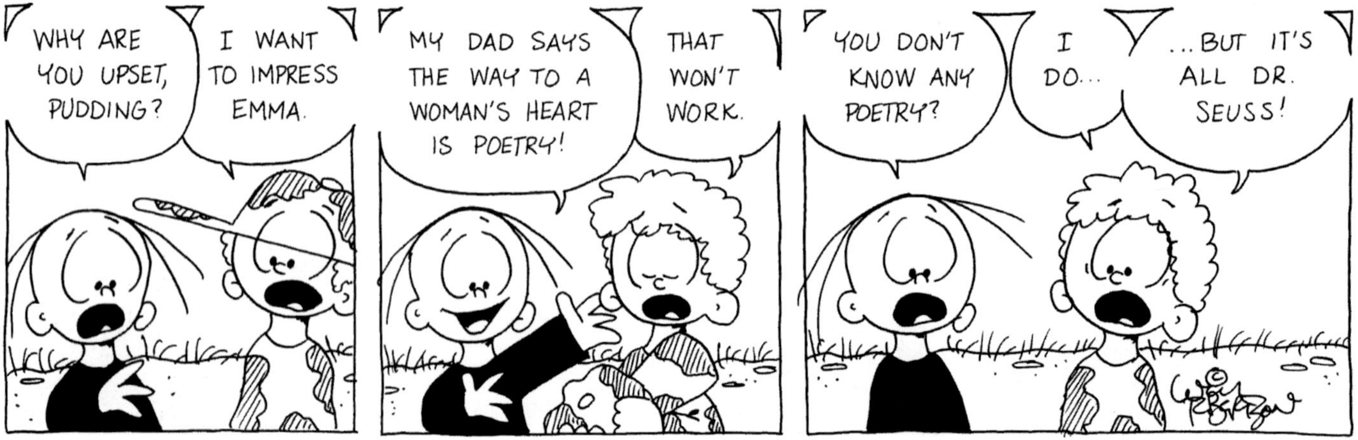
WHY ARE YOU UPSET, PUDDING?
I WANT TO IMPRESS EMMA.
MY DAD SAYS THE WAY TO A WOMAN'S HEART IS POETRY!
THAT WON'T WORK.
YOU DON'T KNOW ANY POETRY?
I DO...
...BUT IT'S ALL DR. SEUSS!

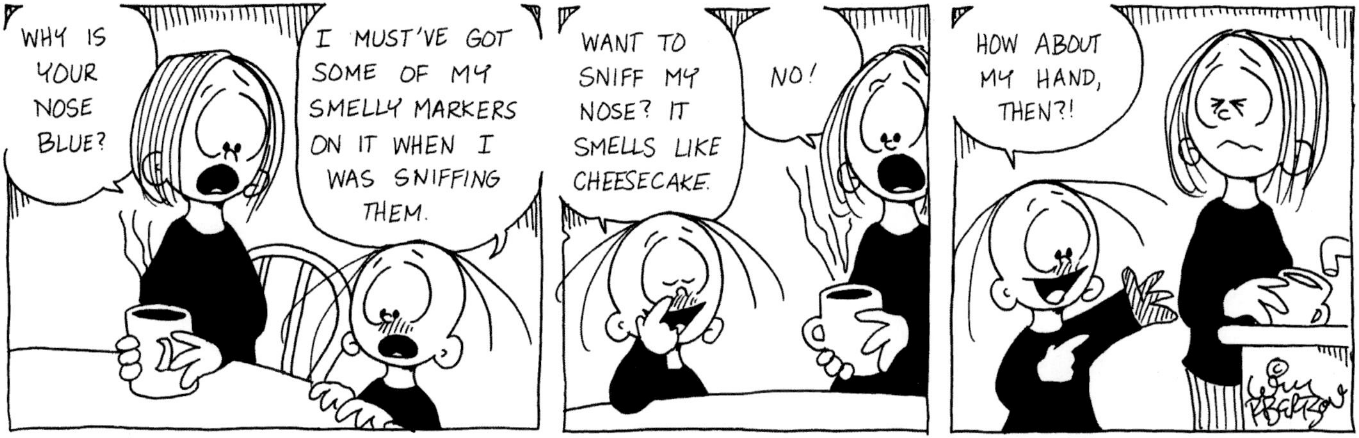
WHY IS YOUR NOSE BLUE?
I MUST'VE GOT SOME OF MY SMELLY MARKERS ON IT WHEN I WAS SNIFFING THEM.
WANT TO SNIFF MY NOSE? IT SMELLS LIKE CHEESECAKE.
NO!
HOW ABOUT MY HAND, THEN?!

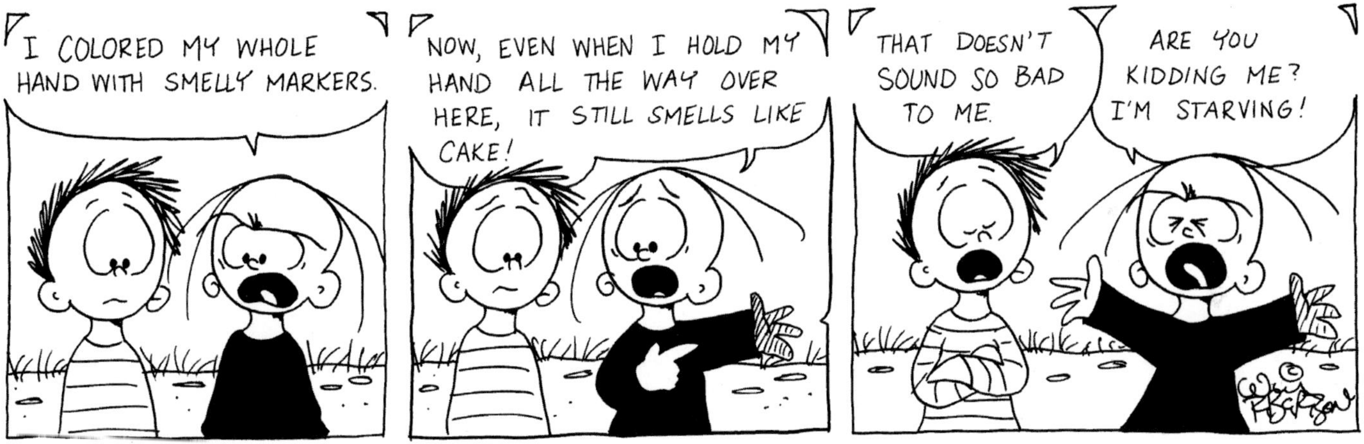
I COLORED MY WHOLE HAND WITH SMELLY MARKERS.
NOW, EVEN WHEN I HOLD MY HAND ALL THE WAY OVER HERE, IT STILL SMELLS LIKE CAKE!
THAT DOESN'T SOUND SO BAD TO ME.
ARE YOU KIDDING ME? I'M STARVING!

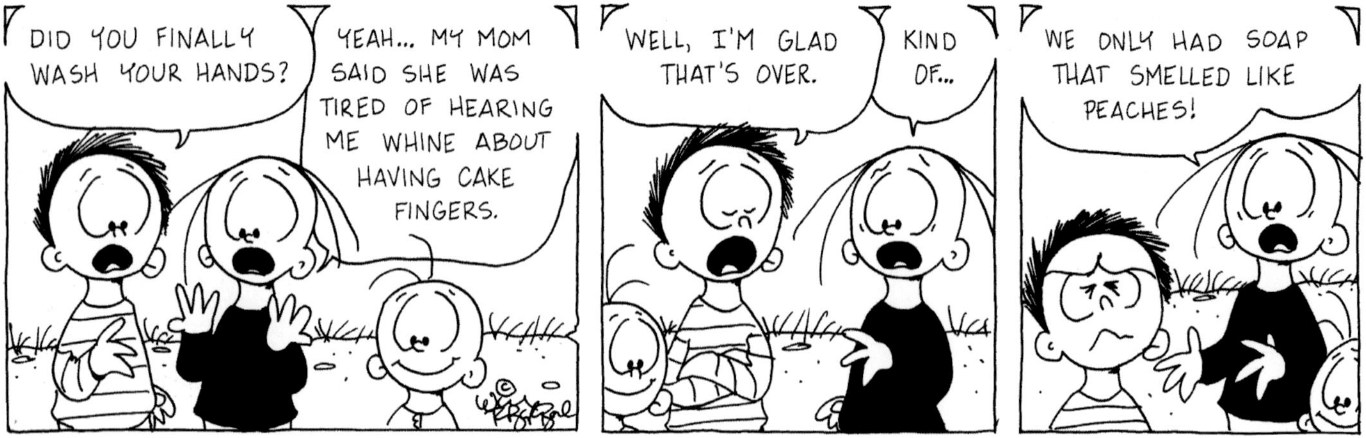
DID YOU FINALLY WASH YOUR HANDS?
YEAH... MY MOM SAID SHE WAS TIRED OF HEARING ME WHINE ABOUT HAVING CAKE FINGERS.
WELL, I'M GLAD THAT'S OVER.
KIND OF...
WE ONLY HAD SOAP THAT SMELLED LIKE PEACHES!

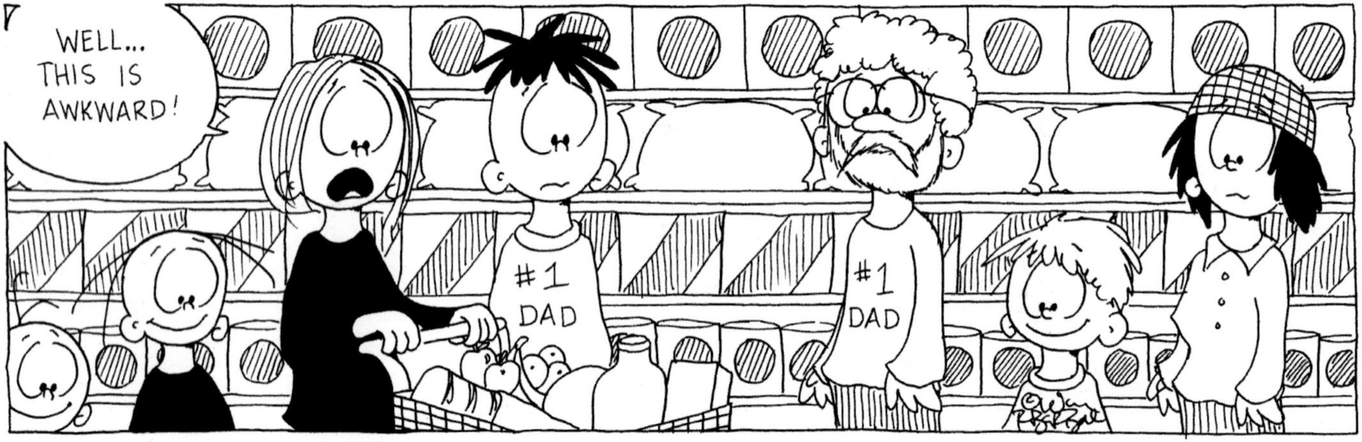
WELL... THIS IS AWKWARD!
#1 DAD
#1 DAD

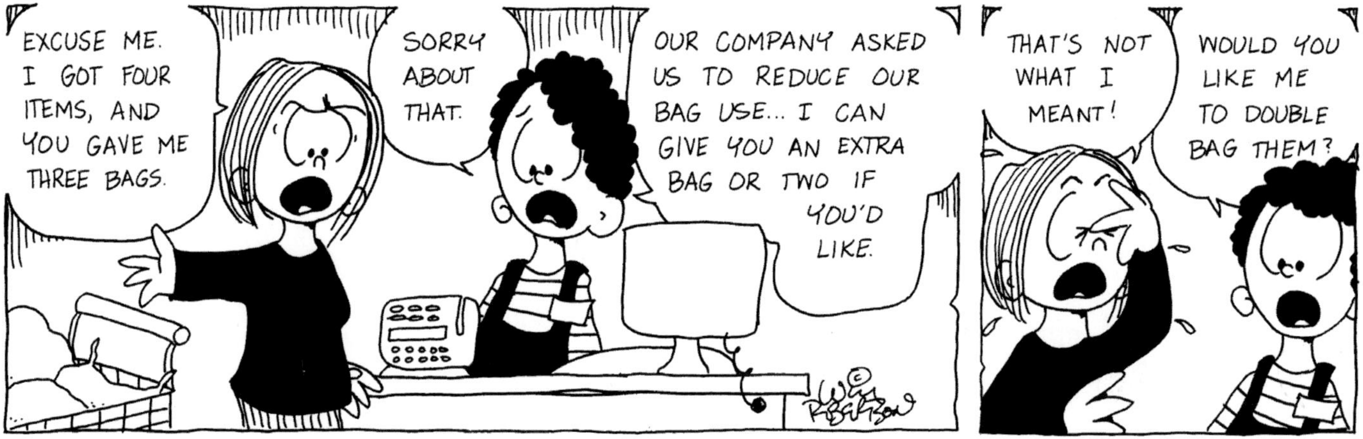
EXCUSE ME. I GOT FOUR ITEMS, AND YOU GAVE ME THREE BAGS.
SORRY ABOUT THAT.
OUR COMPANY ASKED US TO REDUCE OUR BAG USE... I CAN GIVE YOU AN EXTRA BAG OR TWO IF YOU'D LIKE.
THAT'S NOT WHAT I MEANT!
WOULD YOU LIKE ME TO DOUBLE BAG THEM?

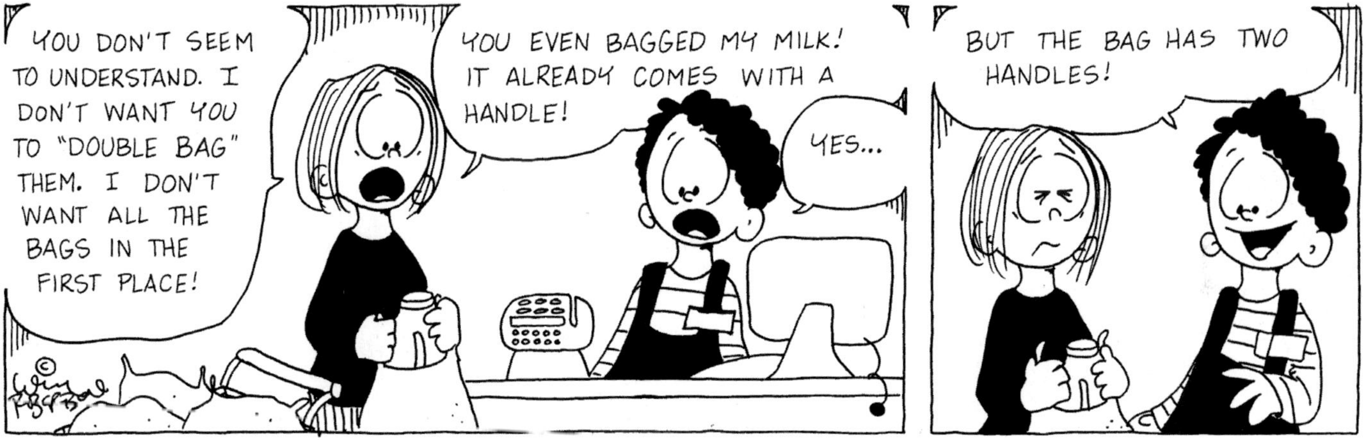
YOU DON'T SEEM TO UNDERSTAND. I DON'T WANT YOU TO "DOUBLE BAG" THEM. I DON'T WANT ALL THE BAGS IN THE FIRST PLACE!
YOU EVEN BAGGED MY MILK! IT ALREADY COMES WITH A HANDLE!
YES...
BUT THE BAG HAS TWO HANDLES!

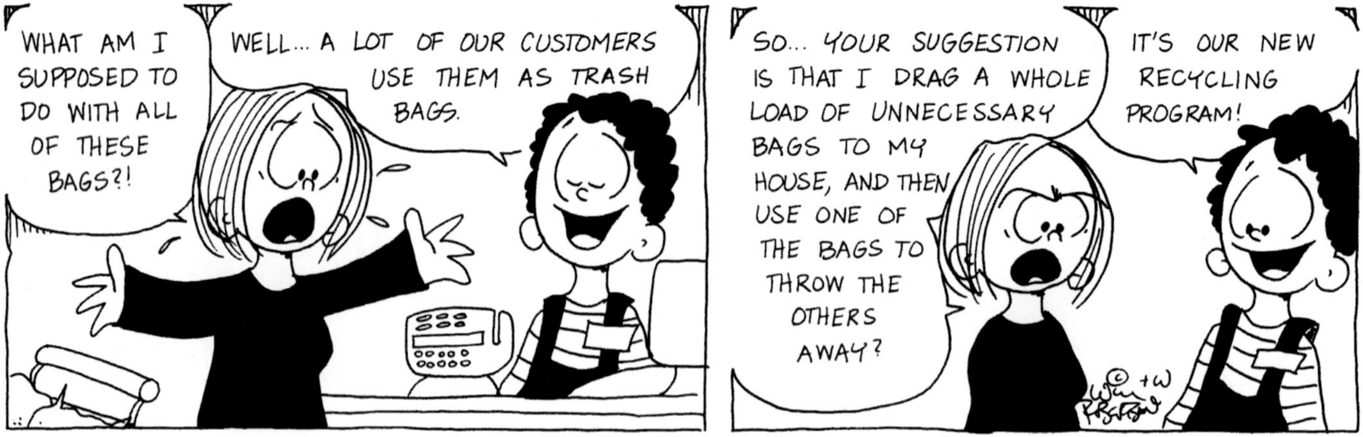
WHAT AM I SUPPOSED TO DO WITH ALL OF THESE BAGS?!
WELL... A LOT OF OUR CUSTOMERS USE THEM AS TRASH BAGS.
SO... YOUR SUGGESTION IS THAT I DRAG A WHOLE LOAD OF UNNECESSARY BAGS TO MY HOUSE, AND THEN USE ONE OF THE BAGS TO THROW THE OTHERS AWAY?
IT'S OUR NEW RECYCLING PROGRAM!

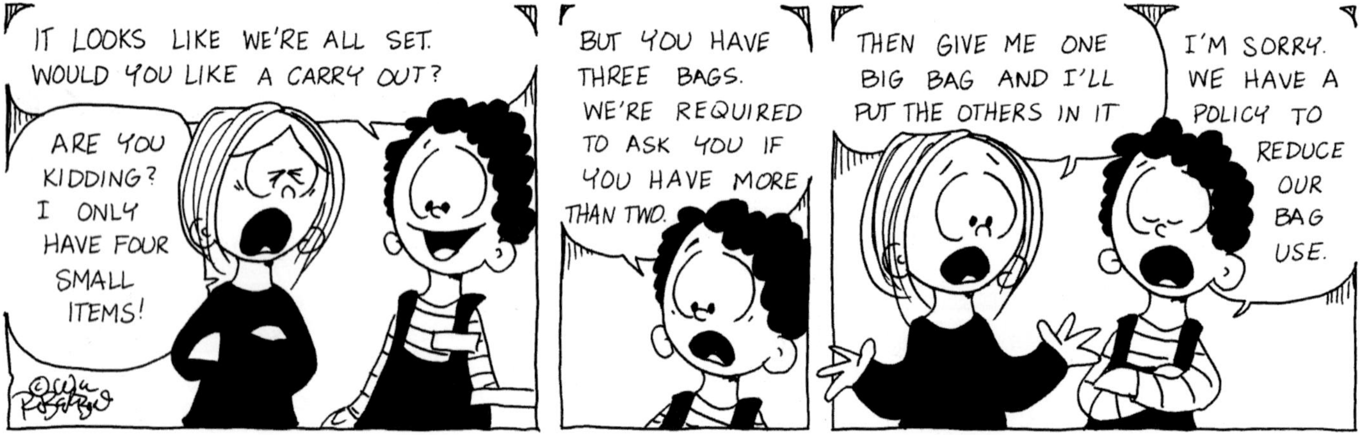
IT LOOKS LIKE WE'RE ALL SET. WOULD YOU LIKE A CARRY OUT?
ARE YOU KIDDING? I ONLY HAVE FOUR SMALL ITEMS!
BUT YOU HAVE THREE BAGS. WE'RE REQUIRED TO ASK YOU IF YOU HAVE MORE THAN TWO.
THEN GIVE ME ONE BIG BAG AND I'LL PUT THE OTHERS IN IT
I'M SORRY. WE HAVE A POLICY TO REDUCE OUR BAG USE.

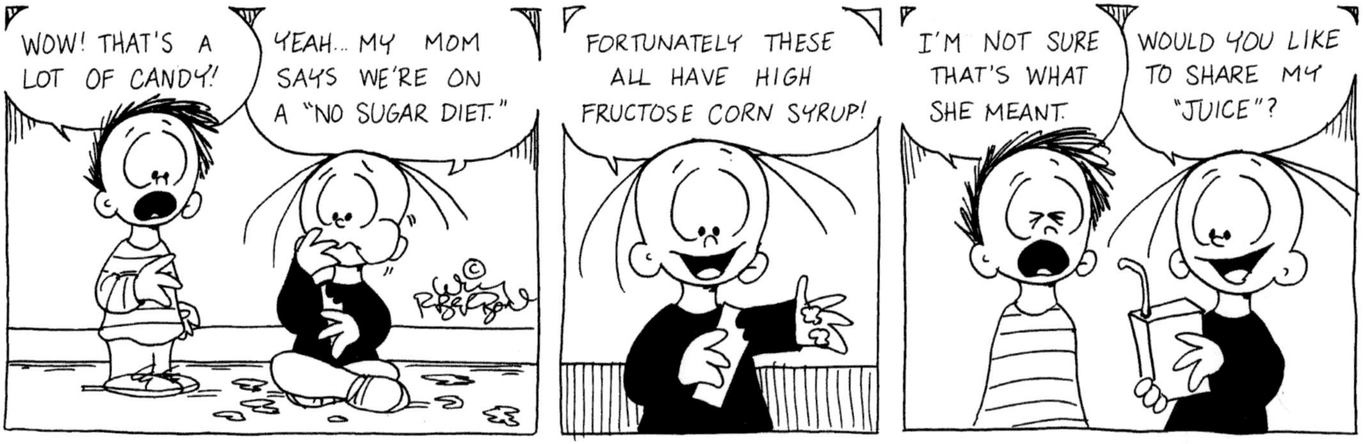
WOW! THAT'S A LOT OF CANDY!
YEAH... MY MOM SAYS WE'RE ON A "NO SUGAR DIET."
FORTUNATELY THESE ALL HAVE HIGH FRUCTOSE CORN SYRUP!
I'M NOT SURE THAT'S WHAT SHE MEANT.
WOULD YOU LIKE TO SHARE MY "JUICE"?

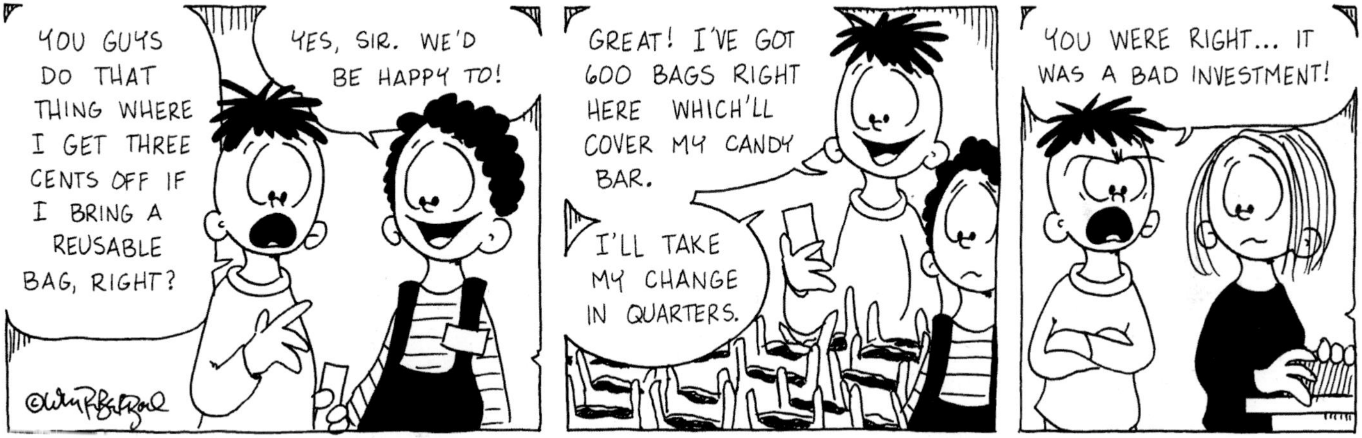
YOU GUYS DO THAT THING WHERE I GET THREE CENTS OFF IF I BRING A REUSABLE BAG, RIGHT?
YES, SIR. WE'D BE HAPPY TO!
GREAT! I'VE GOT 600 BAGS RIGHT HERE WHICH'LL COVER MY CANDY BAR.
I'LL TAKE MY CHANGE IN QUARTERS.
YOU WERE RIGHT... IT WAS A BAD INVESTMENT!

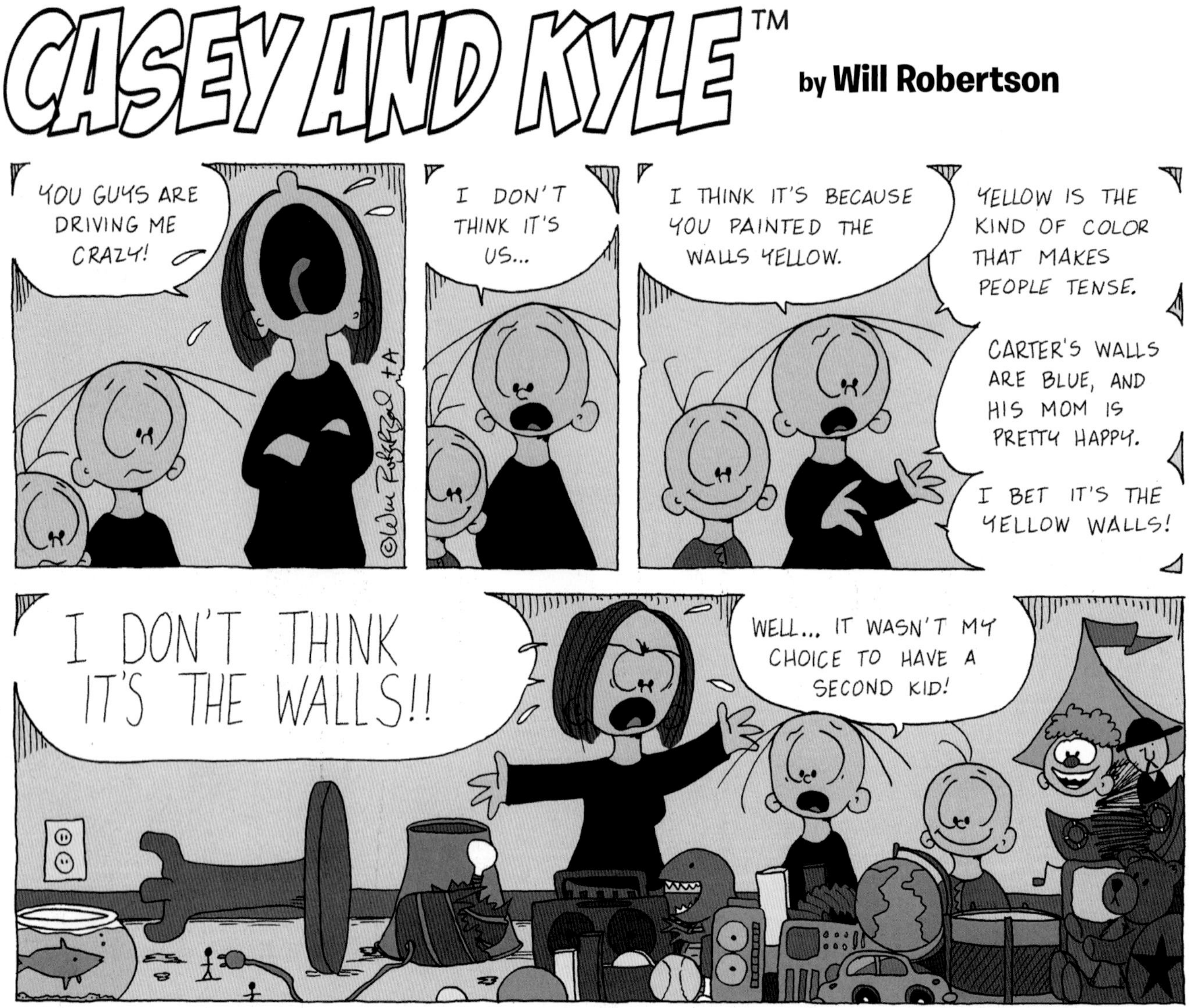
CASEY AND KYLE™
by Will Robertson
YOU GUYS ARE DRIVING ME CRAZY!
I DON'T THINK IT'S US...
I THINK IT'S BECAUSE YOU PAINTED THE WALLS YELLOW.
YELLOW IS THE KIND OF COLOR THAT MAKES PEOPLE TENSE.
CARTER'S WALLS ARE BLUE, AND HIS MOM IS PRETTY HAPPY.
I BET IT'S THE YELLOW WALLS!
I DON'T THINK IT'S THE WALLS!!
WELL... IT WASN'T MY CHOICE TO HAVE A SECOND KID!

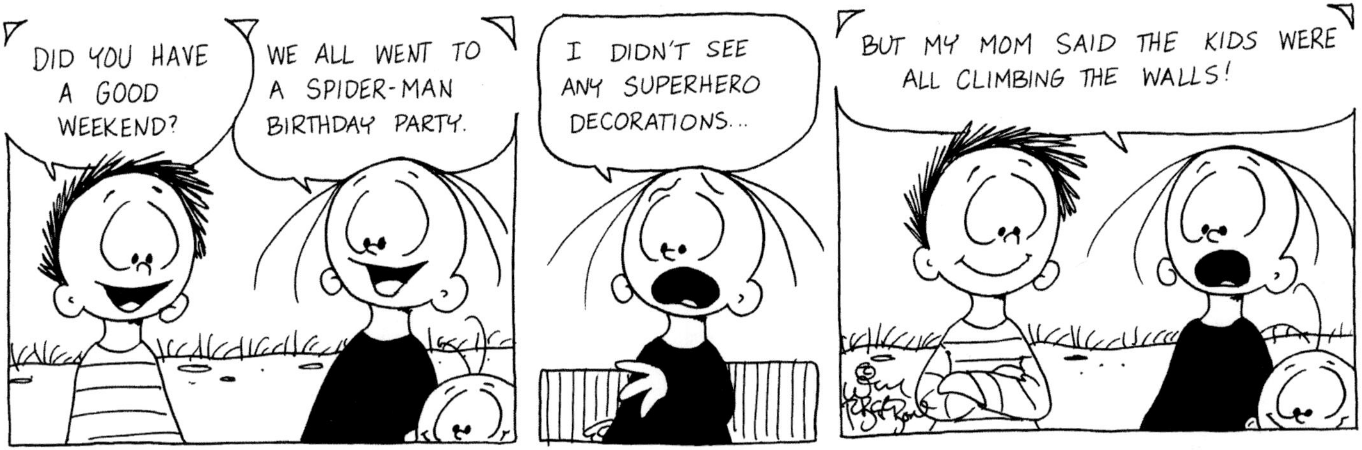
DID YOU HAVE A GOOD WEEKEND?
WE ALL WENT TO A SPIDER-MAN BIRTHDAY PARTY.
I DIDN'T SEE ANY SUPERHERO DECORATIONS...
BUT MY MOM SAID THE KIDS WERE ALL CLIMBING THE WALLS!

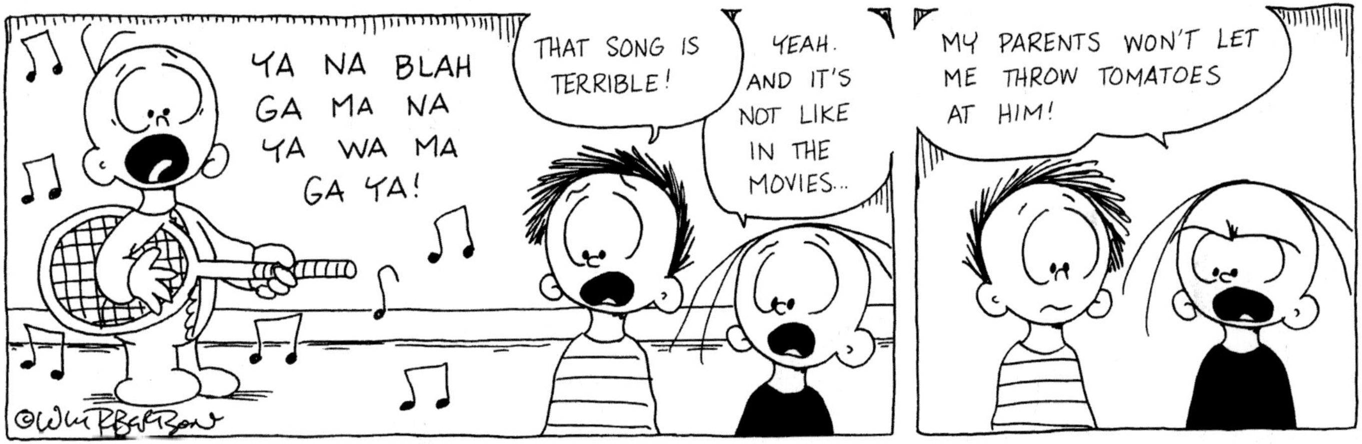
YA NA BLAH GA MA NA YA WA MA GA YA!
THAT SONG IS TERRIBLE!
YEAH. AND IT'S NOT LIKE IN THE MOVIES...
MY PARENTS WON'T LET ME THROW TOMATOES AT HIM!

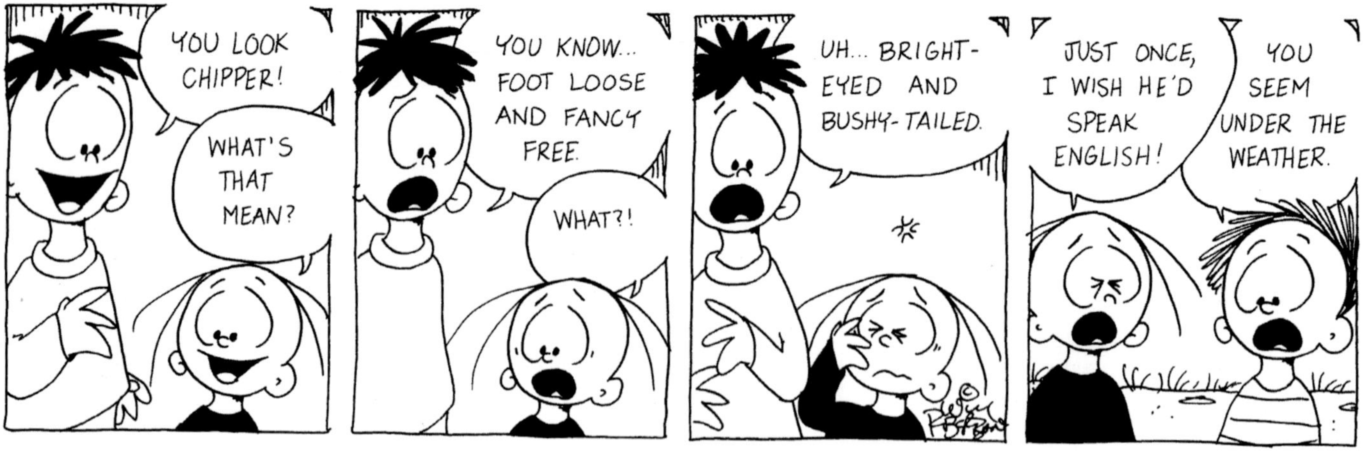
YOU LOOK CHIPPER!
WHAT'S THAT MEAN?
YOU KNOW... FOOT LOOSE AND FANCY FREE.
WHAT?!
UH... BRIGHT-EYED AND BUSHY-TAILED.
JUST ONCE, I WISH HE'D SPEAK ENGLISH!
YOU SEEM UNDER THE WEATHER.

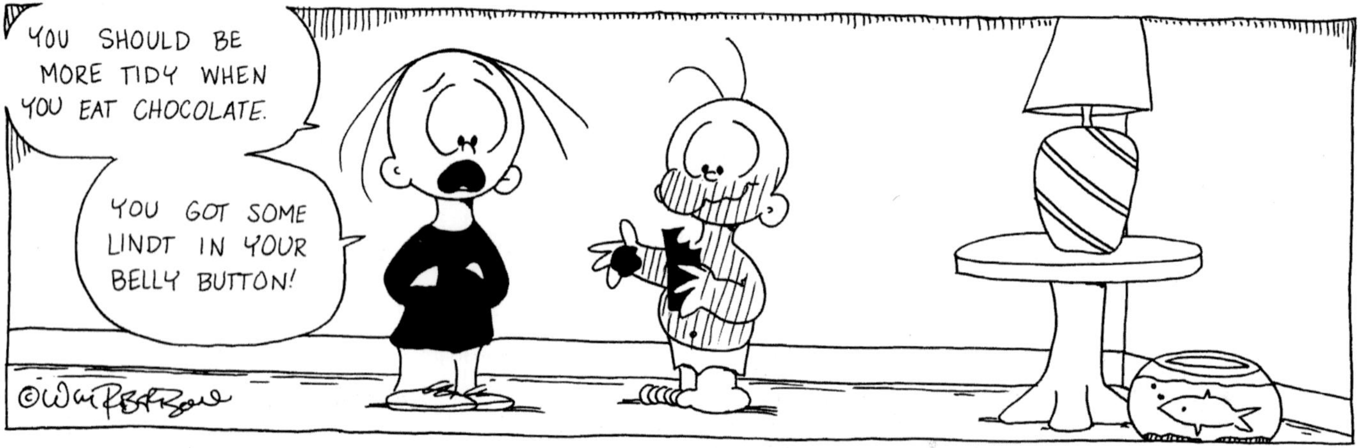
YOU SHOULD BE MORE TIDY WHEN YOU EAT CHOCOLATE.
YOU GOT SOME LINDT IN YOUR BELLY BUTTON!

CASEY AND KYLE™

by **Will Robertson**

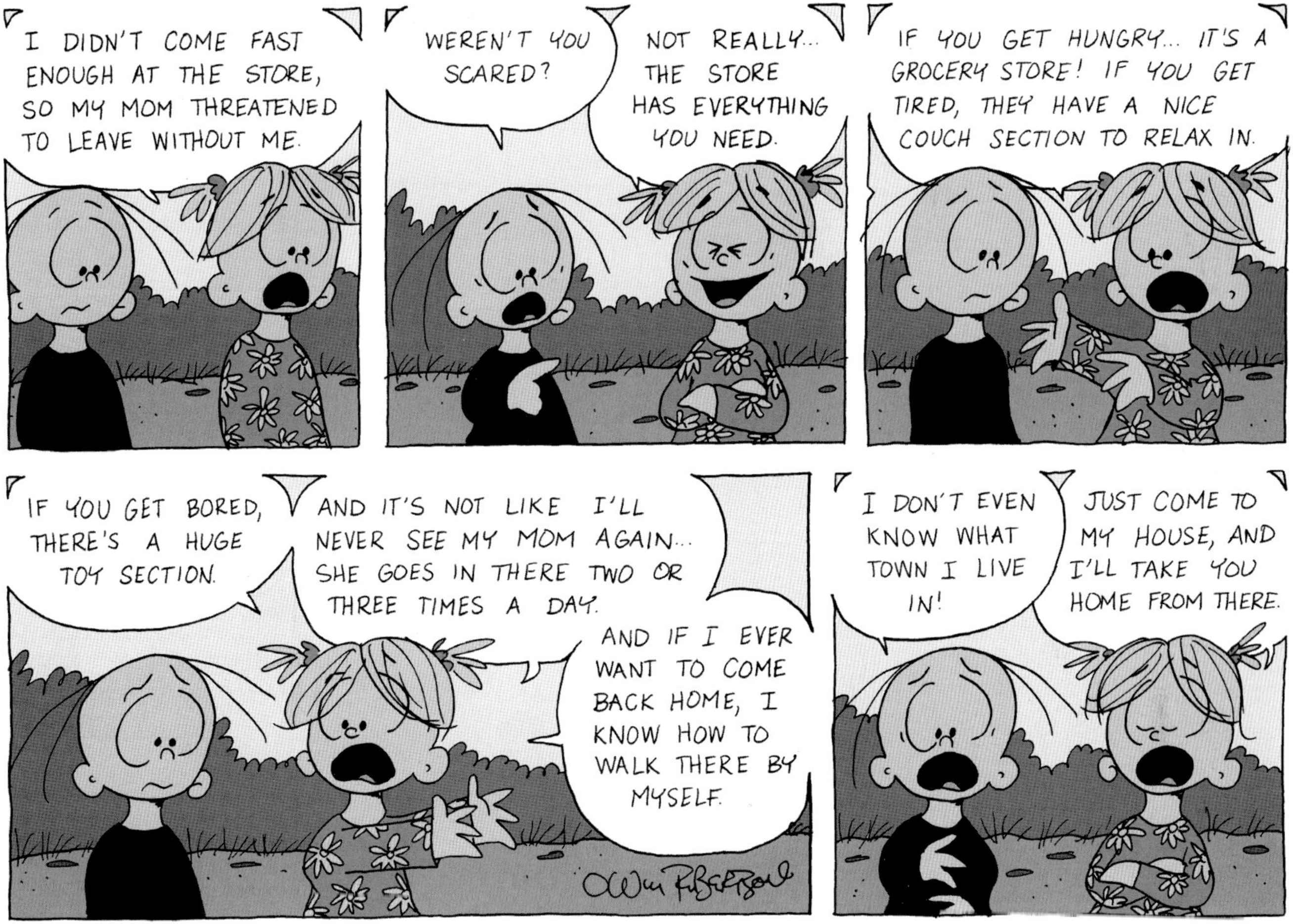
I DIDN'T COME FAST ENOUGH AT THE STORE, SO MY MOM THREATENED TO LEAVE WITHOUT ME.
WEREN'T YOU SCARED?
NOT REALLY... THE STORE HAS EVERYTHING YOU NEED.
IF YOU GET HUNGRY... IT'S A GROCERY STORE! IF YOU GET TIRED, THEY HAVE A NICE COUCH SECTION TO RELAX IN.
IF YOU GET BORED, THERE'S A HUGE TOY SECTION.
AND IT'S NOT LIKE I'LL NEVER SEE MY MOM AGAIN... SHE GOES IN THERE TWO OR THREE TIMES A DAY.
AND IF I EVER WANT TO COME BACK HOME, I KNOW HOW TO WALK THERE BY MYSELF.
I DON'T EVEN KNOW WHAT TOWN I LIVE IN!
JUST COME TO MY HOUSE, AND I'LL TAKE YOU HOME FROM THERE.

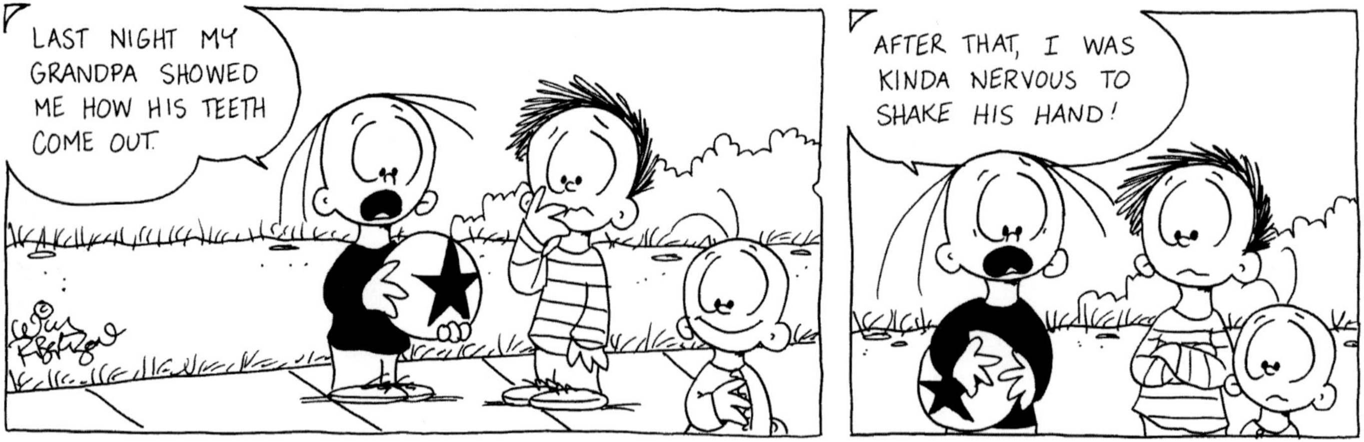
LAST NIGHT MY GRANDPA SHOWED ME HOW HIS TEETH COME OUT.
AFTER THAT, I WAS KINDA NERVOUS TO SHAKE HIS HAND!

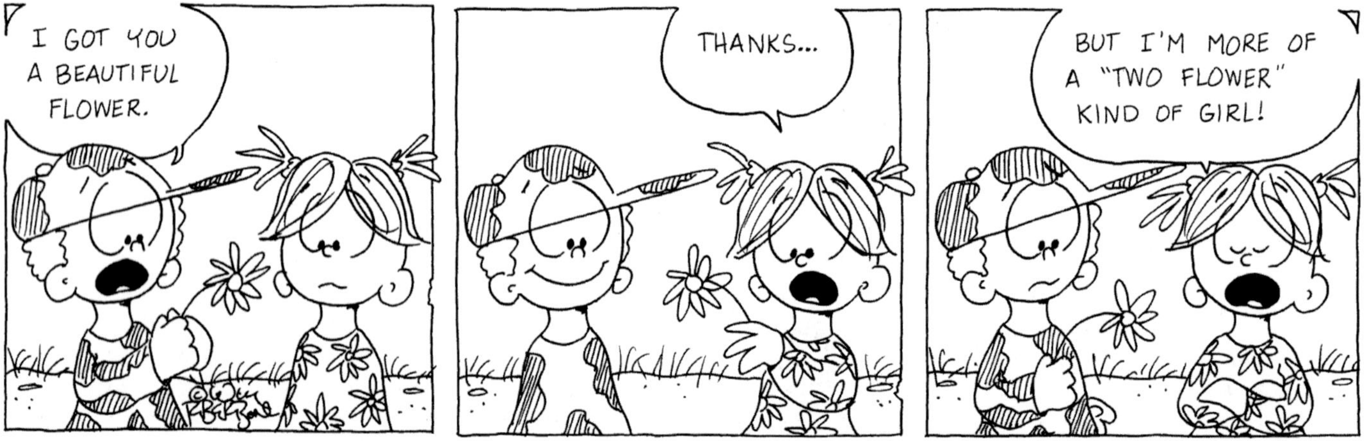
I GOT YOU A BEAUTIFUL FLOWER.
THANKS...
BUT I'M MORE OF A "TWO FLOWER" KIND OF GIRL!

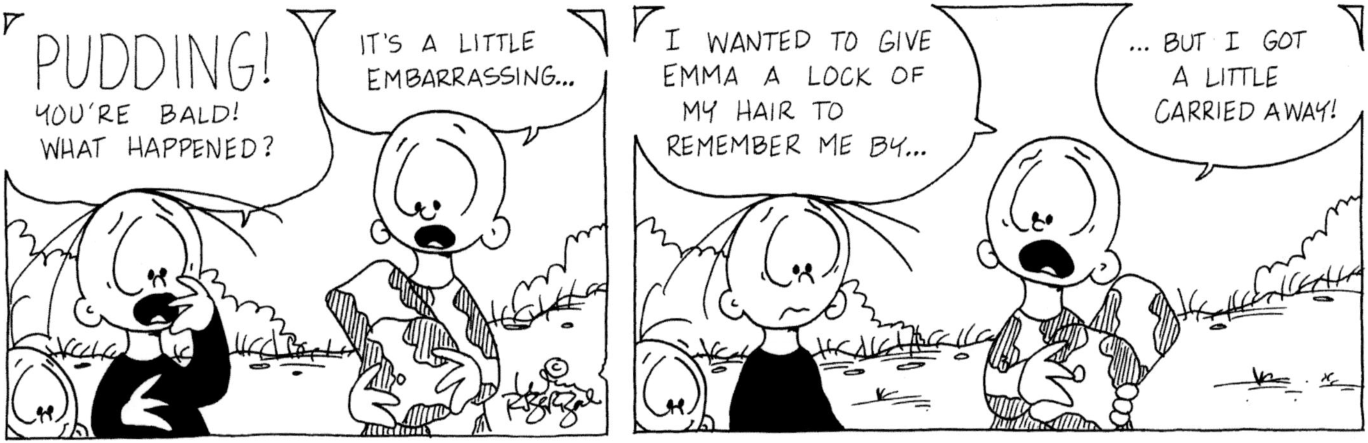
PUDDING! YOU'RE BALD! WHAT HAPPENED?
IT'S A LITTLE EMBARRASSING...
I WANTED TO GIVE EMMA A LOCK OF MY HAIR TO REMEMBER ME BY...
... BUT I GOT A LITTLE CARRIED AWAY!

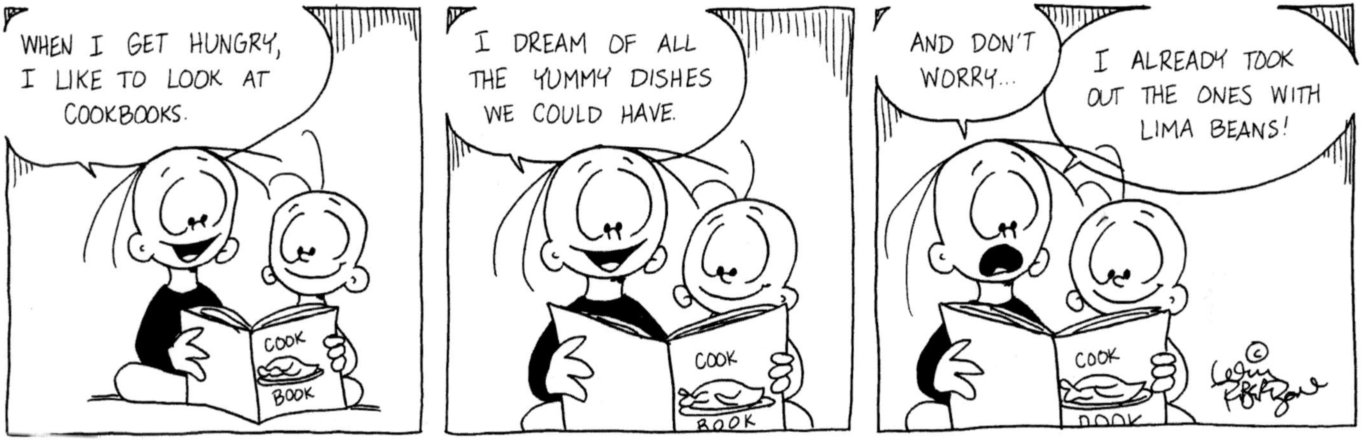
WHEN I GET HUNGRY, I LIKE TO LOOK AT COOKBOOKS.
COOK BOOK
I DREAM OF ALL THE YUMMY DISHES WE COULD HAVE.
COOK BOOK
AND DON'T WORRY...
I ALREADY TOOK OUT THE ONES WITH LIMA BEANS!
COOK

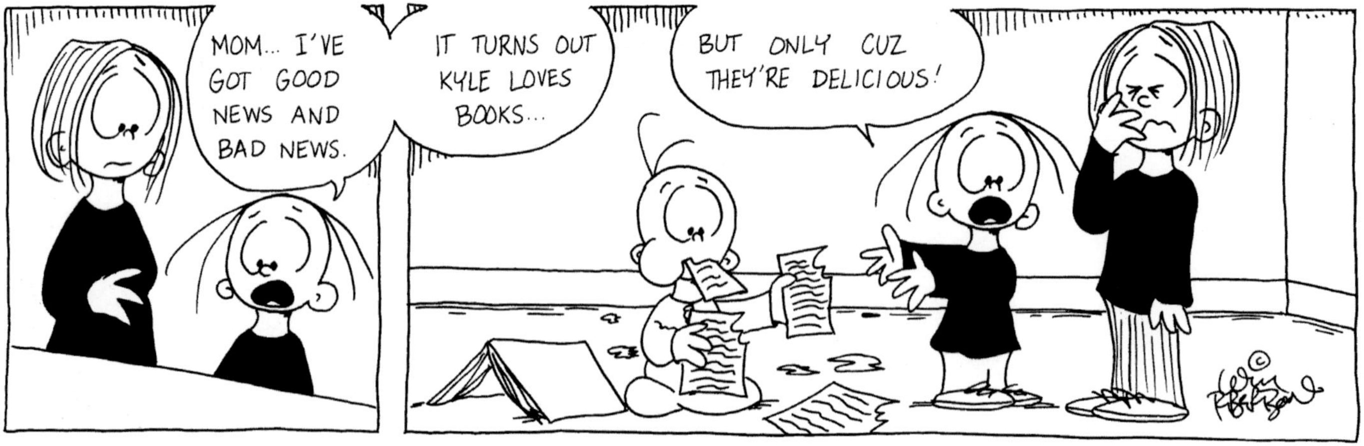
MOM... I'VE GOT GOOD NEWS AND BAD NEWS.
IT TURNS OUT KYLE LOVES BOOKS...
BUT ONLY CUZ THEY'RE DELICIOUS!

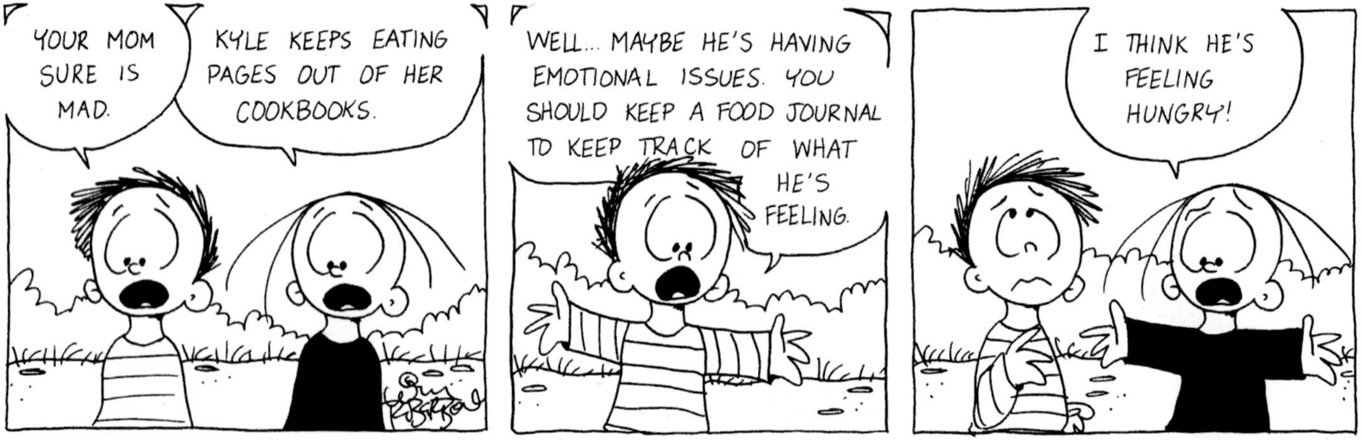
YOUR MOM SURE IS MAD.
KYLE KEEPS EATING PAGES OUT OF HER COOKBOOKS.
WELL... MAYBE HE'S HAVING EMOTIONAL ISSUES. YOU SHOULD KEEP A FOOD JOURNAL TO KEEP TRACK OF WHAT HE'S FEELING.
I THINK HE'S FEELING HUNGRY!

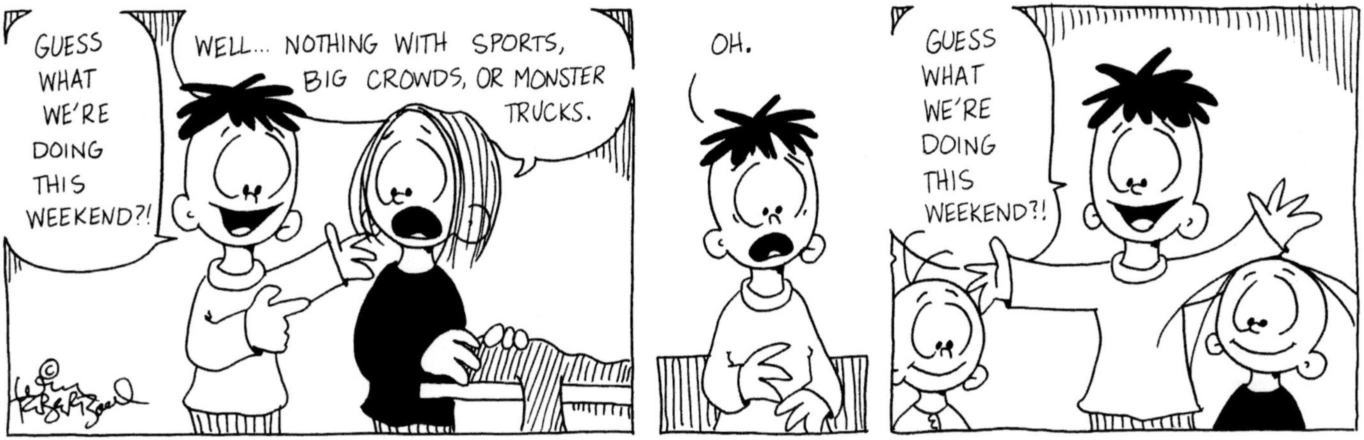
GUESS WHAT WE'RE DOING THIS WEEKEND?!
WELL... NOTHING WITH SPORTS, BIG CROWDS, OR MONSTER TRUCKS.
OH.
GUESS WHAT WE'RE DOING THIS WEEKEND?!

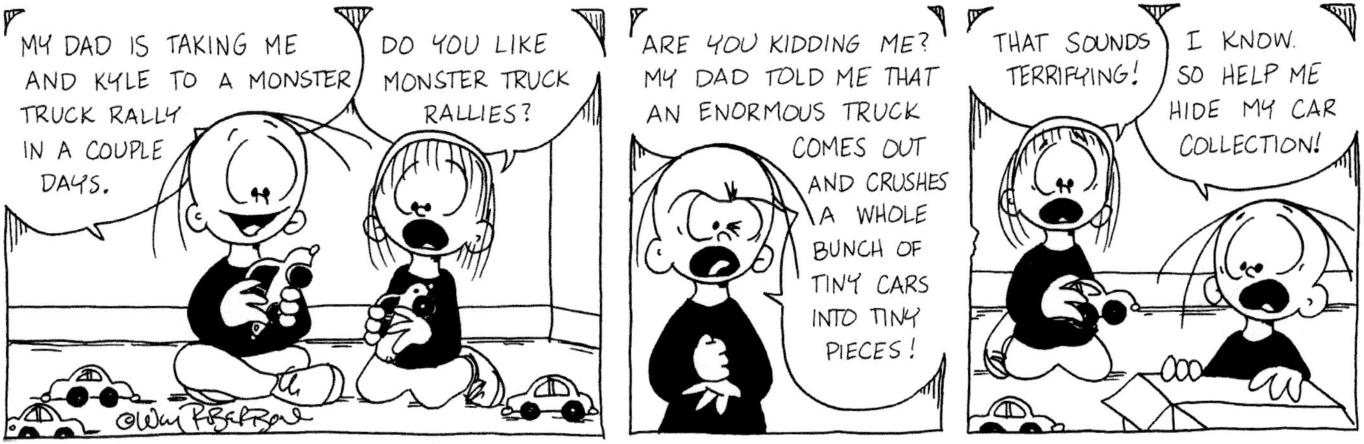
MY DAD IS TAKING ME AND KYLE TO A MONSTER TRUCK RALLY IN A COUPLE DAYS.
DO YOU LIKE MONSTER TRUCK RALLIES?
ARE YOU KIDDING ME? MY DAD TOLD ME THAT AN ENORMOUS TRUCK COMES OUT AND CRUSHES A WHOLE BUNCH OF TINY CARS INTO TINY PIECES!
THAT SOUNDS TERRIFYING!
I KNOW. SO HELP ME HIDE MY CAR COLLECTION!

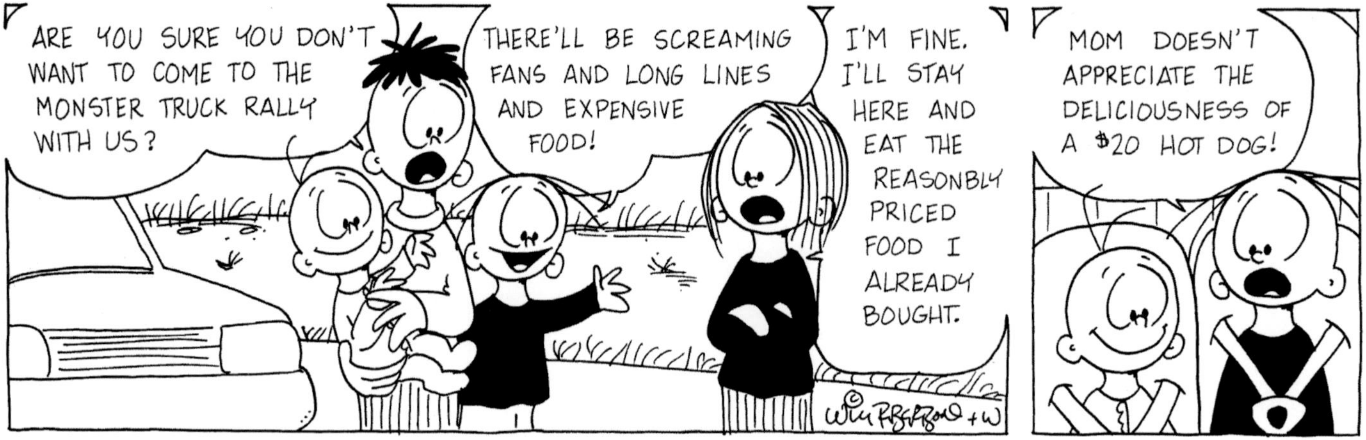
ARE YOU SURE YOU DON'T WANT TO COME TO THE MONSTER TRUCK RALLY WITH US?
THERE'LL BE SCREAMING FANS AND LONG LINES AND EXPENSIVE FOOD!
I'M FINE. I'LL STAY HERE AND EAT THE REASONBLY PRICED FOOD I ALREADY BOUGHT.
MOM DOESN'T APPRECIATE THE DELICIOUSNESS OF A $20 HOT DOG!

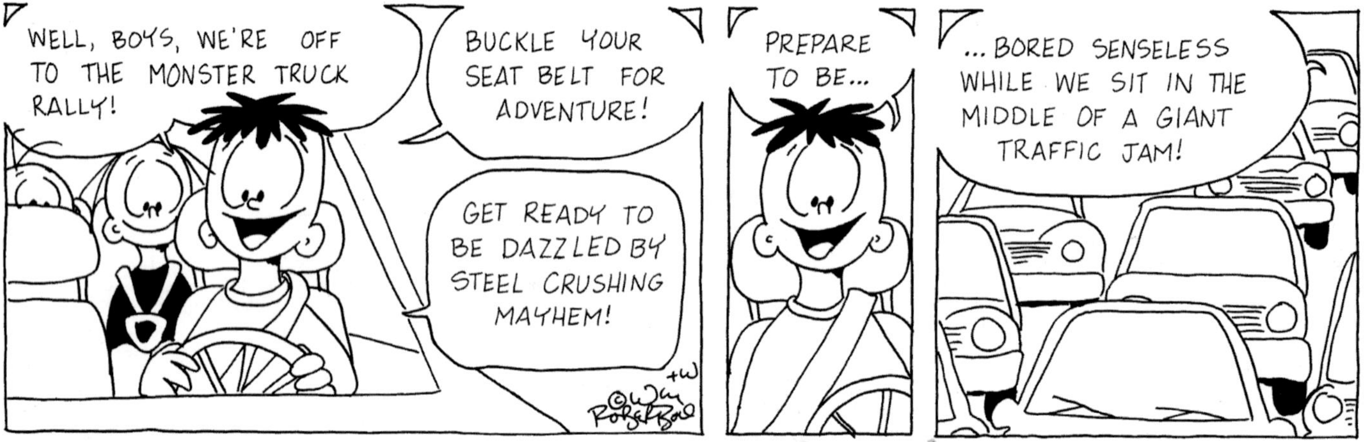
WELL, BOYS, WE'RE OFF TO THE MONSTER TRUCK RALLY!
BUCKLE YOUR SEAT BELT FOR ADVENTURE!
GET READY TO BE DAZZLED BY STEEL CRUSHING MAYHEM!
PREPARE TO BE...
...BORED SENSELESS WHILE WE SIT IN THE MIDDLE OF A GIANT TRAFFIC JAM!

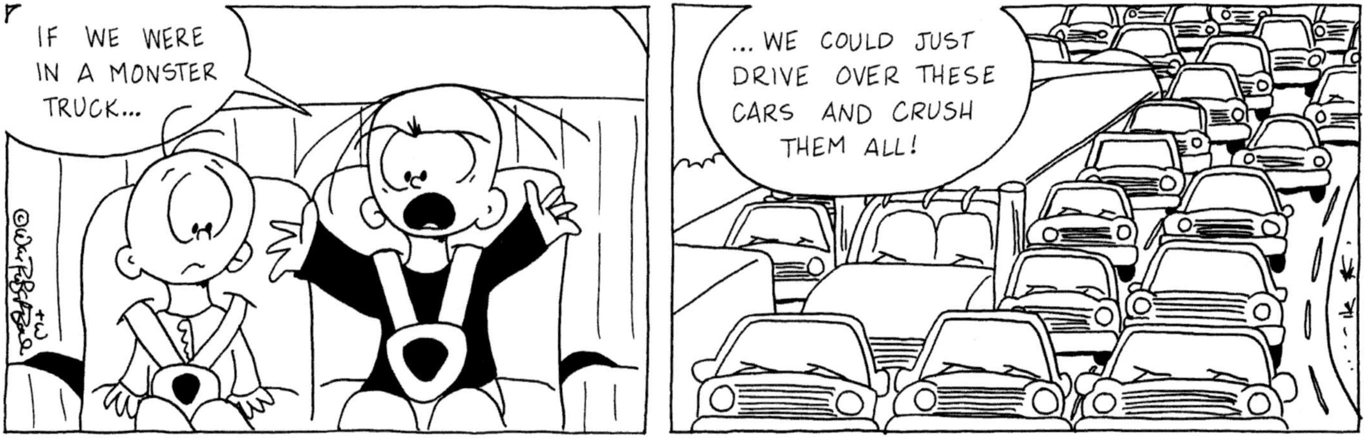
IF WE WERE IN A MONSTER TRUCK...
... WE COULD JUST DRIVE OVER THESE CARS AND CRUSH THEM ALL!

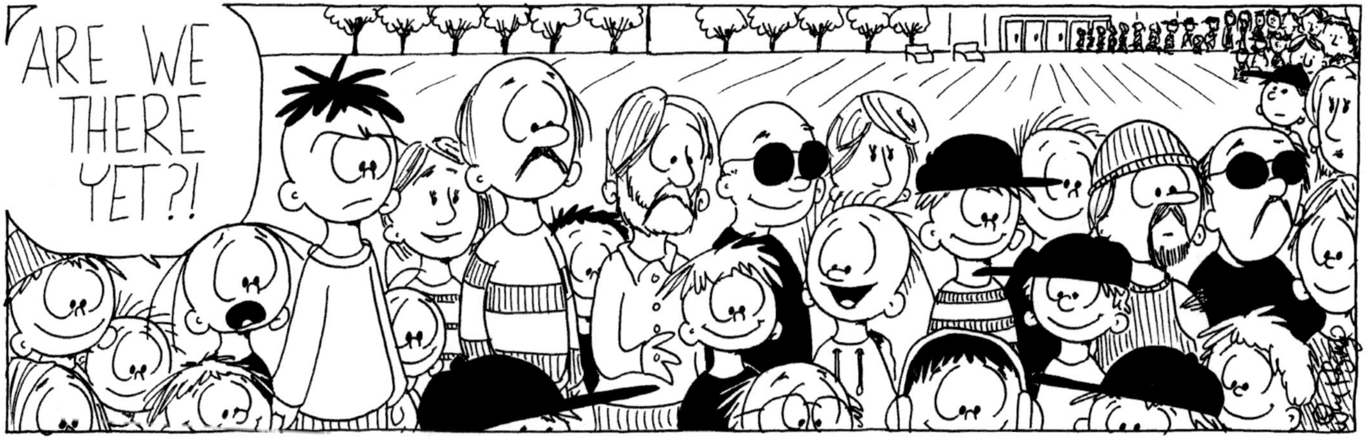
ARE WE THERE YET?!

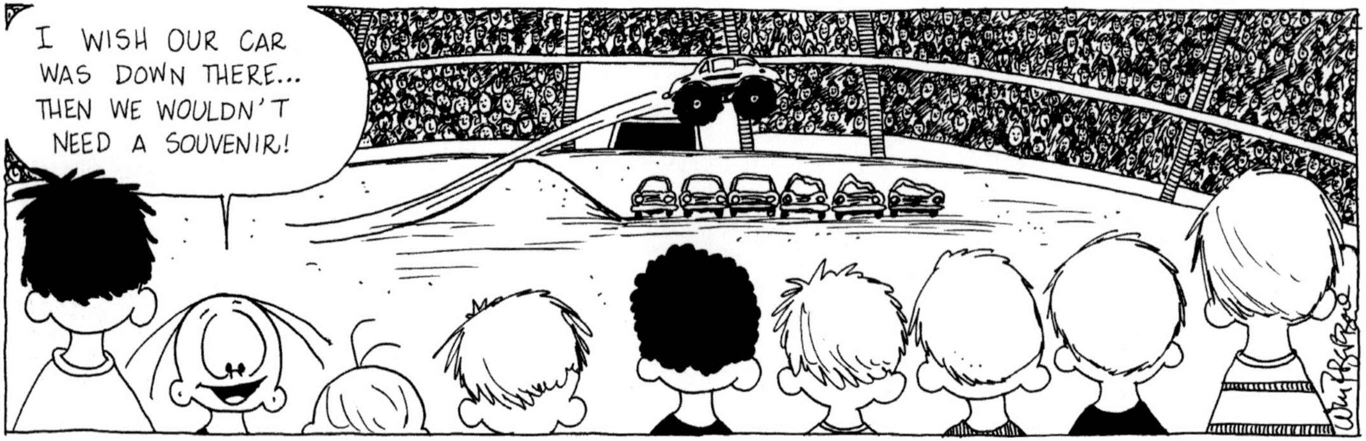
I WISH OUR CAR WAS DOWN THERE... THEN WE WOULDN'T NEED A SOUVENIR!

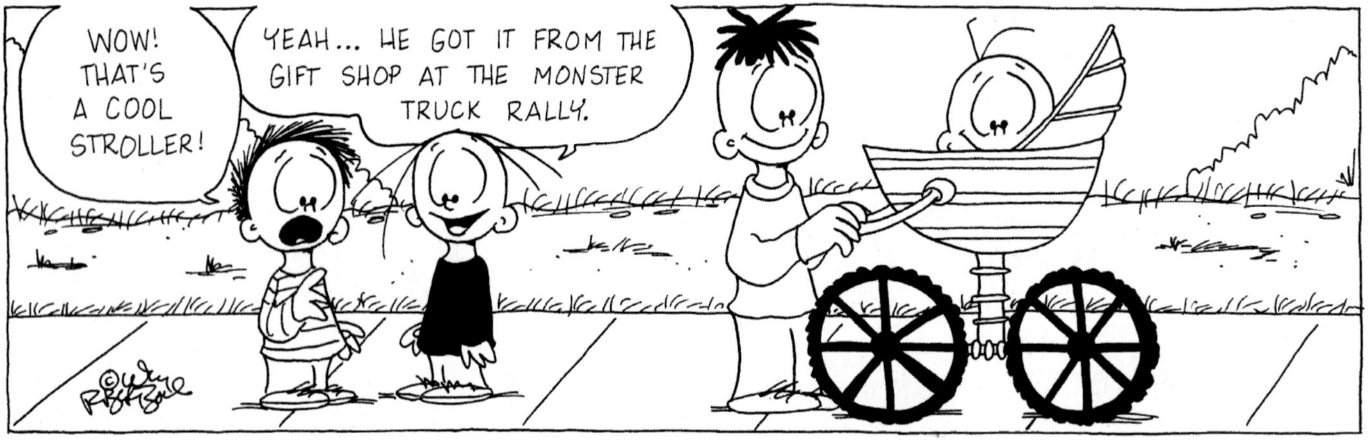
WOW! THAT'S A COOL STROLLER!
YEAH... HE GOT IT FROM THE GIFT SHOP AT THE MONSTER TRUCK RALLY.

CASEY AND KYLE™

by **Will Robertson**

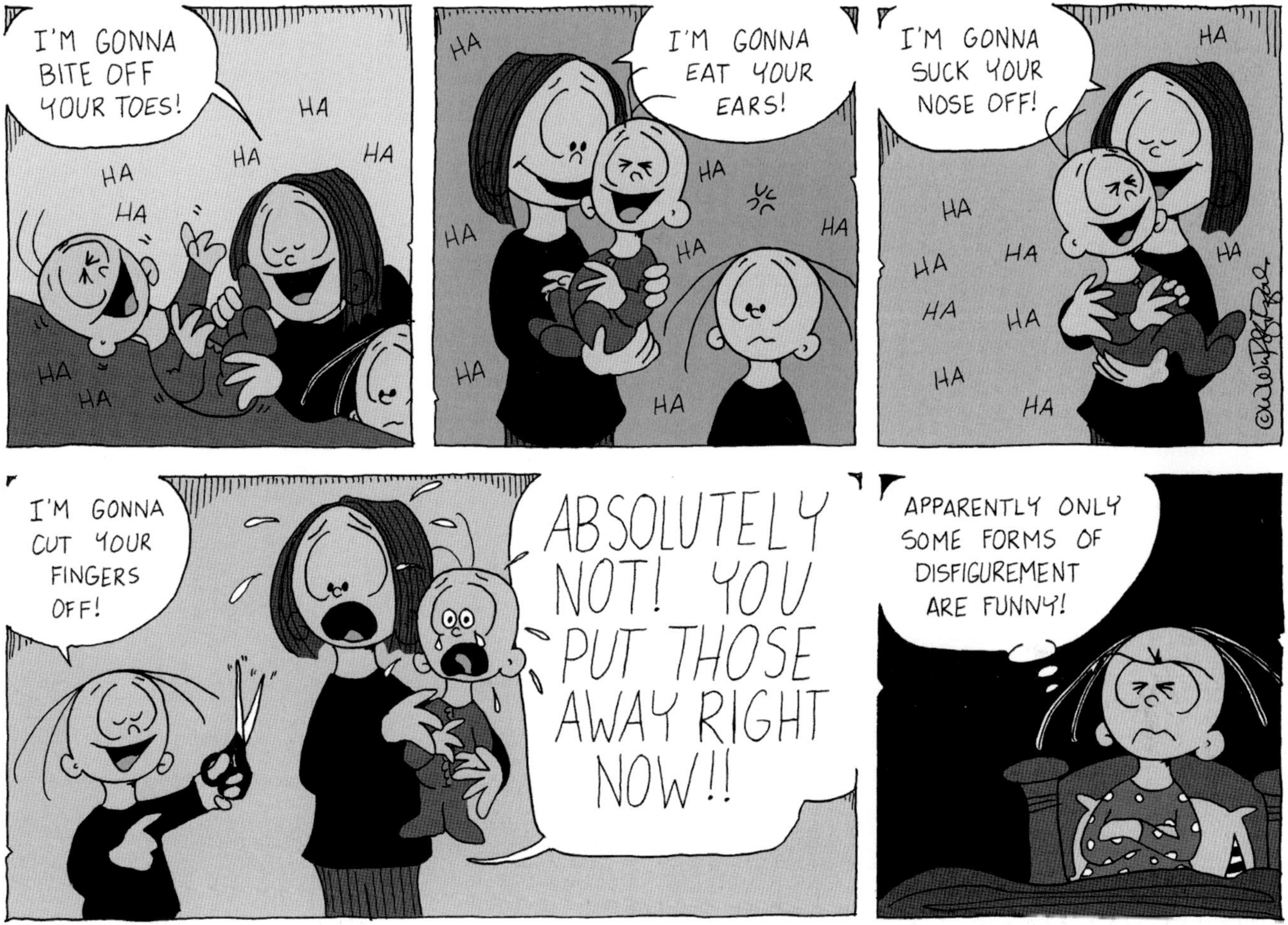

I'M GONNA BITE OFF YOUR TOES!
HA HA HA HA HA HA HA
I'M GONNA EAT YOUR EARS!
HA HA HA HA HA HA
I'M GONNA SUCK YOUR NOSE OFF!
HA HA HA HA HA HA HA HA HA
I'M GONNA CUT YOUR FINGERS OFF!
ABSOLUTELY NOT! YOU PUT THOSE AWAY RIGHT NOW!!
APPARENTLY ONLY SOME FORMS OF DISFIGUREMENT ARE FUNNY!

CASEY AND KYLE™

by Will Robertson

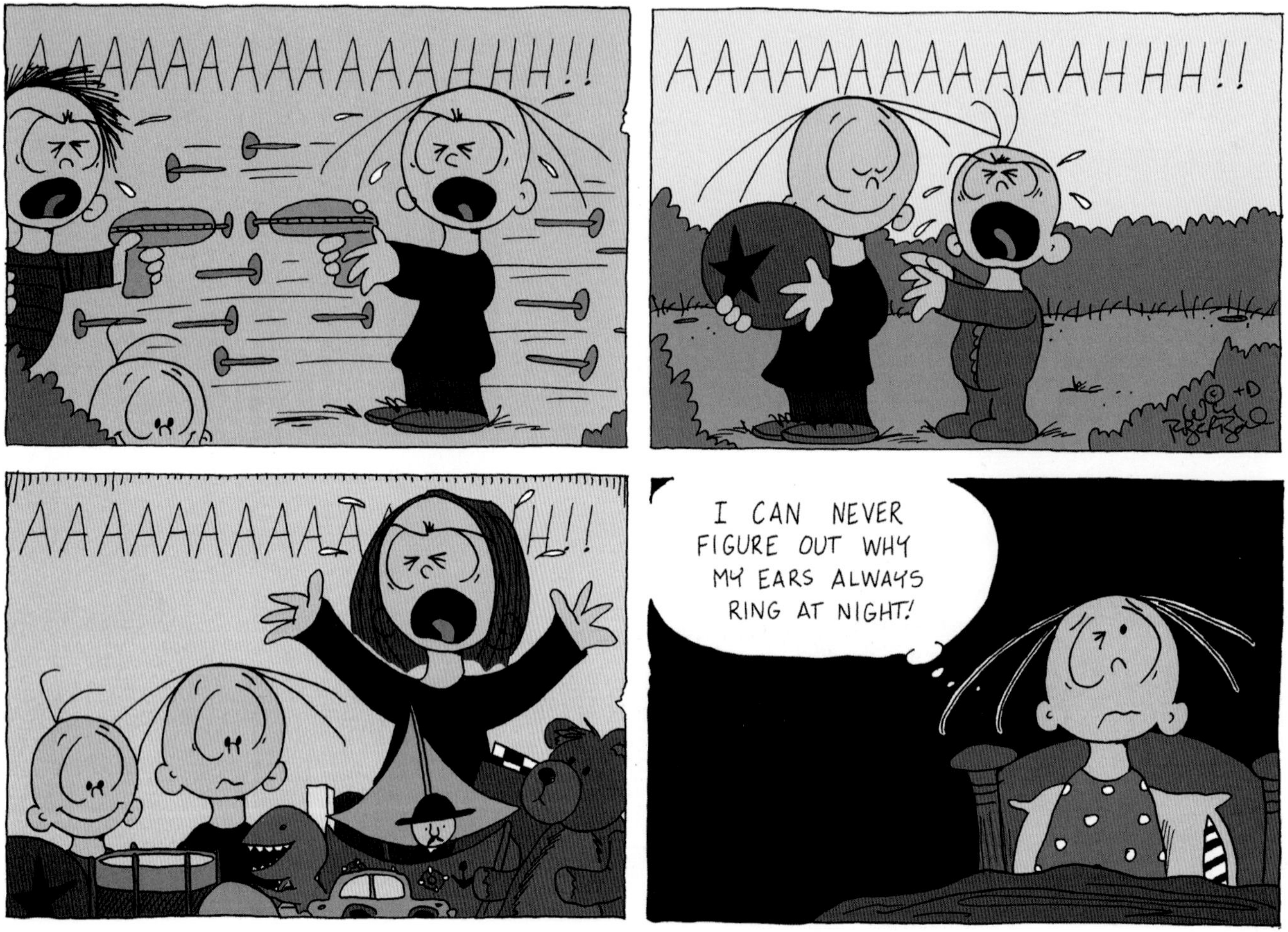

AAAAAAAAAAAAAHHH!!
AAAAAAAAAAAAAHHH!!
AAAAAAAAAA
H!!
I CAN NEVER FIGURE OUT WHY MY EARS ALWAYS RING AT NIGHT!

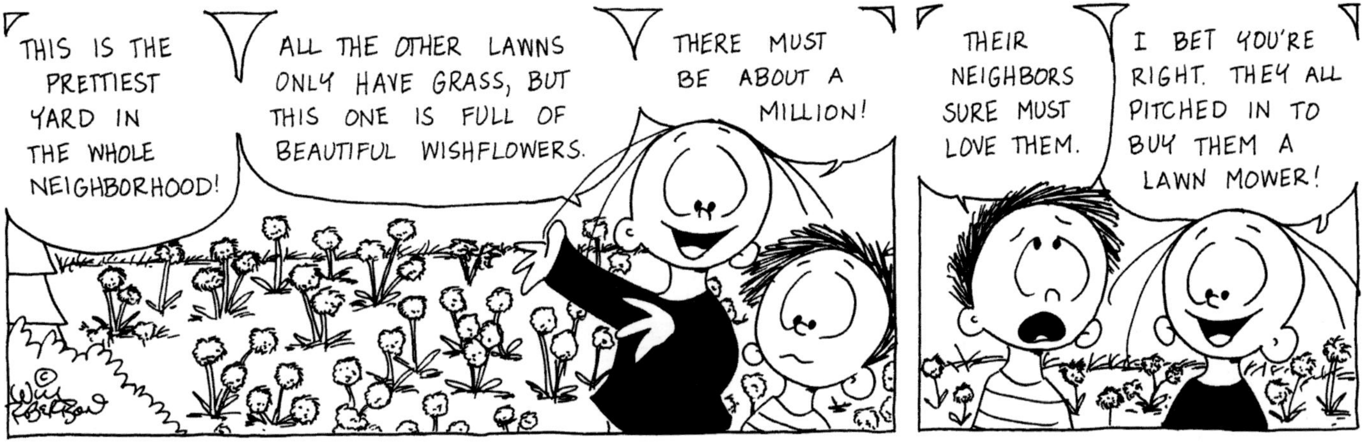
THIS IS THE PRETTIEST YARD IN THE WHOLE NEIGHBORHOOD!
ALL THE OTHER LAWNS ONLY HAVE GRASS, BUT THIS ONE IS FULL OF BEAUTIFUL WISHFLOWERS.
THERE MUST BE ABOUT A MILLION!
THEIR NEIGHBORS SURE MUST LOVE THEM.
I BET YOU'RE RIGHT. THEY ALL PITCHED IN TO BUY THEM A LAWN MOWER!

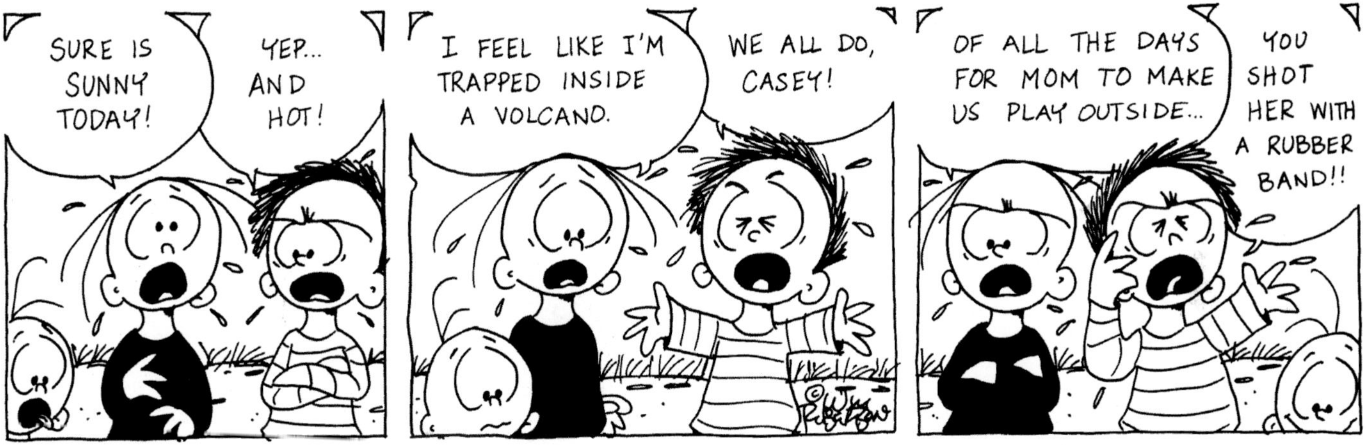
SURE IS SUNNY TODAY!
YEP... AND HOT!
I FEEL LIKE I'M TRAPPED INSIDE A VOLCANO.
WE ALL DO, CASEY!
OF ALL THE DAYS FOR MOM TO MAKE US PLAY OUTSIDE...
YOU SHOT HER WITH A RUBBER BAND!!

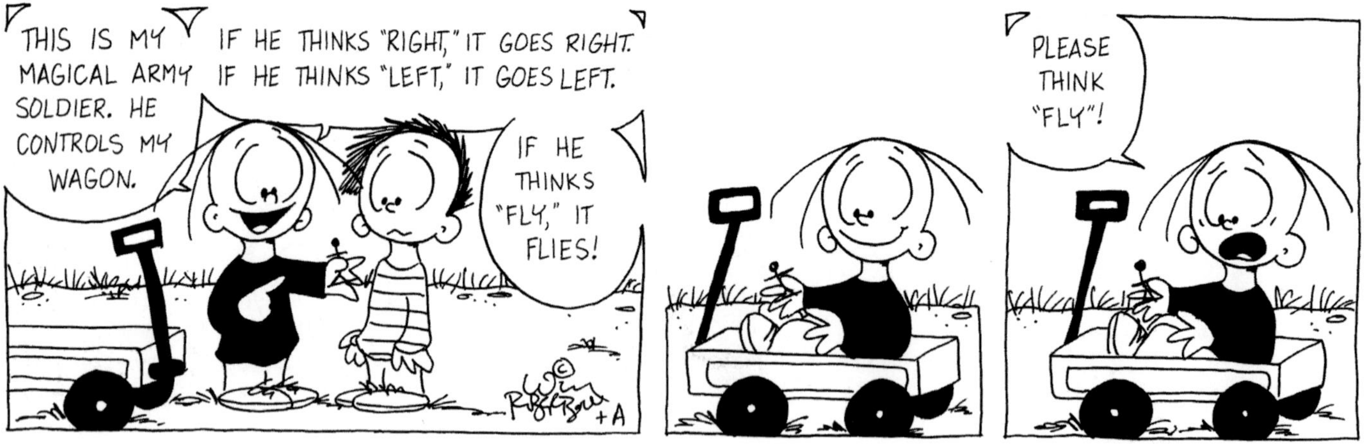
THIS IS MY MAGICAL ARMY SOLDIER. HE CONTROLS MY WAGON.
IF HE THINKS "RIGHT," IT GOES RIGHT. IF HE THINKS "LEFT," IT GOES LEFT.
IF HE THINKS "FLY," IT FLIES!
PLEASE THINK "FLY"!

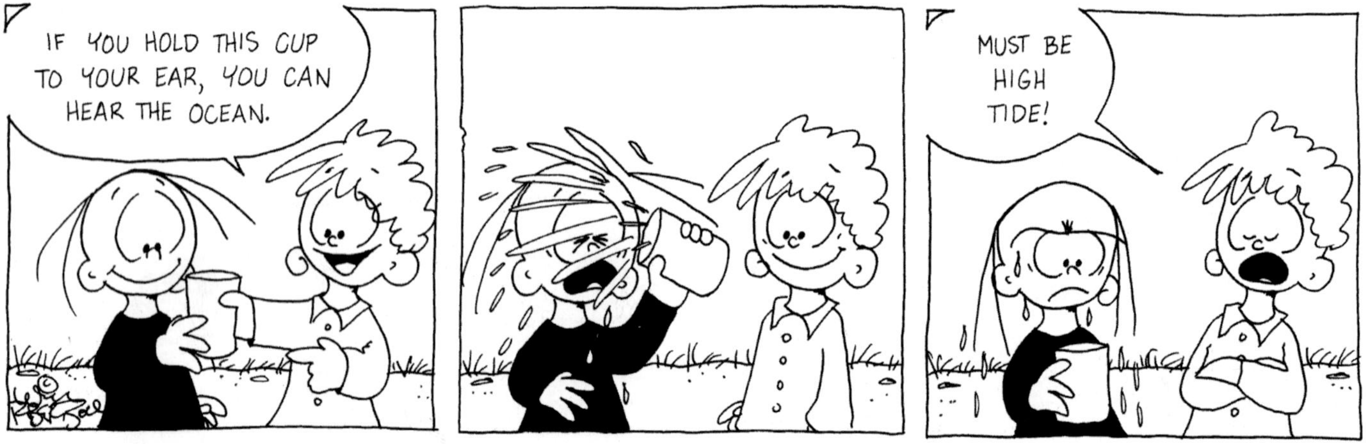
IF YOU HOLD THIS CUP TO YOUR EAR, YOU CAN HEAR THE OCEAN.
MUST BE HIGH TIDE!

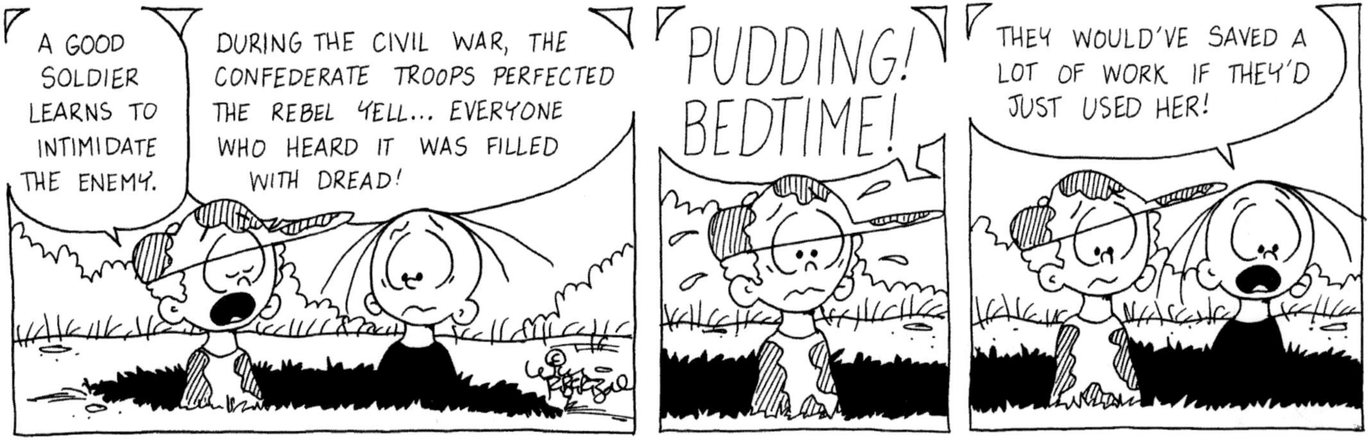
A GOOD SOLDIER LEARNS TO INTIMIDATE THE ENEMY.
DURING THE CIVIL WAR, THE CONFEDERATE TROOPS PERFECTED THE REBEL YELL... EVERYONE WHO HEARD IT WAS FILLED WITH DREAD!
PUDDING! BEDTIME!
THEY WOULD'VE SAVED A LOT OF WORK IF THEY'D JUST USED HER!

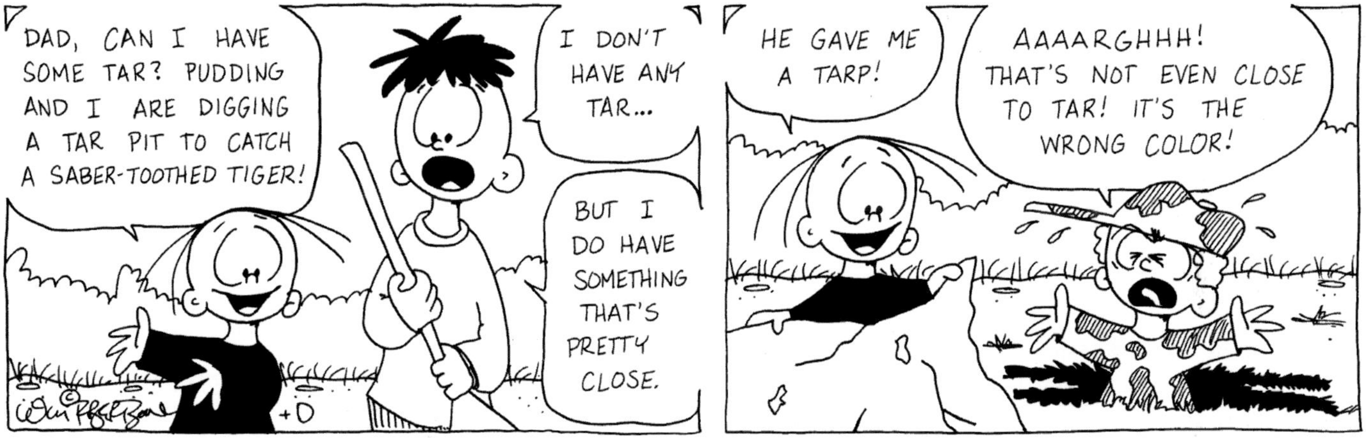
DAD, CAN I HAVE SOME TAR? PUDDING AND I ARE DIGGING A TAR PIT TO CATCH A SABER-TOOTHED TIGER!
I DON'T HAVE ANY TAR...
BUT I DO HAVE SOMETHING THAT'S PRETTY CLOSE.
HE GAVE ME A TARP!
AAAARGHHH! THAT'S NOT EVEN CLOSE TO TAR! IT'S THE WRONG COLOR!

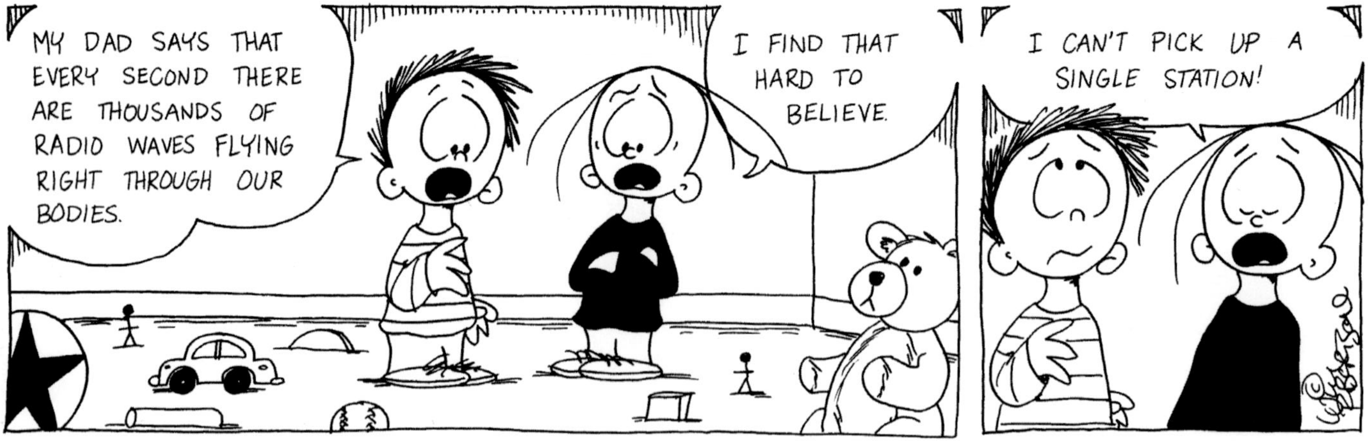
MY DAD SAYS THAT EVERY SECOND THERE ARE THOUSANDS OF RADIO WAVES FLYING RIGHT THROUGH OUR BODIES.
I FIND THAT HARD TO BELIEVE.
I CAN'T PICK UP A SINGLE STATION!

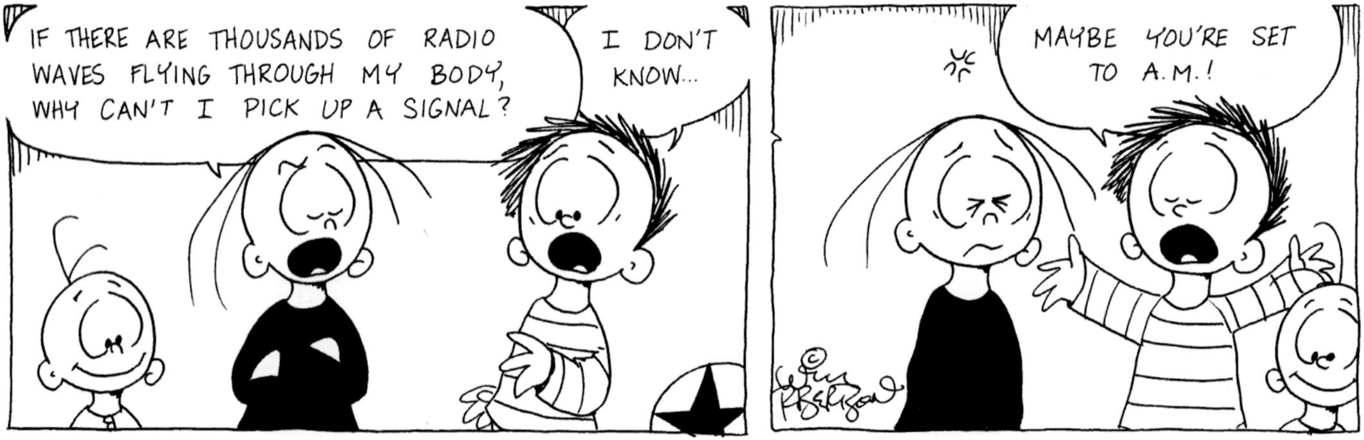
IF THERE ARE THOUSANDS OF RADIO WAVES FLYING THROUGH MY BODY, WHY CAN'T I PICK UP A SIGNAL?
I DON'T KNOW...
MAYBE YOU'RE SET TO A.M.!

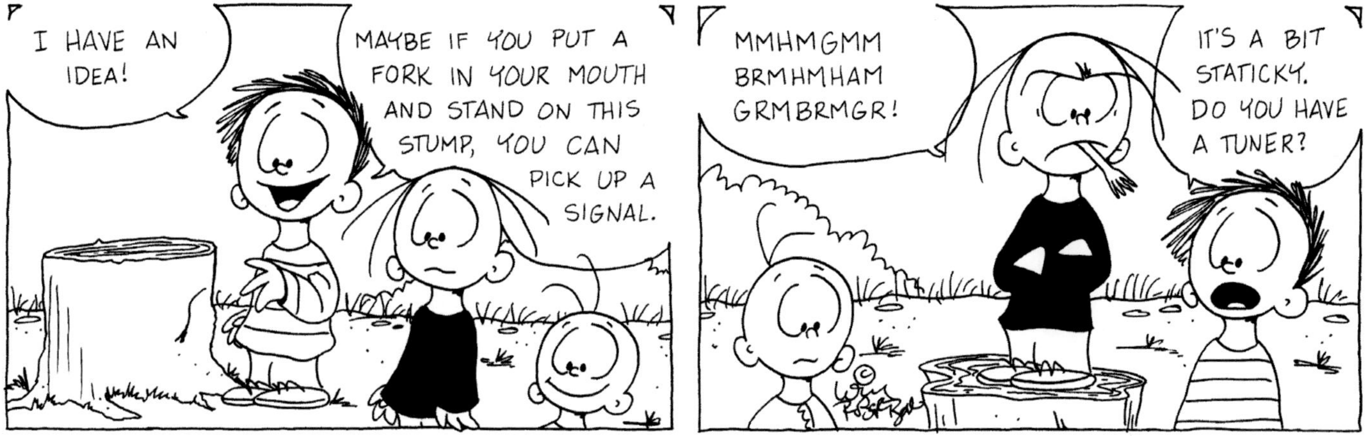
I HAVE AN IDEA!
MAYBE IF YOU PUT A FORK IN YOUR MOUTH AND STAND ON THIS STUMP, YOU CAN PICK UP A SIGNAL.
MMHMGMM BRMHMHAM GRMBRMGR!
IT'S A BIT STATICKY. DO YOU HAVE A TUNER?

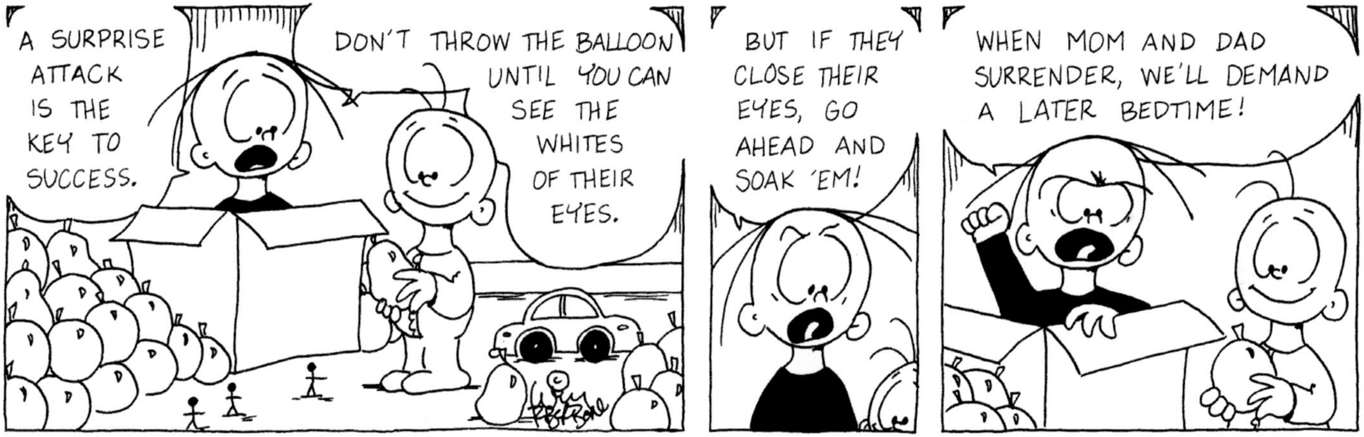
A SURPRISE ATTACK IS THE KEY TO SUCCESS.
DON'T THROW THE BALLOON UNTIL YOU CAN SEE THE WHITES OF THEIR EYES.
BUT IF THEY CLOSE THEIR EYES, GO AHEAD AND SOAK 'EM!
WHEN MOM AND DAD SURRENDER, WE'LL DEMAND A LATER BEDTIME!

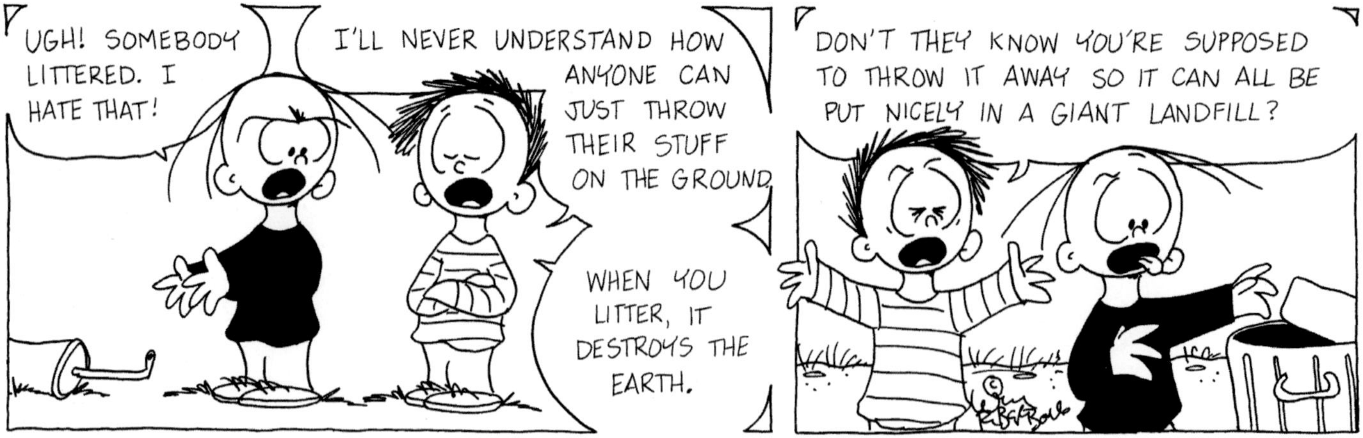
UGH! SOMEBODY LITTERED. I HATE THAT!
I'LL NEVER UNDERSTAND HOW ANYONE CAN JUST THROW THEIR STUFF ON THE GROUND.
WHEN YOU LITTER, IT DESTROYS THE EARTH.
DON'T THEY KNOW YOU'RE SUPPOSED TO THROW IT AWAY SO IT CAN ALL BE PUT NICELY IN A GIANT LANDFILL?

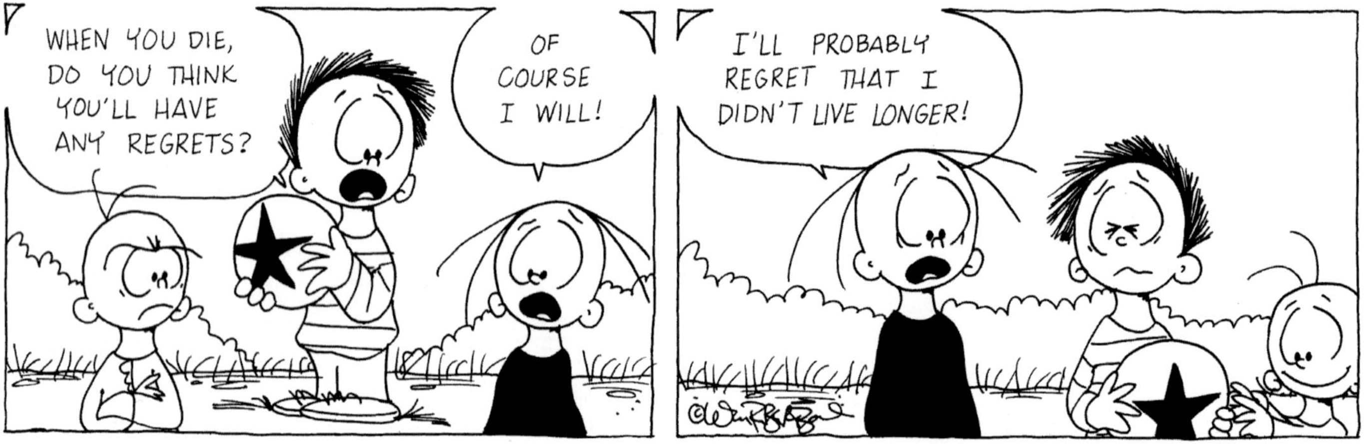
WHEN YOU DIE, DO YOU THINK YOU'LL HAVE ANY REGRETS?
OF COURSE I WILL!
I'LL PROBABLY REGRET THAT I DIDN'T LIVE LONGER!

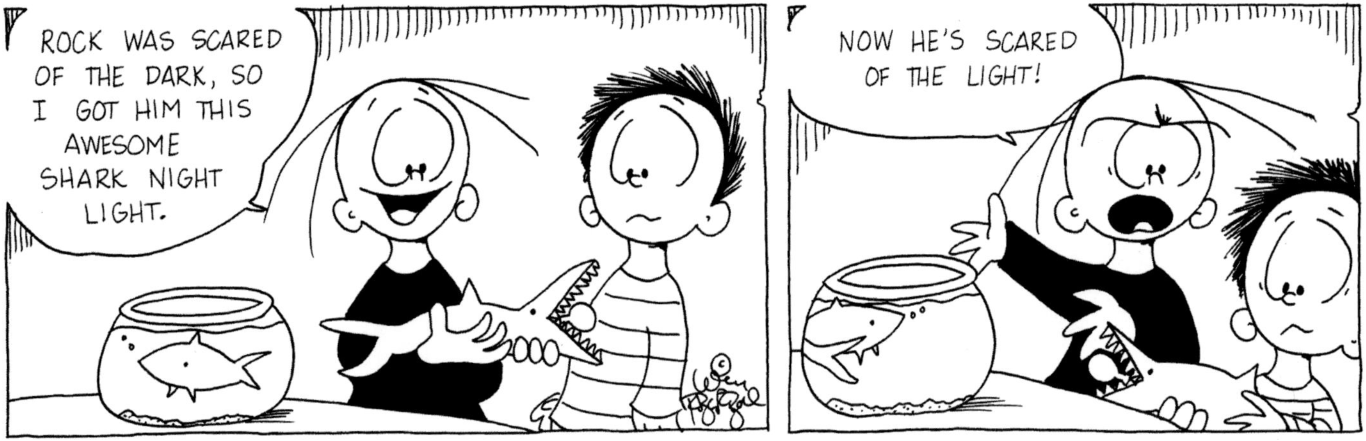
ROCK WAS SCARED OF THE DARK, SO I GOT HIM THIS AWESOME SHARK NIGHT LIGHT.
NOW HE'S SCARED OF THE LIGHT!

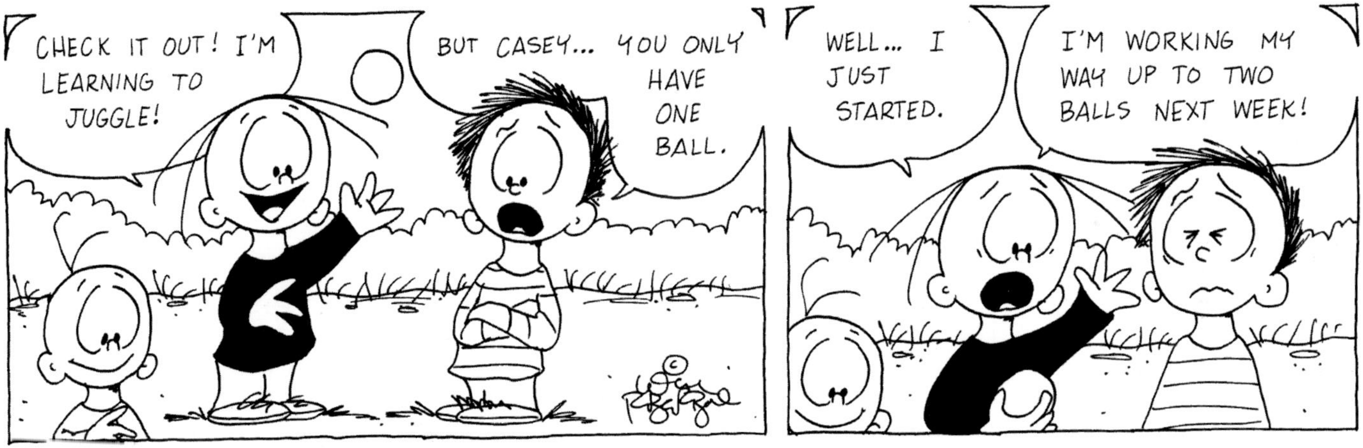
CHECK IT OUT! I'M LEARNING TO JUGGLE!
BUT CASEY... YOU ONLY HAVE ONE BALL.
WELL... I JUST STARTED.
I'M WORKING MY WAY UP TO TWO BALLS NEXT WEEK!

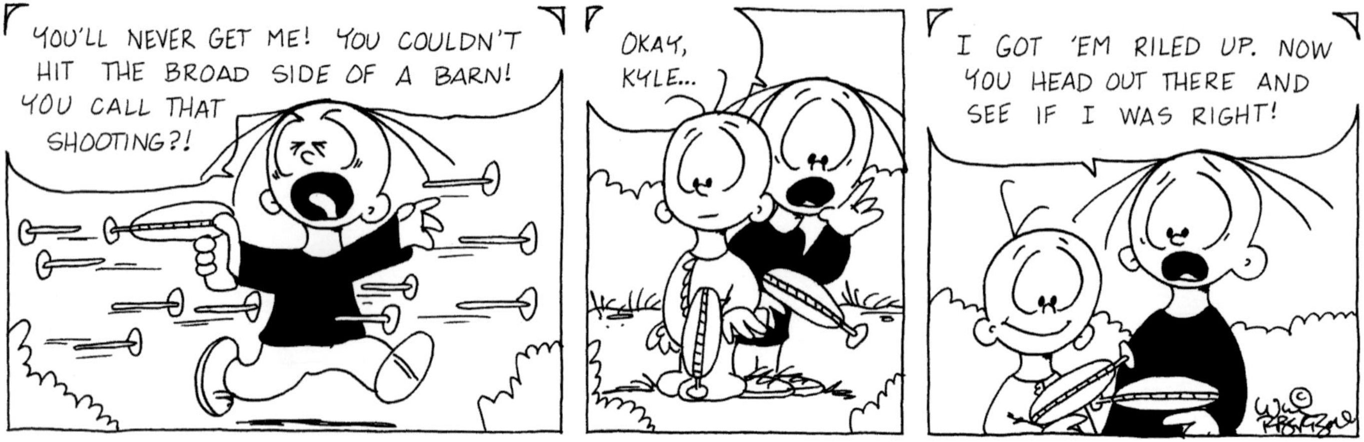
YOU'LL NEVER GET ME! YOU COULDN'T HIT THE BROAD SIDE OF A BARN! YOU CALL THAT SHOOTING?!
OKAY, KYLE...
I GOT 'EM RILED UP. NOW YOU HEAD OUT THERE AND SEE IF I WAS RIGHT!

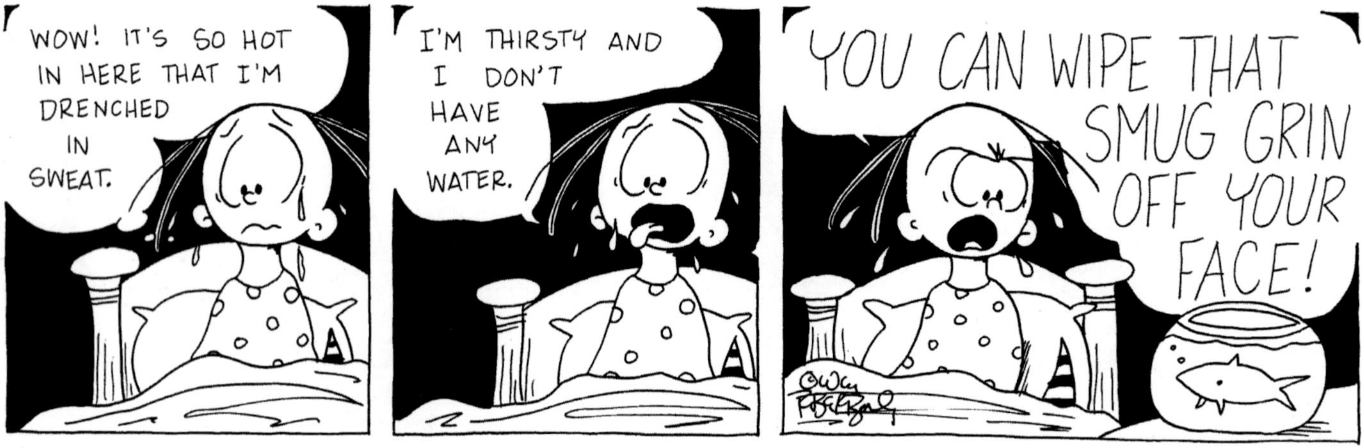
WOW! IT'S SO HOT IN HERE THAT I'M DRENCHED IN SWEAT.
I'M THIRSTY AND I DON'T HAVE ANY WATER.
YOU CAN WIPE THAT SMUG GRIN OFF YOUR FACE!

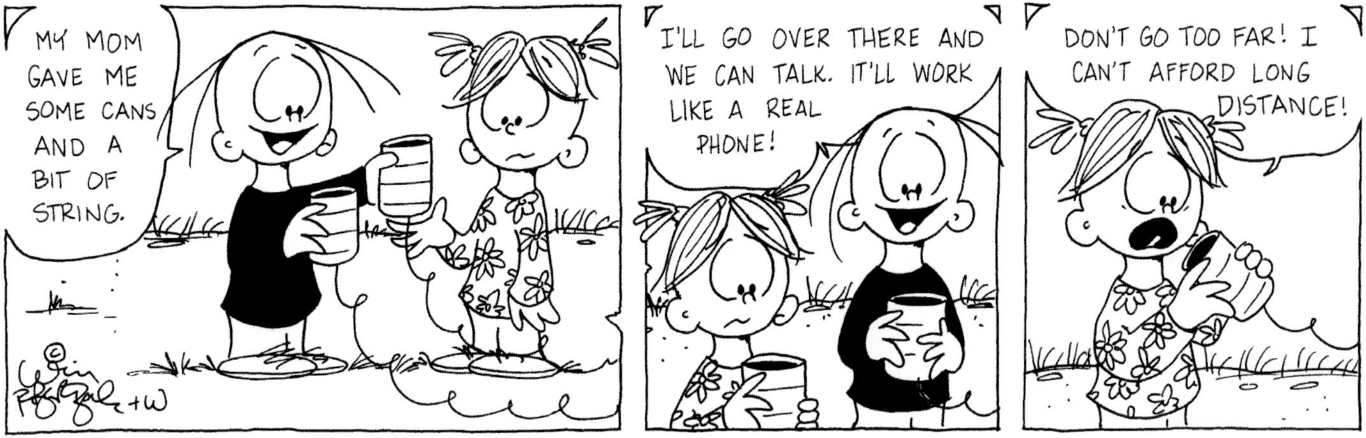
MY MOM GAVE ME SOME CANS AND A BIT OF STRING.
I'LL GO OVER THERE AND WE CAN TALK. IT'LL WORK LIKE A REAL PHONE!
DON'T GO TOO FAR! I CAN'T AFFORD LONG DISTANCE!

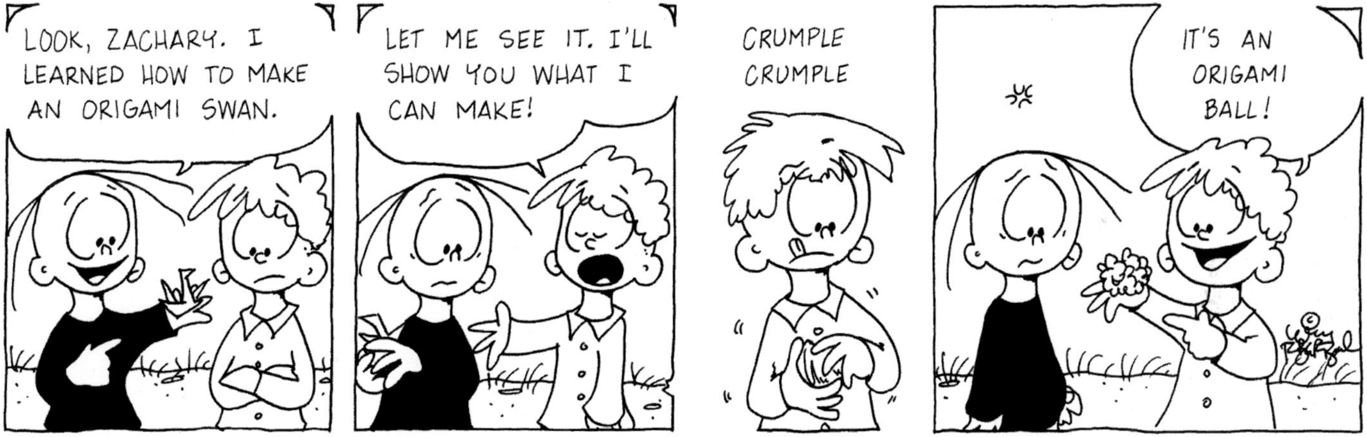
LOOK, ZACHARY. I LEARNED HOW TO MAKE AN ORIGAMI SWAN.
LET ME SEE IT. I'LL SHOW YOU WHAT I CAN MAKE!
CRUMPLE CRUMPLE
IT'S AN ORIGAMI BALL!

CASEY AND KYLE™

by **Will Robertson**

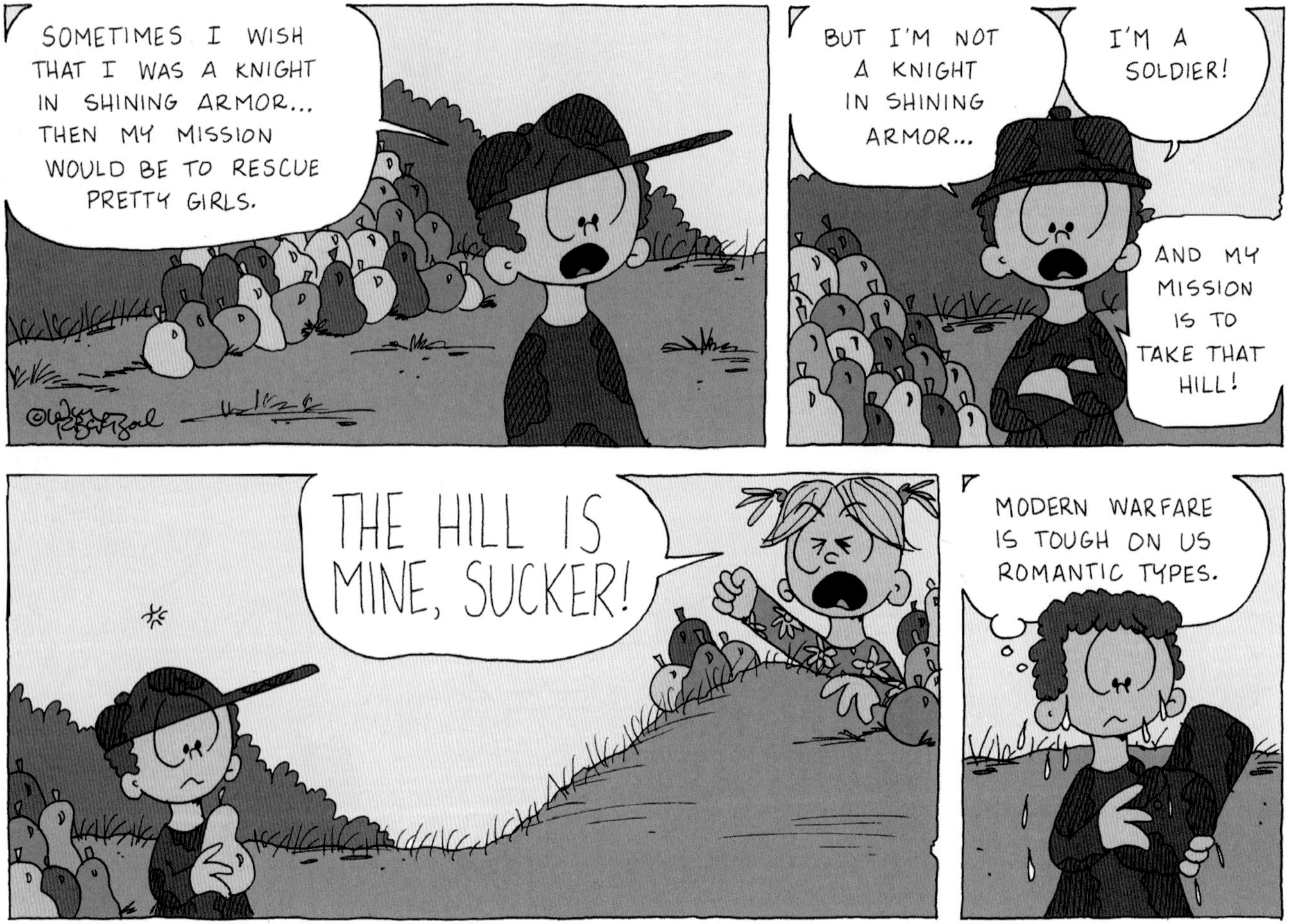
SOMETIMES I WISH THAT I WAS A KNIGHT IN SHINING ARMOR... THEN MY MISSION WOULD BE TO RESCUE PRETTY GIRLS.
BUT I'M NOT A KNIGHT IN SHINING ARMOR...
I'M A SOLDIER!
AND MY MISSION IS TO TAKE THAT HILL!
THE HILL IS MINE, SUCKER!
MODERN WARFARE IS TOUGH ON US ROMANTIC TYPES.

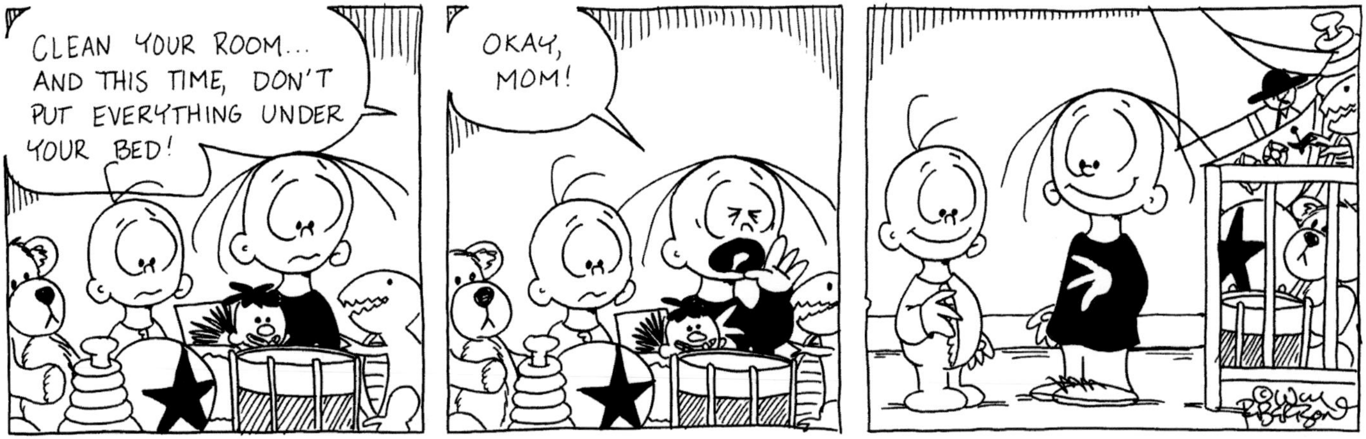
CLEAN YOUR ROOM... AND THIS TIME, DON'T PUT EVERYTHING UNDER YOUR BED!
OKAY, MOM!

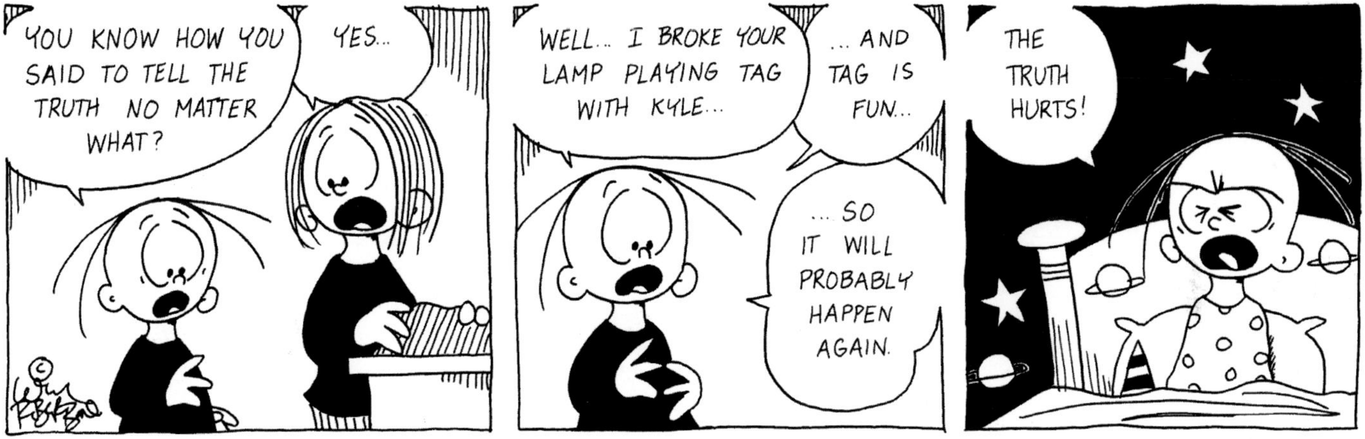
YOU KNOW HOW YOU SAID TO TELL THE TRUTH NO MATTER WHAT?
YES...
WELL... I BROKE YOUR LAMP PLAYING TAG WITH KYLE...
...AND TAG IS FUN...
...SO IT WILL PROBABLY HAPPEN AGAIN.
THE TRUTH HURTS!

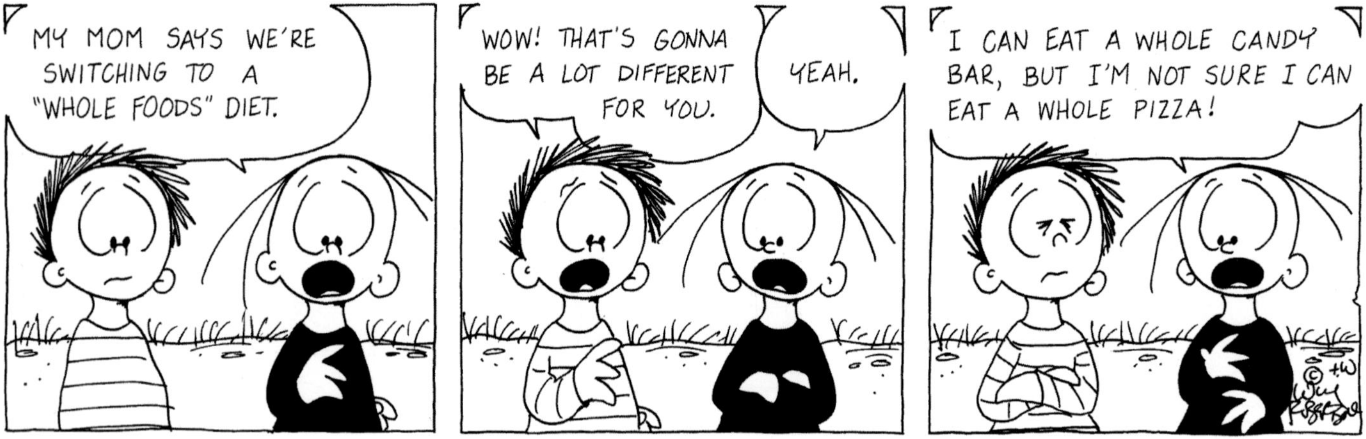
MY MOM SAYS WE'RE SWITCHING TO A "WHOLE FOODS" DIET.
WOW! THAT'S GONNA BE A LOT DIFFERENT FOR YOU.
YEAH.
I CAN EAT A WHOLE CANDY BAR, BUT I'M NOT SURE I CAN EAT A WHOLE PIZZA!

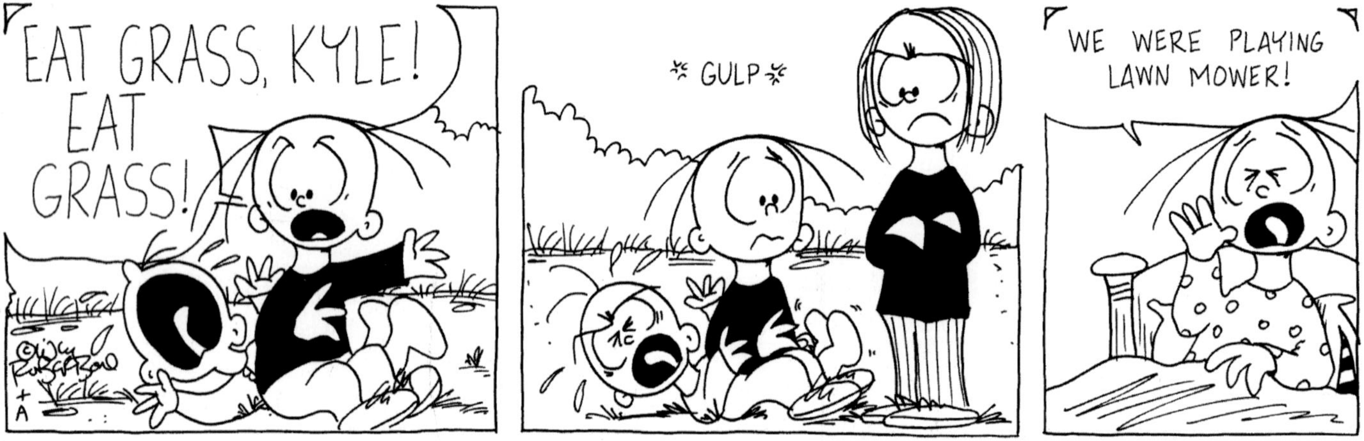
EAT GRASS, KYLE! EAT GRASS!
GULP
WE WERE PLAYING LAWN MOWER!

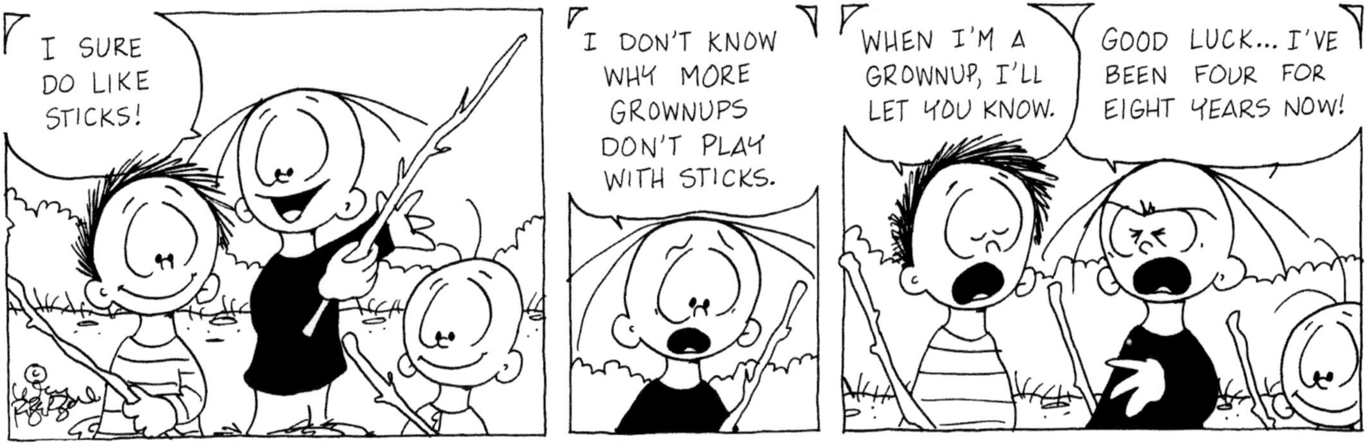
I SURE DO LIKE STICKS!
I DON'T KNOW WHY MORE GROWNUPS DON'T PLAY WITH STICKS.
WHEN I'M A GROWNUP, I'LL LET YOU KNOW.
GOOD LUCK... I'VE BEEN FOUR FOR EIGHT YEARS NOW!

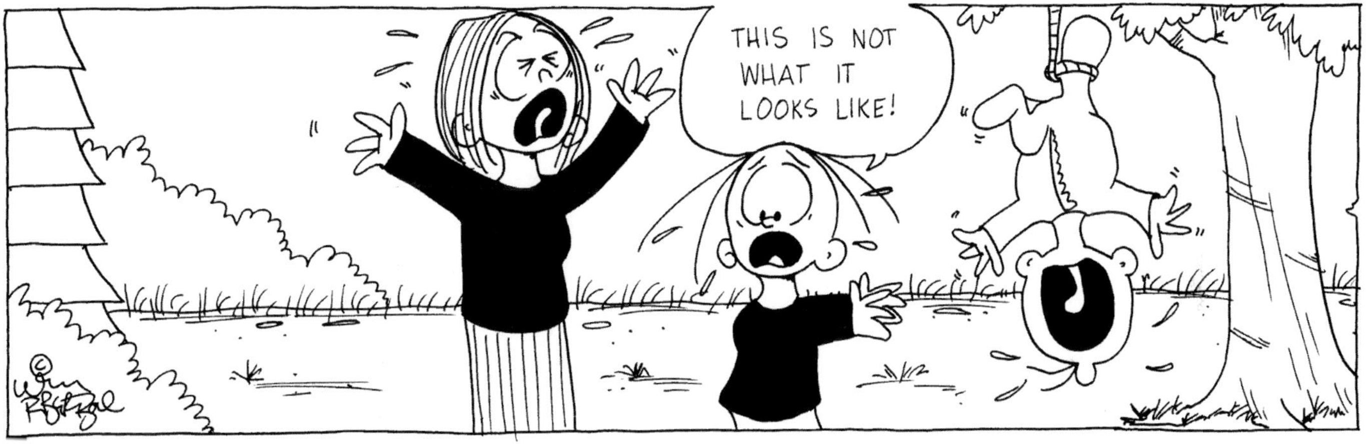
THIS IS NOT WHAT IT LOOKS LIKE!

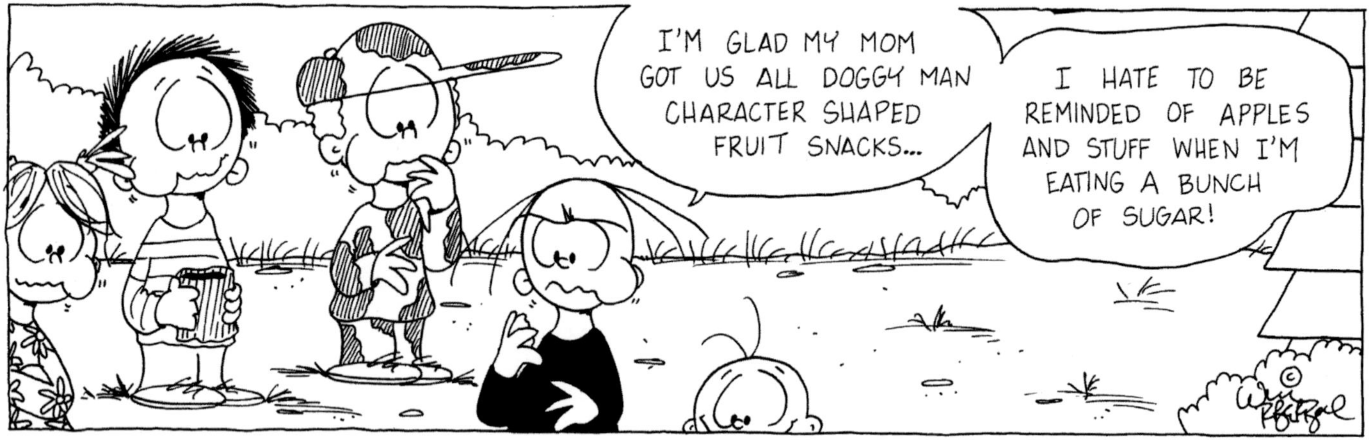
I'M GLAD MY MOM GOT US ALL DOGGY MAN CHARACTER SHAPED FRUIT SNACKS...
I HATE TO BE REMINDED OF APPLES AND STUFF WHEN I'M EATING A BUNCH OF SUGAR!

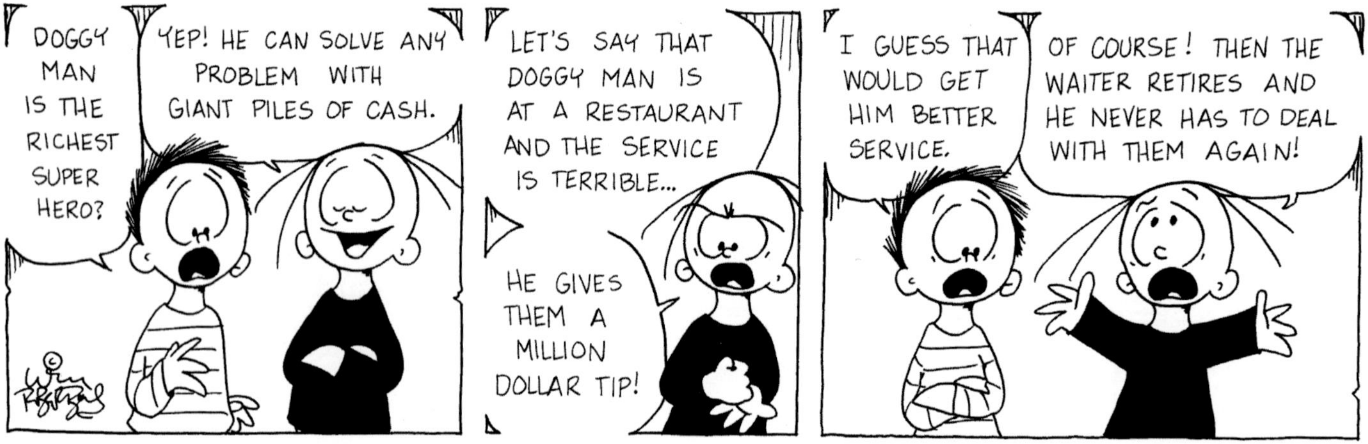
DOGGY MAN IS THE RICHEST SUPER HERO?
YEP! HE CAN SOLVE ANY PROBLEM WITH GIANT PILES OF CASH.
LET'S SAY THAT DOGGY MAN IS AT A RESTAURANT AND THE SERVICE IS TERRIBLE...
HE GIVES THEM A MILLION DOLLAR TIP!
I GUESS THAT WOULD GET HIM BETTER SERVICE.
OF COURSE! THEN THE WAITER RETIRES AND HE NEVER HAS TO DEAL WITH THEM AGAIN!

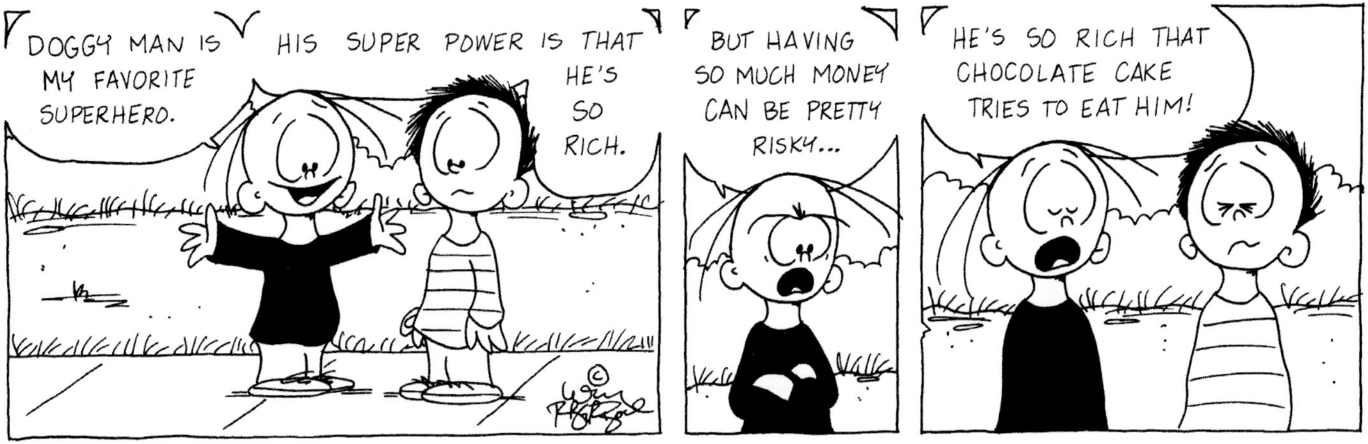
DOGGY MAN IS MY FAVORITE SUPERHERO.
HIS SUPER POWER IS THAT HE'S SO RICH.
BUT HAVING SO MUCH MONEY CAN BE PRETTY RISKY...
HE'S SO RICH THAT CHOCOLATE CAKE TRIES TO EAT HIM!

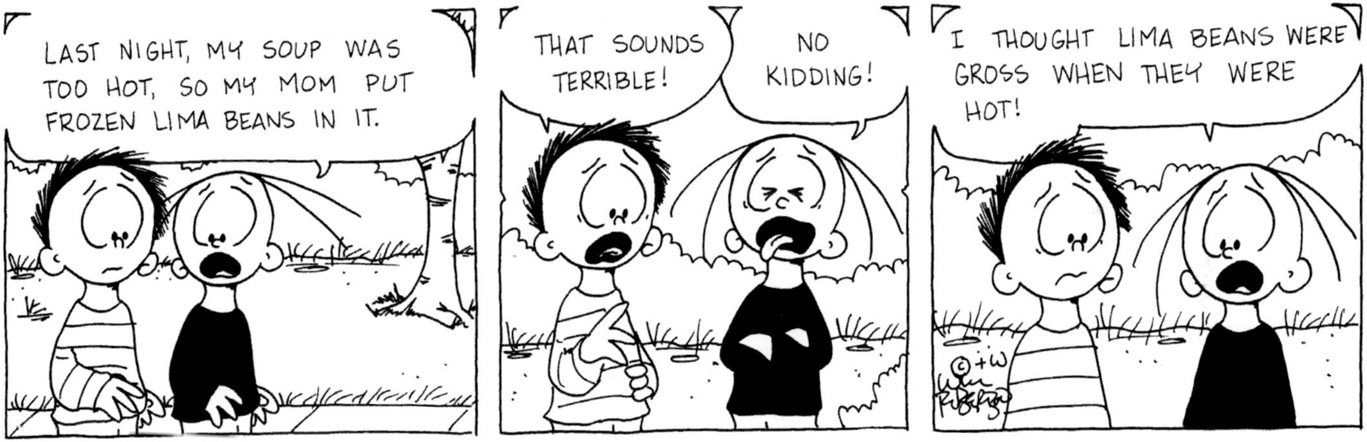
LAST NIGHT, MY SOUP WAS TOO HOT, SO MY MOM PUT FROZEN LIMA BEANS IN IT.
THAT SOUNDS TERRIBLE!
NO KIDDING!
I THOUGHT LIMA BEANS WERE GROSS WHEN THEY WERE HOT!

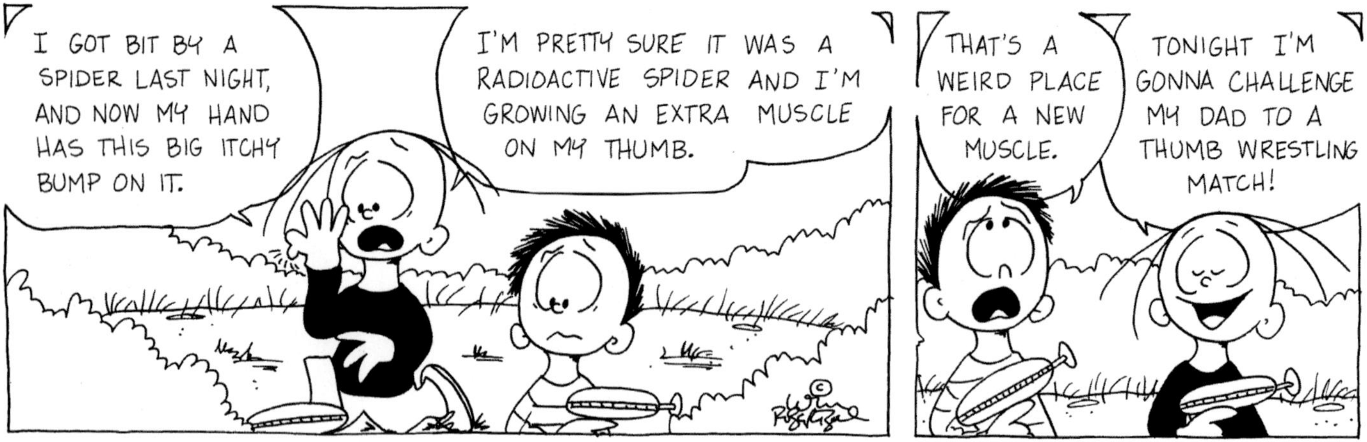
I GOT BIT BY A SPIDER LAST NIGHT, AND NOW MY HAND HAS THIS BIG ITCHY BUMP ON IT.
I'M PRETTY SURE IT WAS A RADIOACTIVE SPIDER AND I'M GROWING AN EXTRA MUSCLE ON MY THUMB.
THAT'S A WEIRD PLACE FOR A NEW MUSCLE.
TONIGHT I'M GONNA CHALLENGE MY DAD TO A THUMB WRESTLING MATCH!

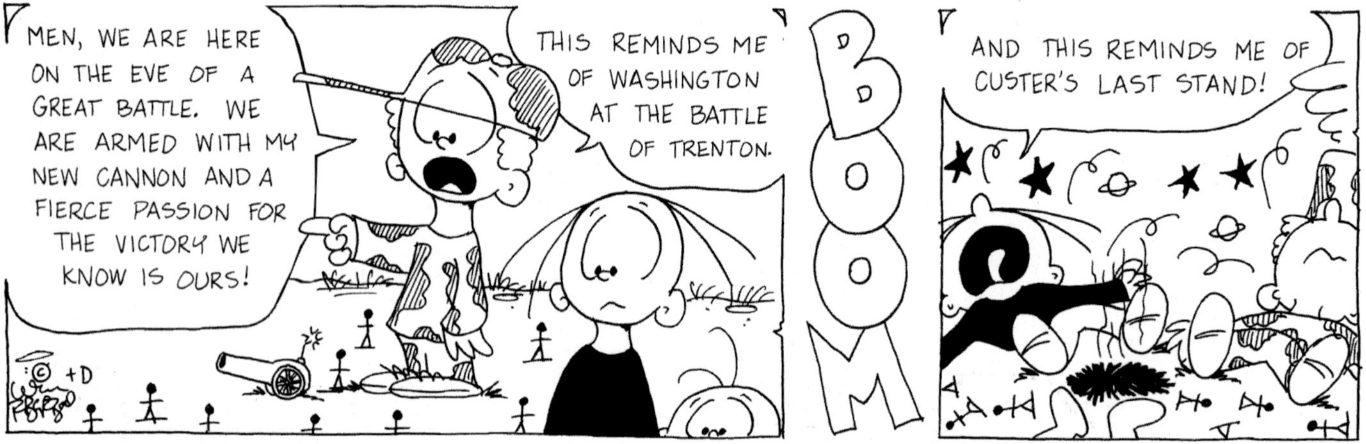
MEN, WE ARE HERE ON THE EVE OF A GREAT BATTLE. WE ARE ARMED WITH MY NEW CANNON AND A FIERCE PASSION FOR THE VICTORY WE KNOW IS OURS!
THIS REMINDS ME OF WASHINGTON AT THE BATTLE OF TRENTON.
BOOOM
AND THIS REMINDS ME OF CUSTER'S LAST STAND!

CASEY AND KYLE™ by Will Robertson

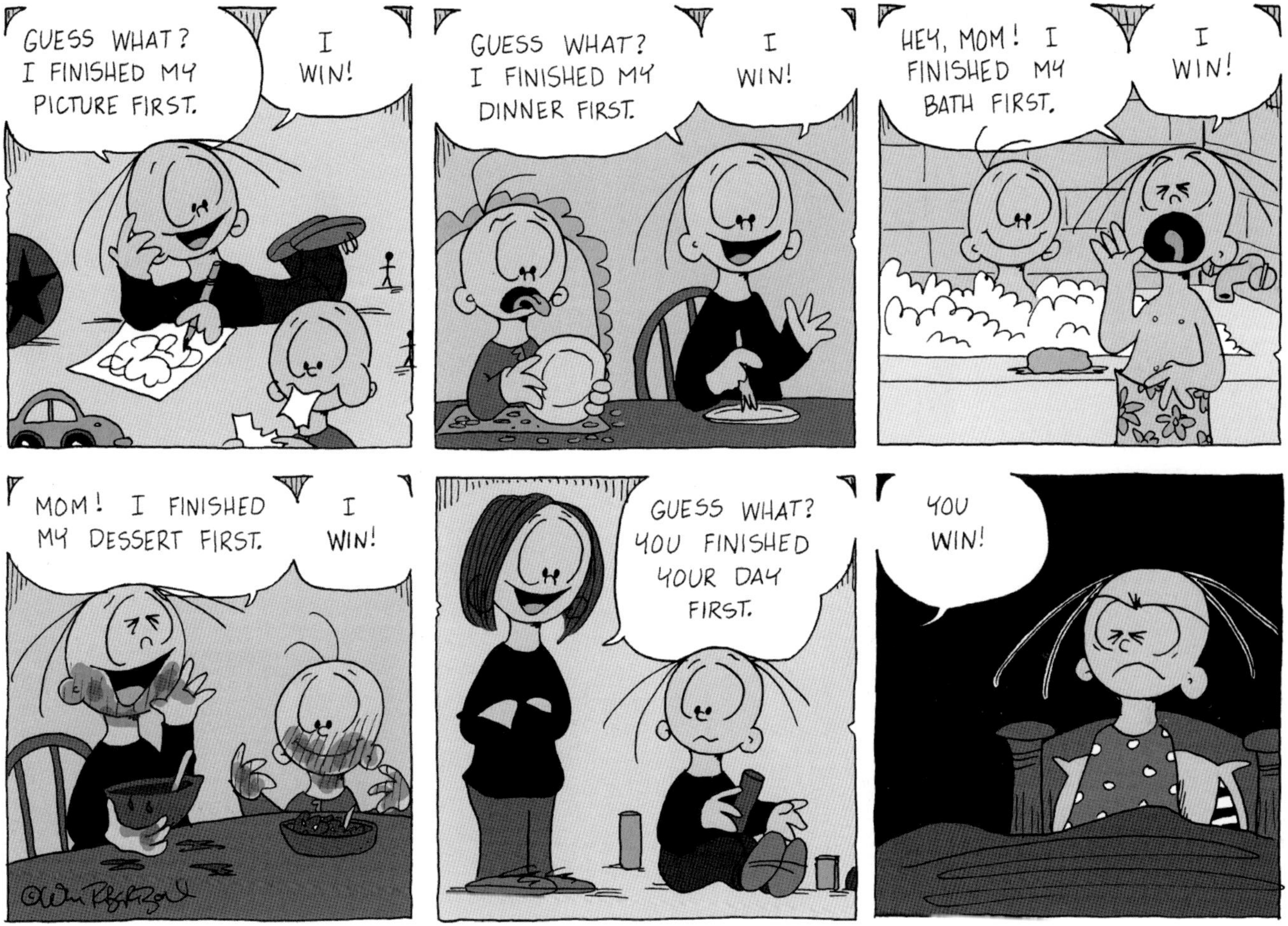

GUESS WHAT? I FINISHED MY PICTURE FIRST.
I WIN!
GUESS WHAT? I FINISHED MY DINNER FIRST.
I WIN!
HEY, MOM! I FINISHED MY BATH FIRST.
I WIN!
MOM! I FINISHED MY DESSERT FIRST.
I WIN!
GUESS WHAT? YOU FINISHED YOUR DAY FIRST.
YOU WIN!

CASEY AND KYLE™

by **Will Robertson**

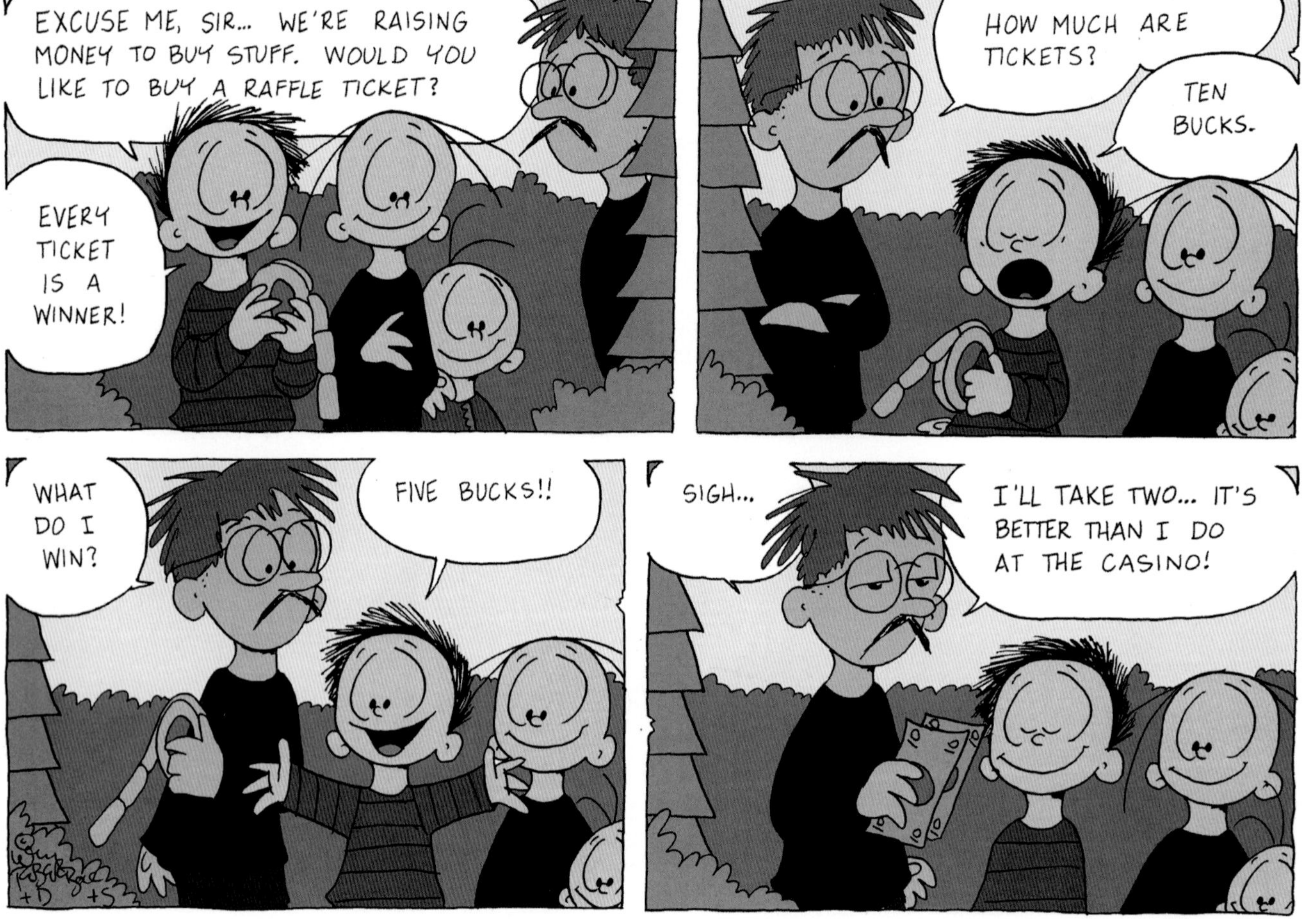

EXCUSE ME, SIR... WE'RE RAISING MONEY TO BUY STUFF. WOULD YOU LIKE TO BUY A RAFFLE TICKET?
EVERY TICKET IS A WINNER!
HOW MUCH ARE TICKETS?
TEN BUCKS.
WHAT DO I WIN?
FIVE BUCKS!!
SIGH...
I'LL TAKE TWO... IT'S BETTER THAN I DO AT THE CASINO!

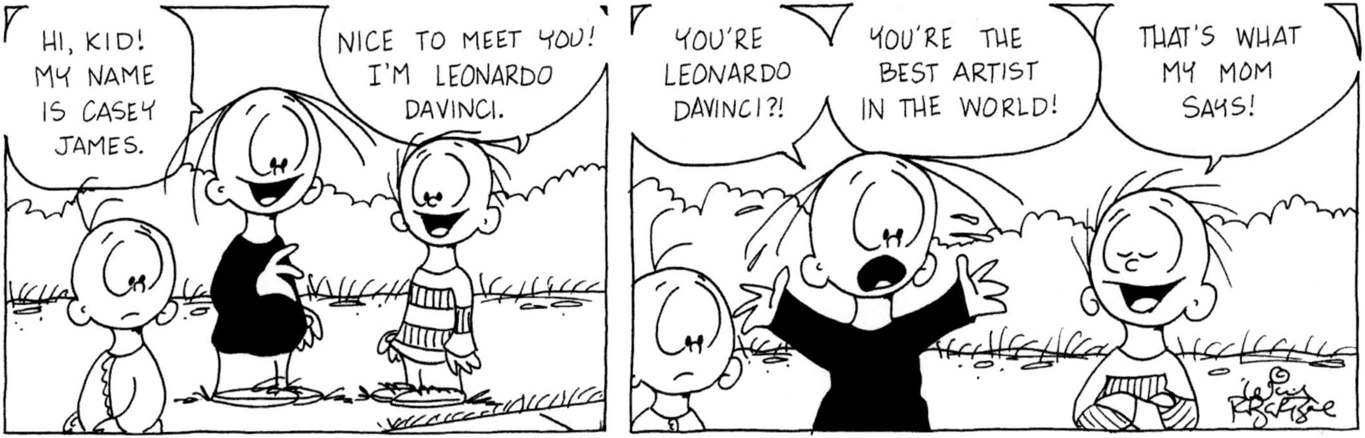
HI, KID! MY NAME IS CASEY JAMES.
NICE TO MEET YOU! I'M LEONARDO DAVINCI.
YOU'RE LEONARDO DAVINCI?!
YOU'RE THE BEST ARTIST IN THE WORLD!
THAT'S WHAT MY MOM SAYS!

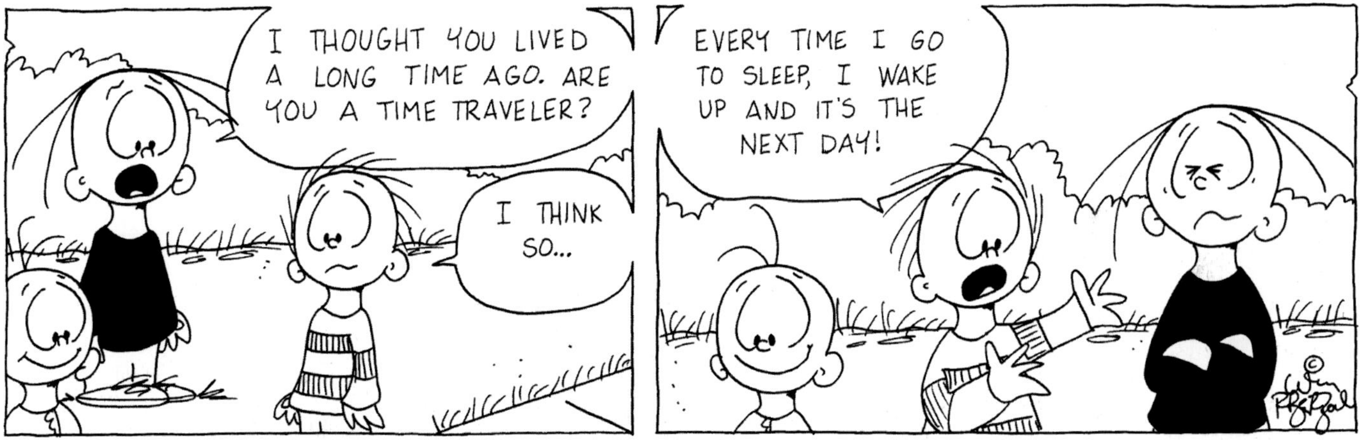
I THOUGHT YOU LIVED A LONG TIME AGO. ARE YOU A TIME TRAVELER?
I THINK SO...
EVERY TIME I GO TO SLEEP, I WAKE UP AND IT'S THE NEXT DAY!

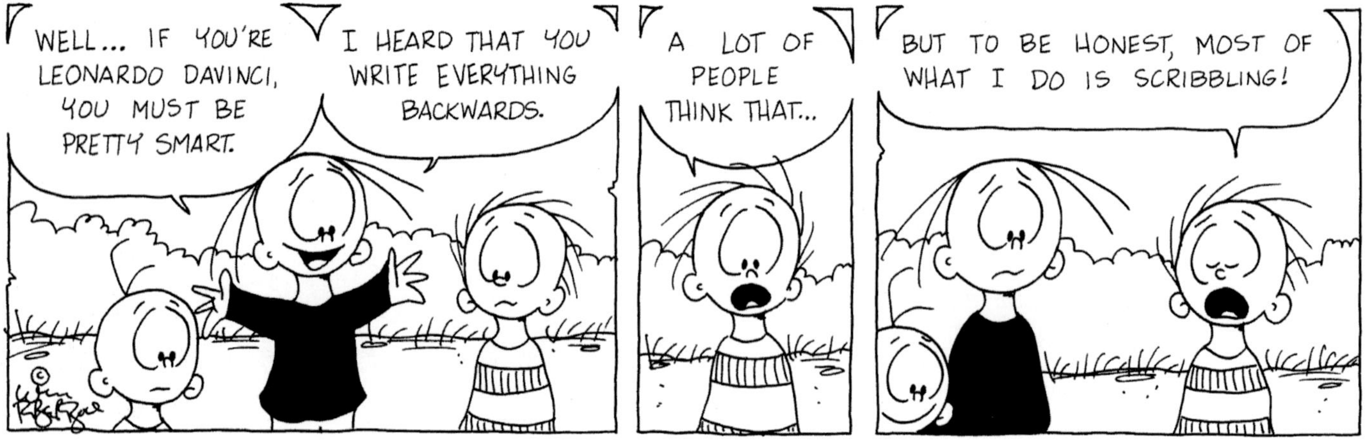
WELL... IF YOU'RE LEONARDO DAVINCI, YOU MUST BE PRETTY SMART.
I HEARD THAT YOU WRITE EVERYTHING BACKWARDS.
A LOT OF PEOPLE THINK THAT...
BUT TO BE HONEST, MOST OF WHAT I DO IS SCRIBBLING!

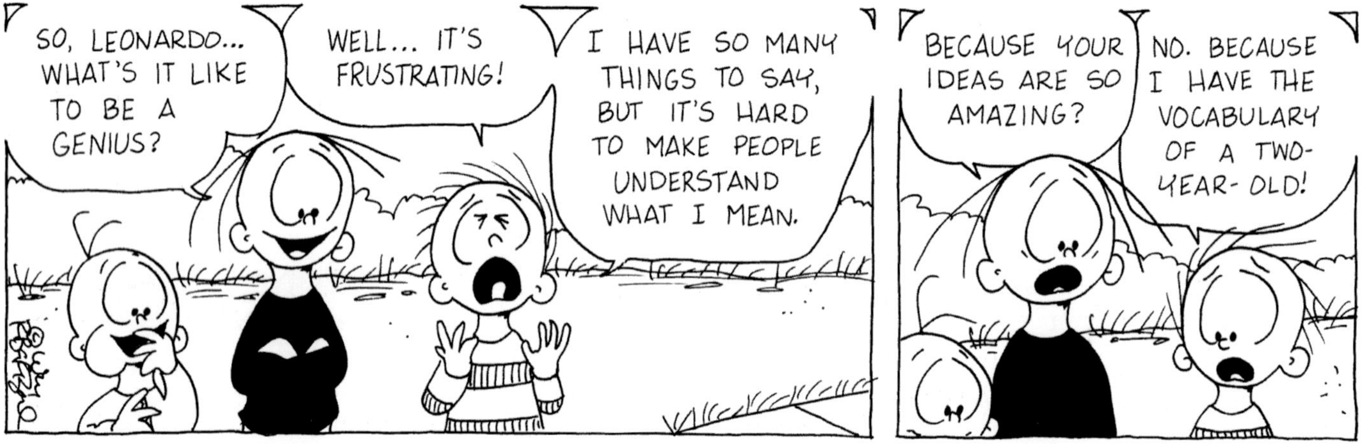
SO, LEONARDO... WHAT'S IT LIKE TO BE A GENIUS?
WELL... IT'S FRUSTRATING!
I HAVE SO MANY THINGS TO SAY, BUT IT'S HARD TO MAKE PEOPLE UNDERSTAND WHAT I MEAN.
BECAUSE YOUR IDEAS ARE SO AMAZING?
NO. BECAUSE I HAVE THE VOCABULARY OF A TWO-YEAR-OLD!

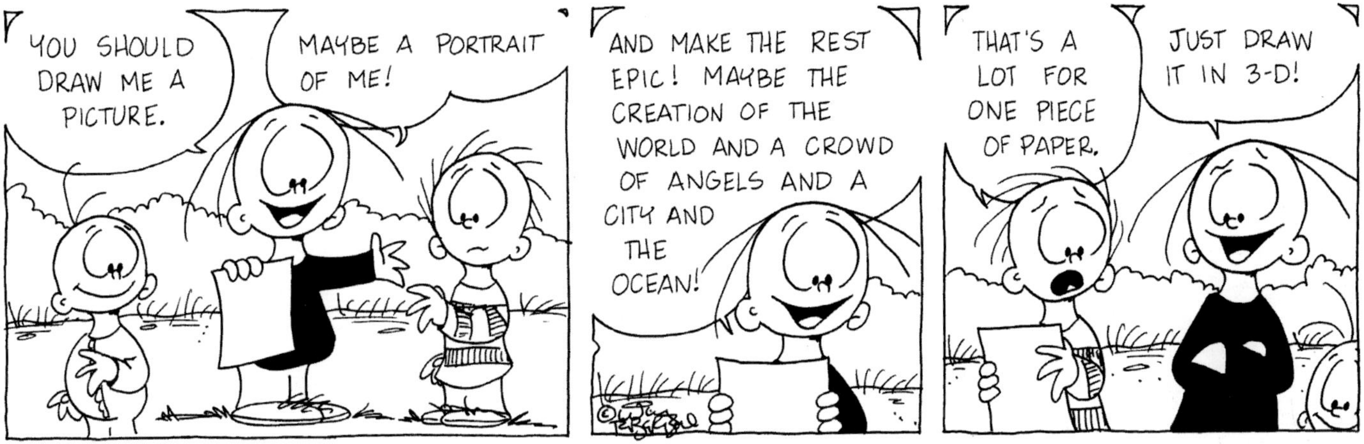
YOU SHOULD DRAW ME A PICTURE.
MAYBE A PORTRAIT OF ME!
AND MAKE THE REST EPIC! MAYBE THE CREATION OF THE WORLD AND A CROWD OF ANGELS AND A CITY AND THE OCEAN!
THAT'S A LOT FOR ONE PIECE OF PAPER.
JUST DRAW IT IN 3-D!

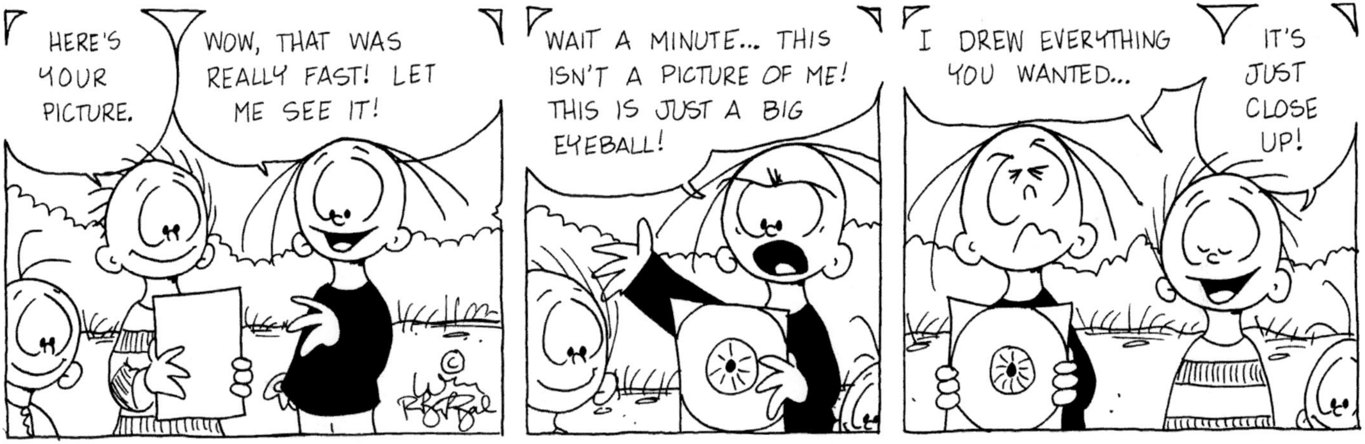
HERE'S YOUR PICTURE.
WOW, THAT WAS REALLY FAST! LET ME SEE IT!
WAIT A MINUTE... THIS ISN'T A PICTURE OF ME! THIS IS JUST A BIG EYEBALL!
I DREW EVERYTHING YOU WANTED...
IT'S JUST CLOSE UP!

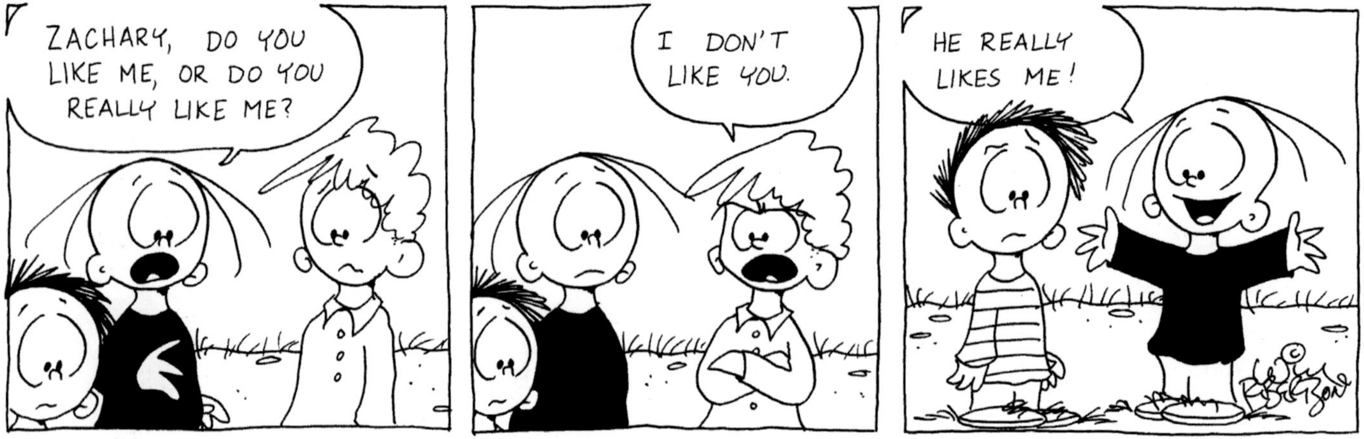
ZACHARY, DO YOU LIKE ME, OR DO YOU REALLY LIKE ME?
I DON'T LIKE YOU.
HE REALLY LIKES ME!

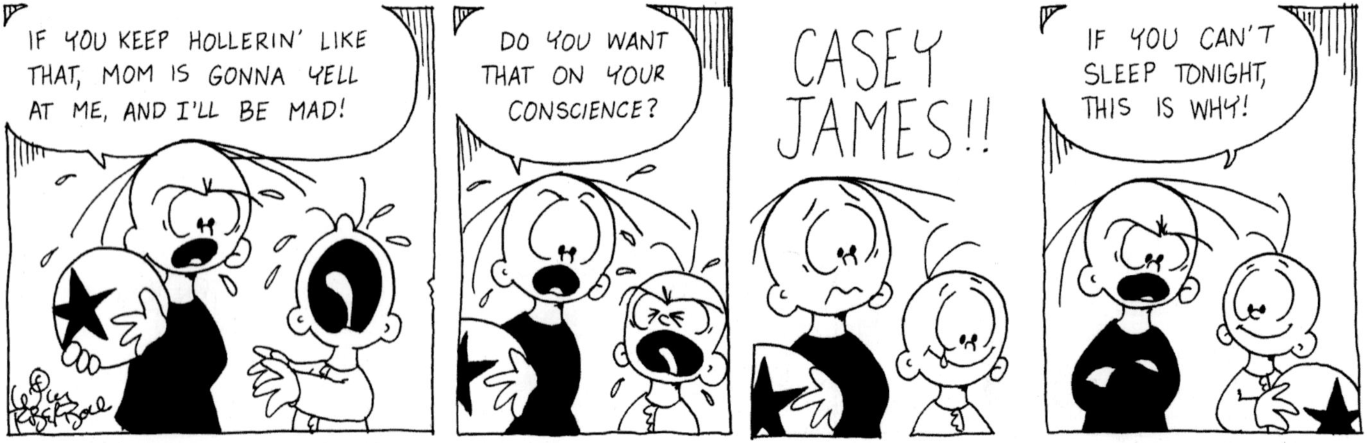
IF YOU KEEP HOLLERIN' LIKE THAT, MOM IS GONNA YELL AT ME, AND I'LL BE MAD!
DO YOU WANT THAT ON YOUR CONSCIENCE?
CASEY JAMES!!
IF YOU CAN'T SLEEP TONIGHT, THIS IS WHY!

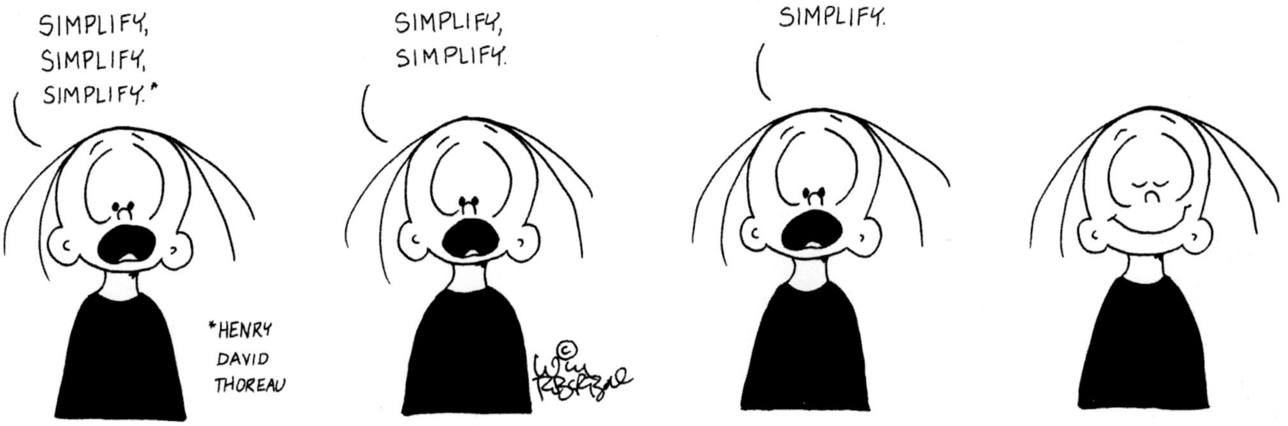
SIMPLIFY, SIMPLIFY, SIMPLIFY.*
*HENRY DAVID THOREAU
SIMPLIFY, SIMPLIFY.
SIMPLIFY.

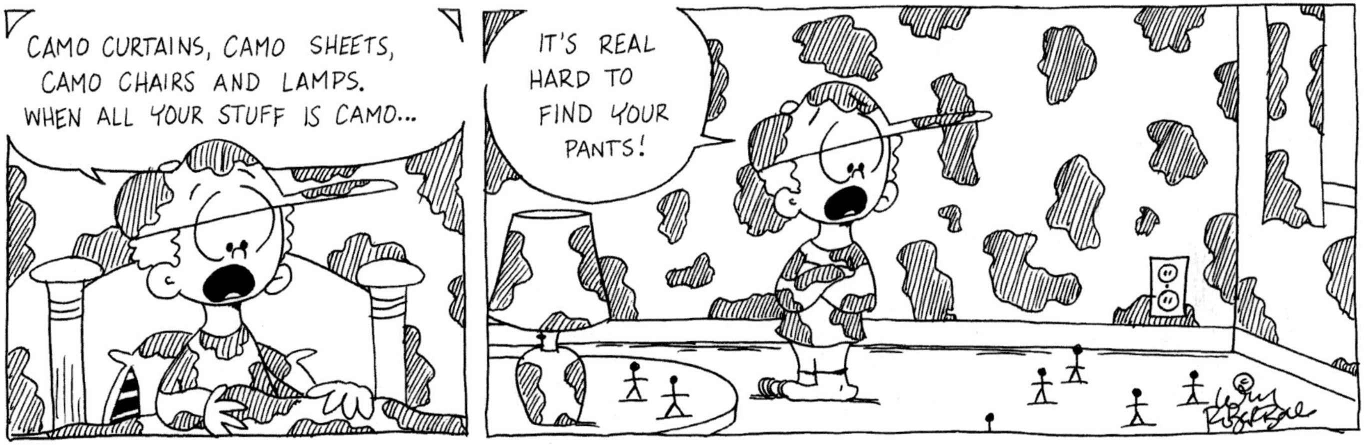
CAMO CURTAINS, CAMO SHEETS, CAMO CHAIRS AND LAMPS. WHEN ALL YOUR STUFF IS CAMO...
IT'S REAL HARD TO FIND YOUR PANTS!

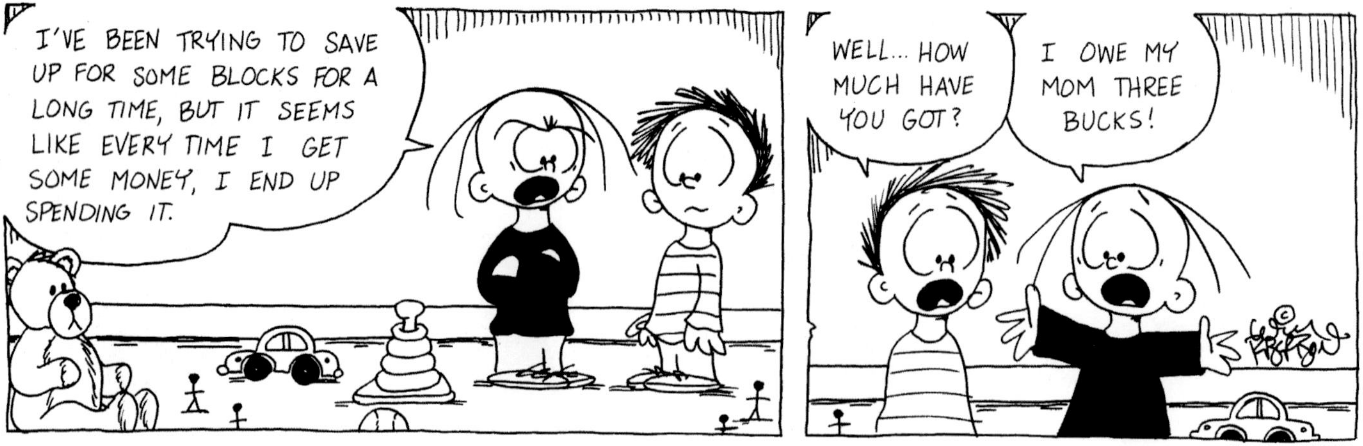
I'VE BEEN TRYING TO SAVE UP FOR SOME BLOCKS FOR A LONG TIME, BUT IT SEEMS LIKE EVERY TIME I GET SOME MONEY, I END UP SPENDING IT.
WELL... HOW MUCH HAVE YOU GOT?
I OWE MY MOM THREE BUCKS!

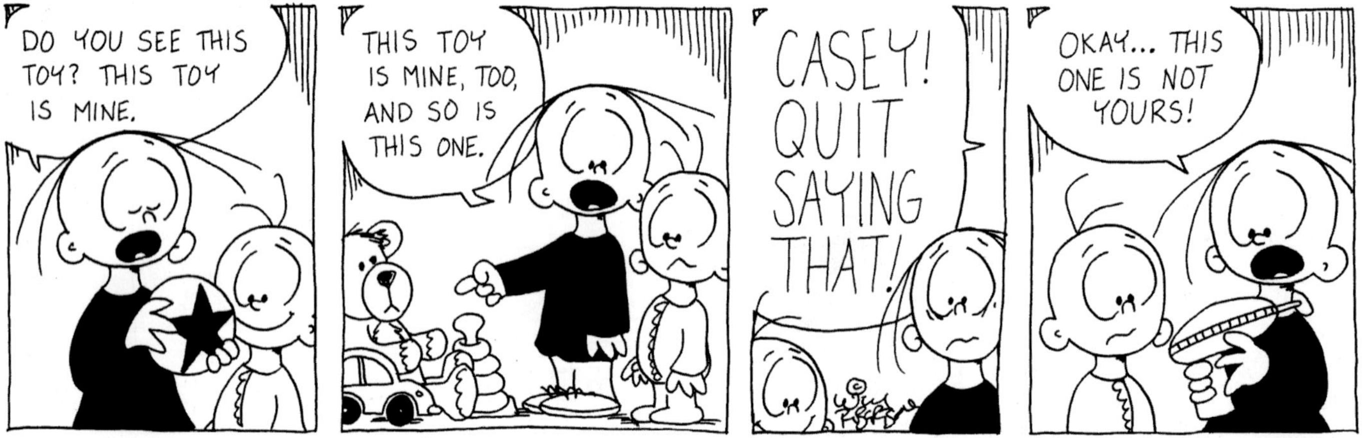
DO YOU SEE THIS TOY? THIS TOY IS MINE.
THIS TOY IS MINE, TOO, AND SO IS THIS ONE.
CASEY! QUIT SAYING THAT!
OKAY... THIS ONE IS NOT YOURS!

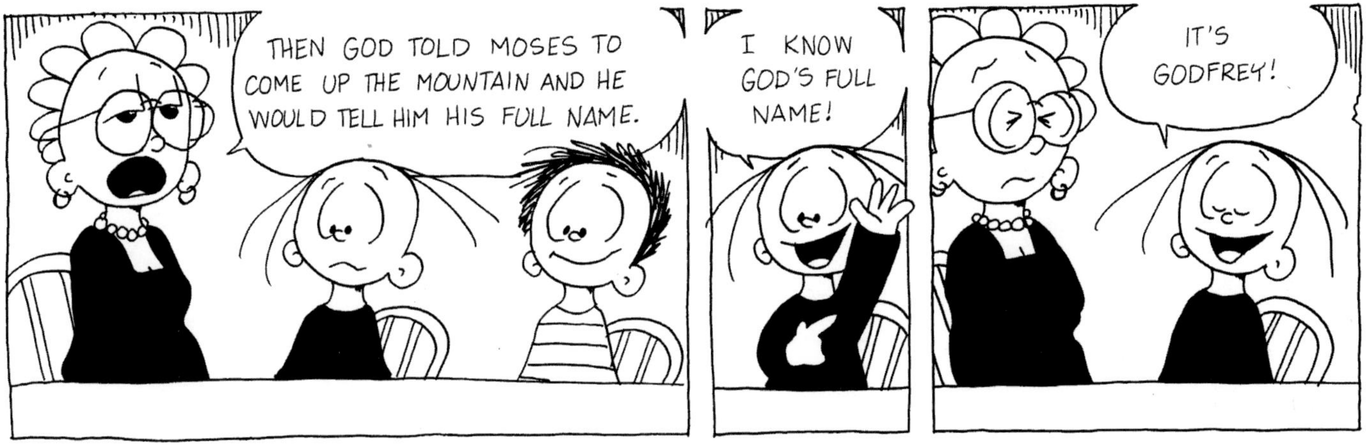
THEN GOD TOLD MOSES TO COME UP THE MOUNTAIN AND HE WOULD TELL HIM HIS FULL NAME.
I KNOW GOD'S FULL NAME!
IT'S GODFREY!

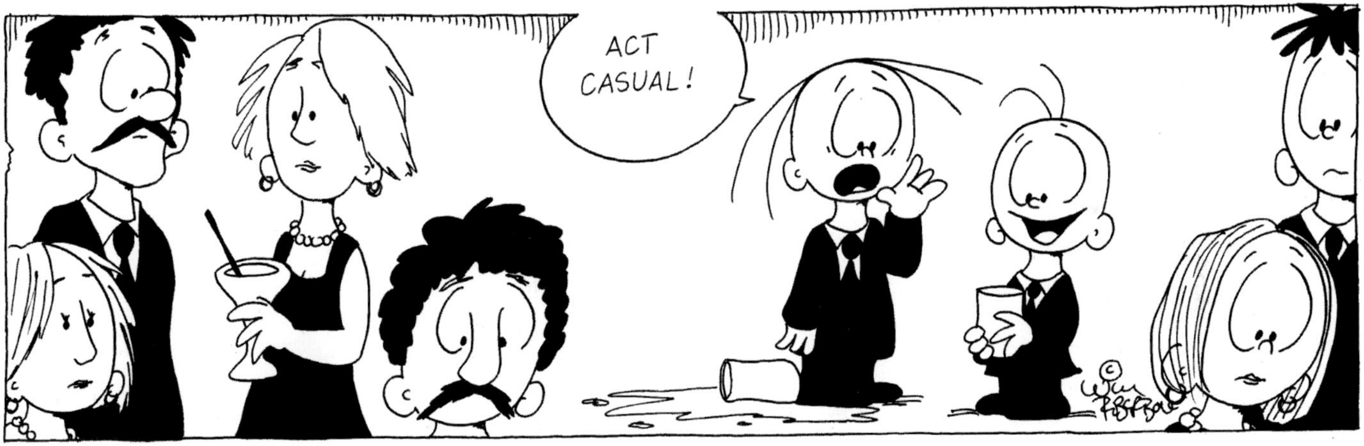
ACT CASUAL!

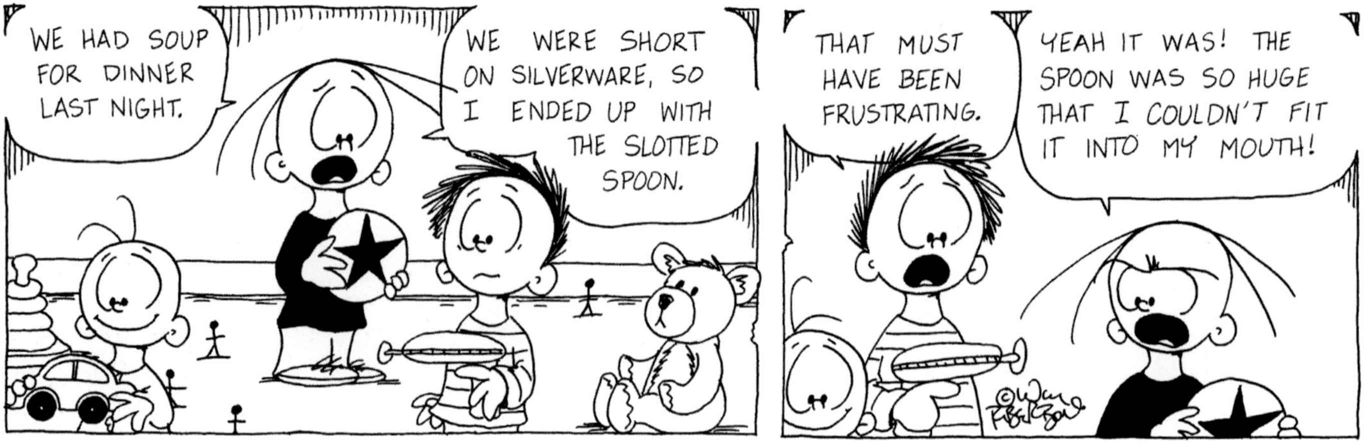
WE HAD SOUP FOR DINNER LAST NIGHT.
WE WERE SHORT ON SILVERWARE, SO I ENDED UP WITH THE SLOTTED SPOON.
THAT MUST HAVE BEEN FRUSTRATING.
YEAH IT WAS! THE SPOON WAS SO HUGE THAT I COULDN'T FIT IT INTO MY MOUTH!

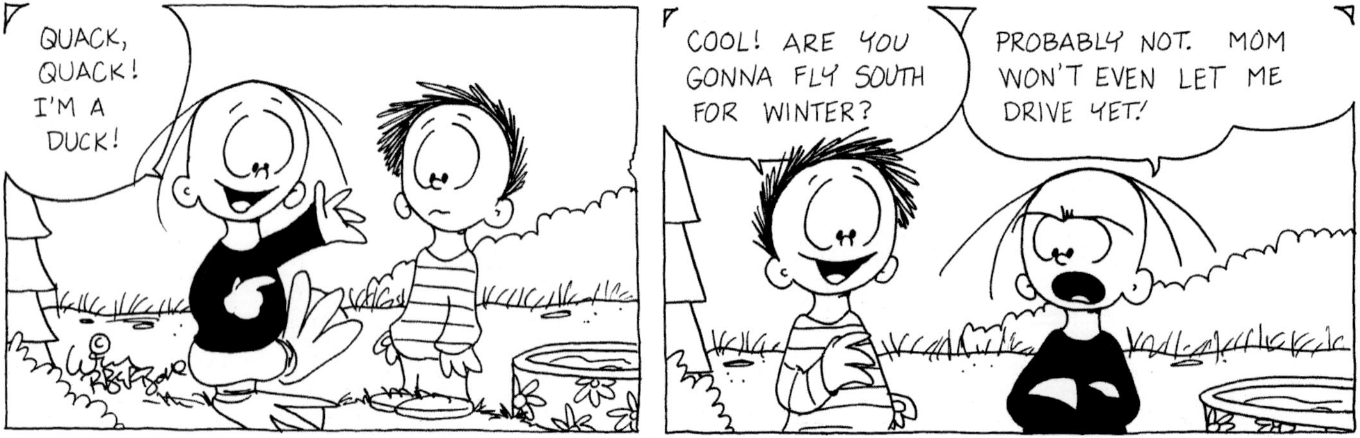
QUACK, QUACK! I'M A DUCK!
COOL! ARE YOU GONNA FLY SOUTH FOR WINTER?
PROBABLY NOT. MOM WON'T EVEN LET ME DRIVE YET!

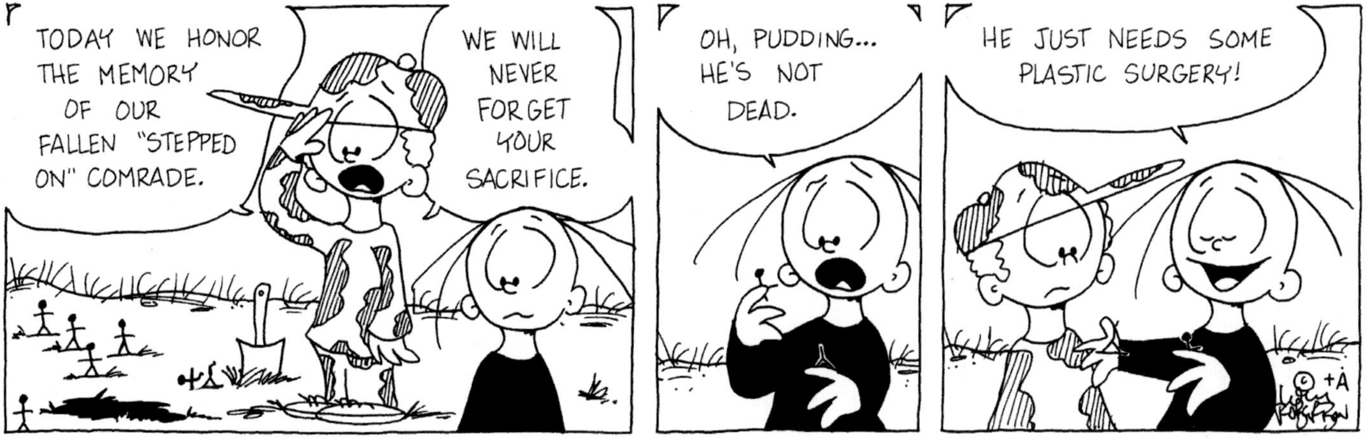
TODAY WE HONOR THE MEMORY OF OUR FALLEN "STEPPED ON" COMRADE.
WE WILL NEVER FORGET YOUR SACRIFICE.
OH, PUDDING... HE'S NOT DEAD.
HE JUST NEEDS SOME PLASTIC SURGERY!

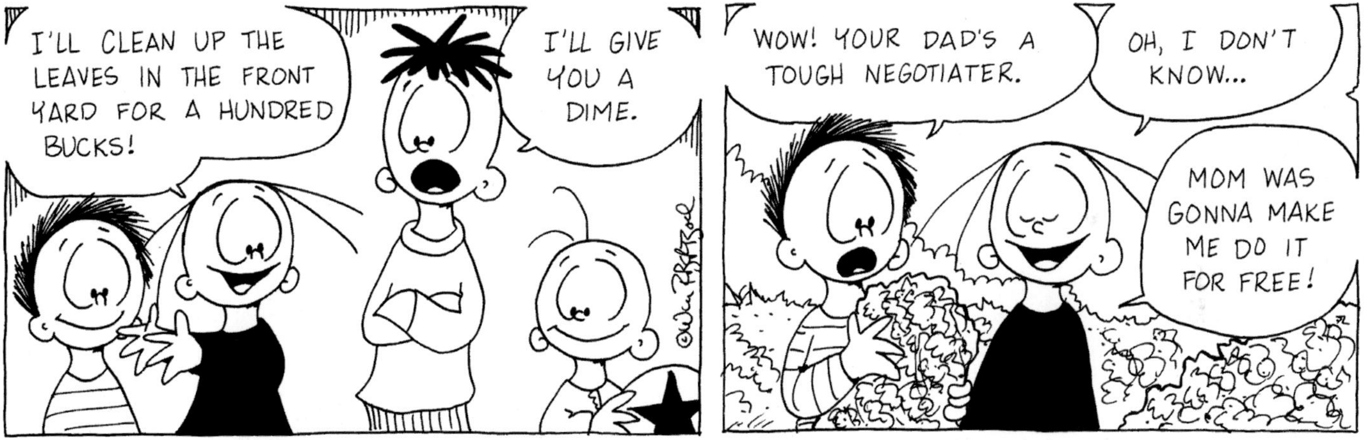
I'LL CLEAN UP THE LEAVES IN THE FRONT YARD FOR A HUNDRED BUCKS!
I'LL GIVE YOU A DIME.
WOW! YOUR DAD'S A TOUGH NEGOTIATER.
OH, I DON'T KNOW...
MOM WAS GONNA MAKE ME DO IT FOR FREE!

CASEY AND KYLE™

by Will Robertson

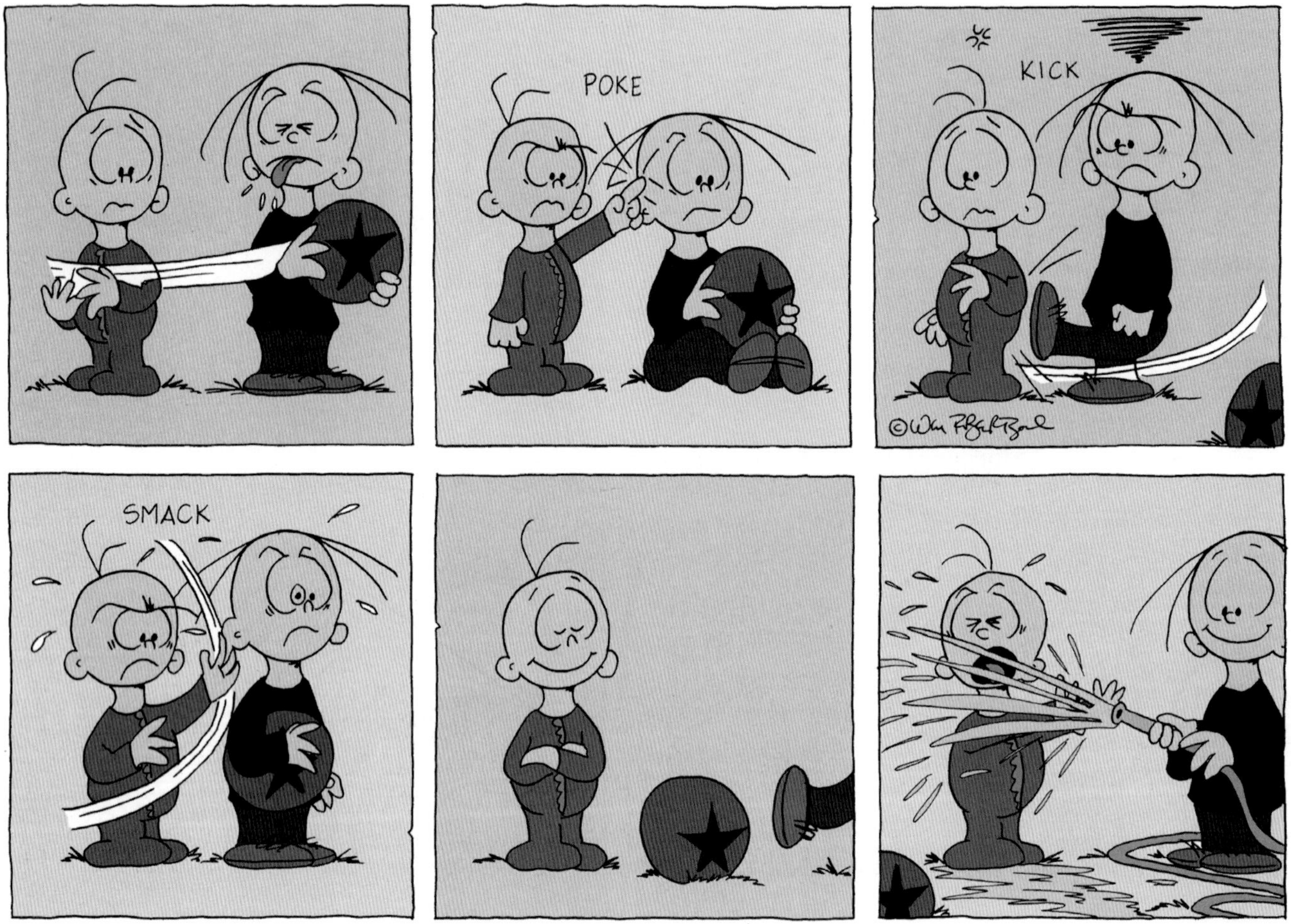
POKE
KICK
SMACK

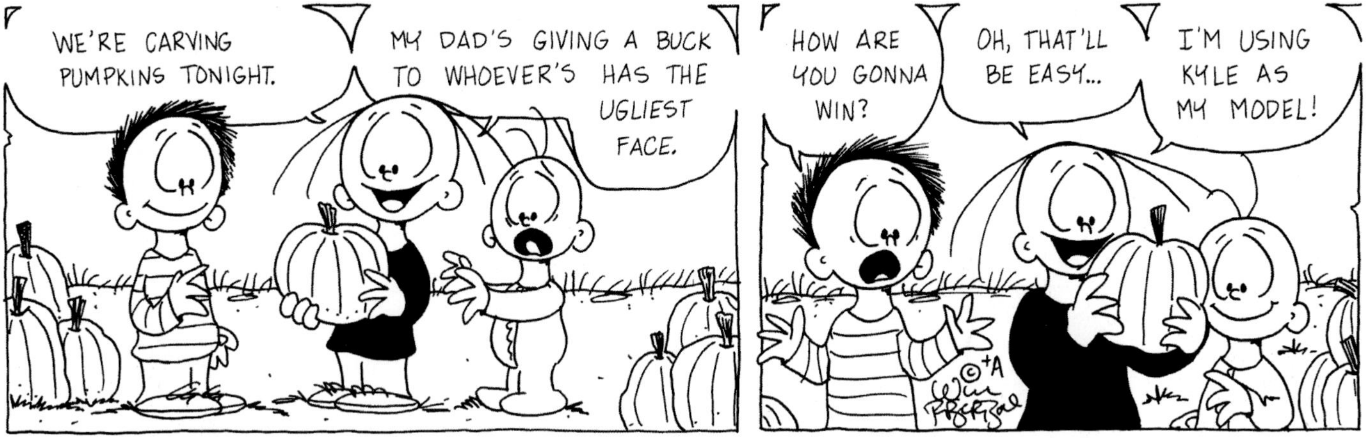
WE'RE CARVING PUMPKINS TONIGHT.
MY DAD'S GIVING A BUCK TO WHOEVER'S HAS THE UGLIEST FACE.
HOW ARE YOU GONNA WIN?
OH, THAT'LL BE EASY...
I'M USING KYLE AS MY MODEL!

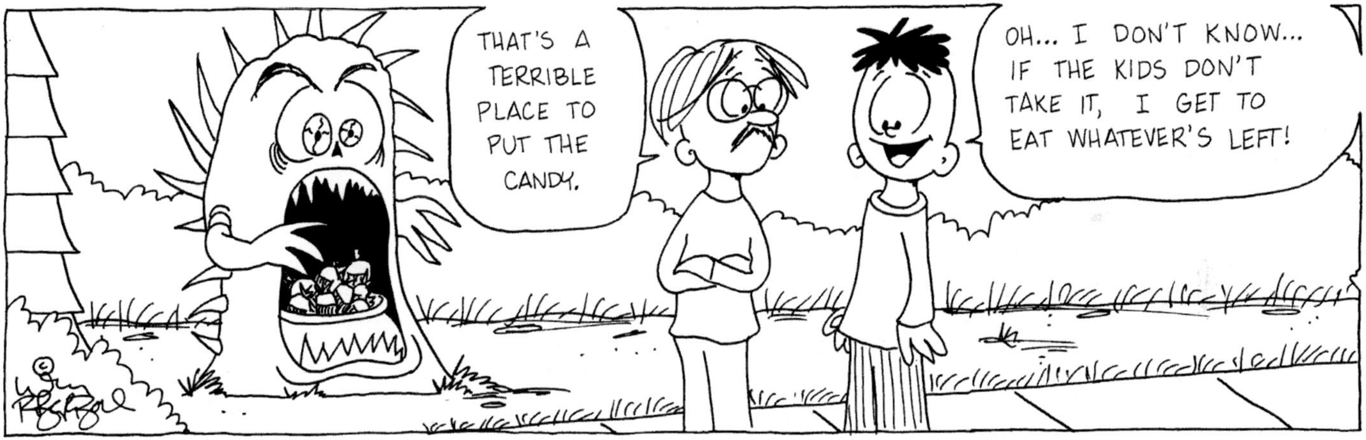
THAT'S A TERRIBLE PLACE TO PUT THE CANDY.
OH... I DON'T KNOW... IF THE KIDS DON'T TAKE IT, I GET TO EAT WHATEVER'S LEFT!

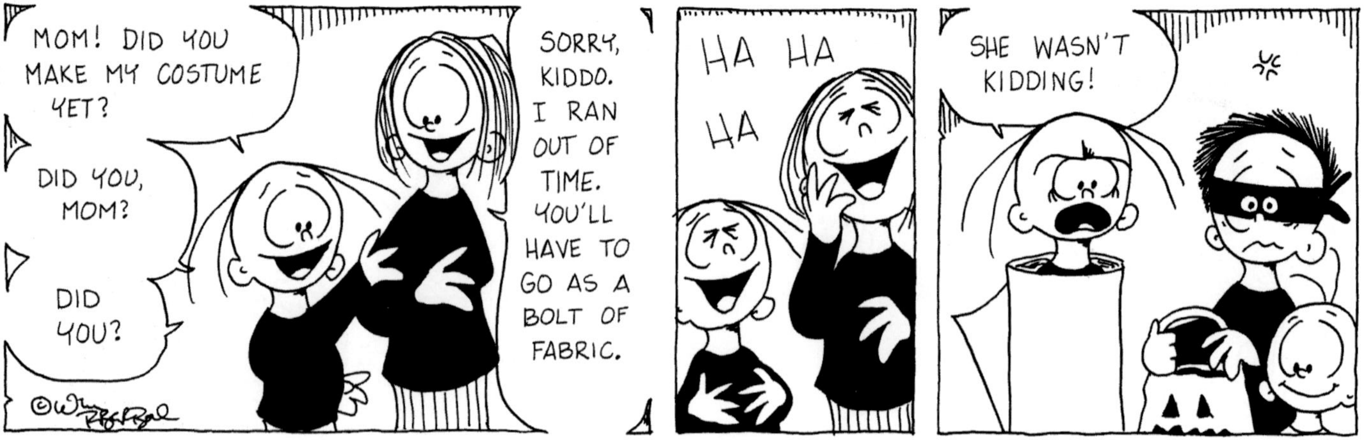
MOM! DID YOU MAKE MY COSTUME YET?
DID YOU, MOM?
DID YOU?
SORRY, KIDDO. I RAN OUT OF TIME. YOU'LL HAVE TO GO AS A BOLT OF FABRIC.
HA HA HA
SHE WASN'T KIDDING!

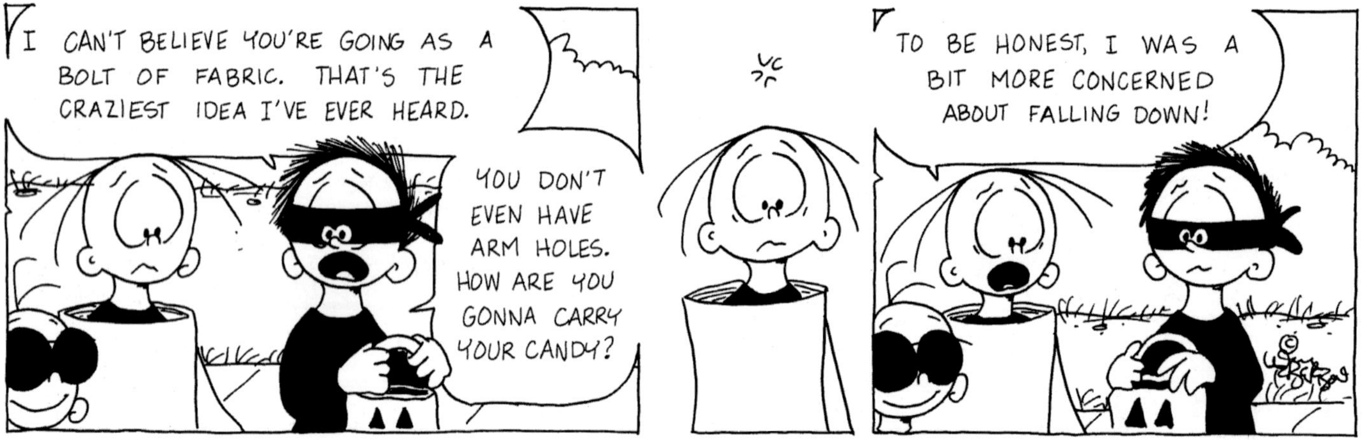
I CAN'T BELIEVE YOU'RE GOING AS A BOLT OF FABRIC. THAT'S THE CRAZIEST IDEA I'VE EVER HEARD.
YOU DON'T EVEN HAVE ARM HOLES. HOW ARE YOU GONNA CARRY YOUR CANDY?
TO BE HONEST, I WAS A BIT MORE CONCERNED ABOUT FALLING DOWN!

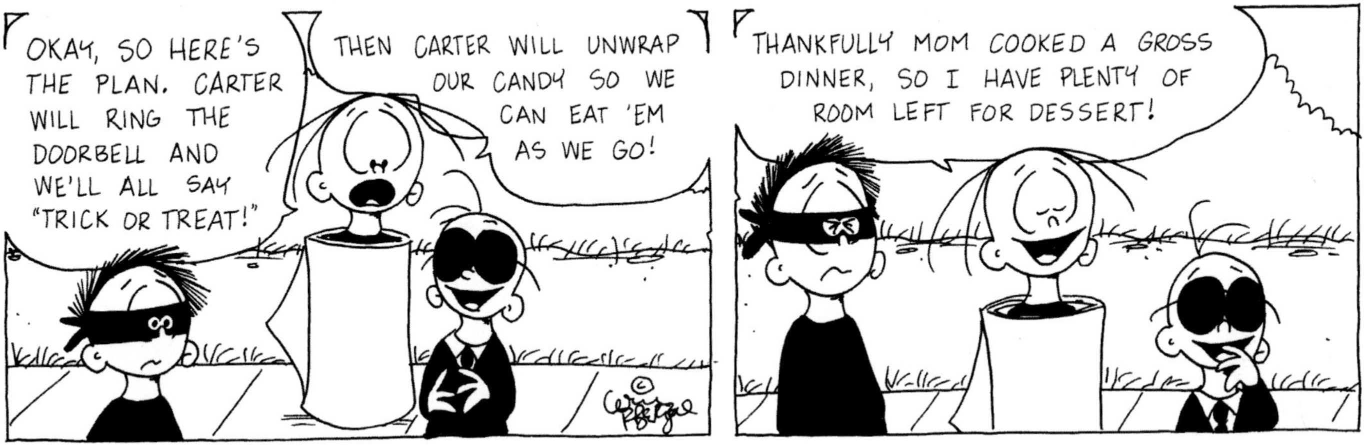
OKAY, SO HERE'S THE PLAN. CARTER WILL RING THE DOORBELL AND WE'LL ALL SAY "TRICK OR TREAT!"
THEN CARTER WILL UNWRAP OUR CANDY SO WE CAN EAT 'EM AS WE GO!
THANKFULLY MOM COOKED A GROSS DINNER, SO I HAVE PLENTY OF ROOM LEFT FOR DESSERT!

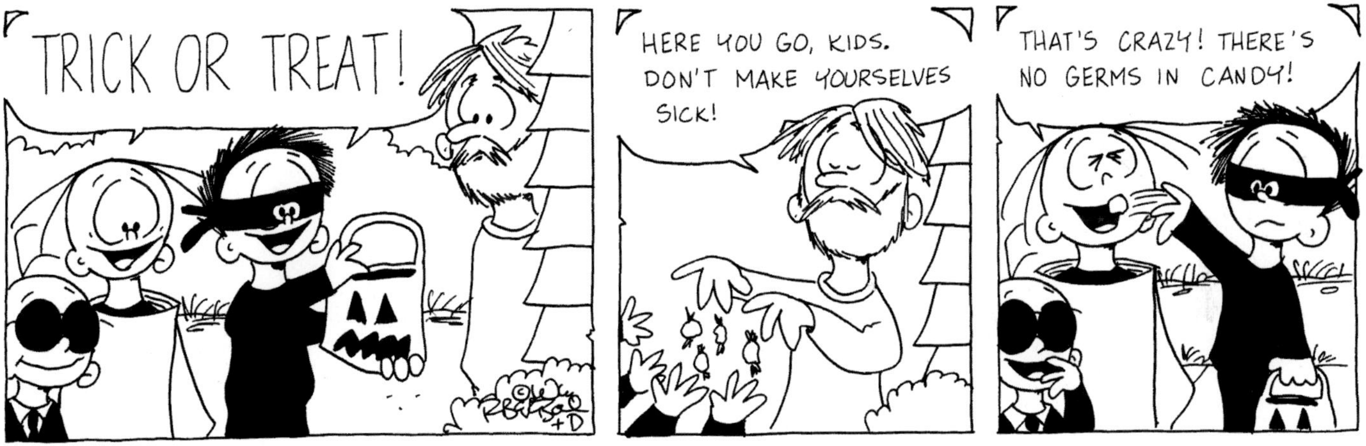
TRICK OR TREAT!
HERE YOU GO, KIDS. DON'T MAKE YOURSELVES SICK!
THAT'S CRAZY! THERE'S NO GERMS IN CANDY!

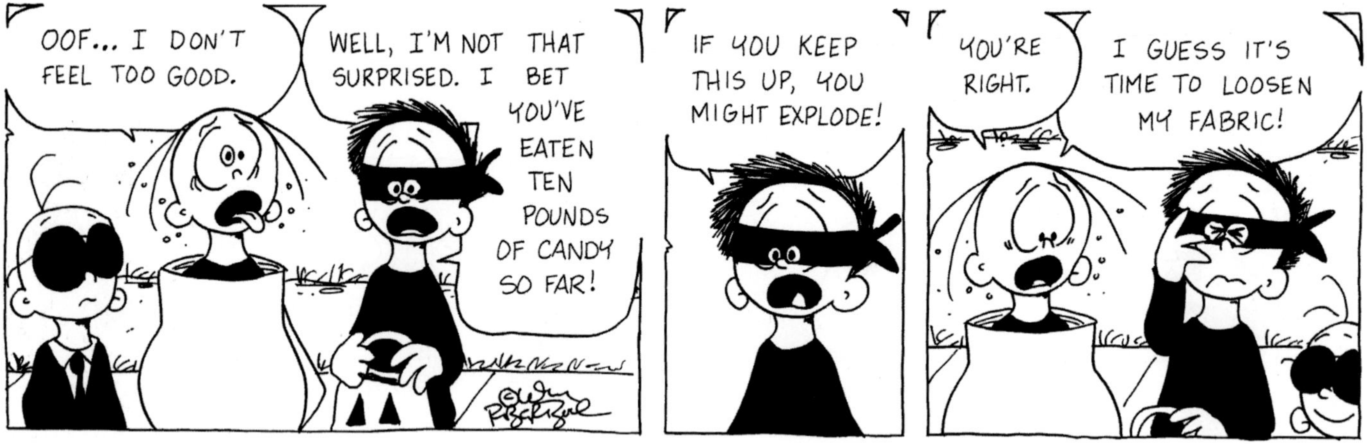
OOF... I DON'T FEEL TOO GOOD.
WELL, I'M NOT THAT SURPRISED. I BET YOU'VE EATEN TEN POUNDS OF CANDY SO FAR!
IF YOU KEEP THIS UP, YOU MIGHT EXPLODE!
YOU'RE RIGHT.
I GUESS IT'S TIME TO LOOSEN MY FABRIC!

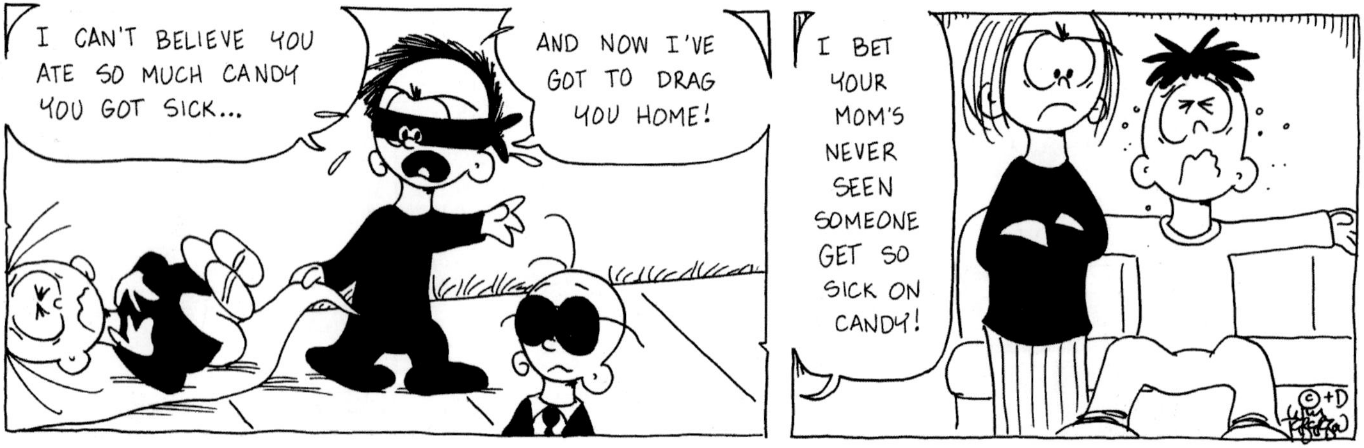
I CAN'T BELIEVE YOU ATE SO MUCH CANDY YOU GOT SICK...
AND NOW I'VE GOT TO DRAG YOU HOME!
I BET YOUR MOM'S NEVER SEEN SOMEONE GET SO SICK ON CANDY!

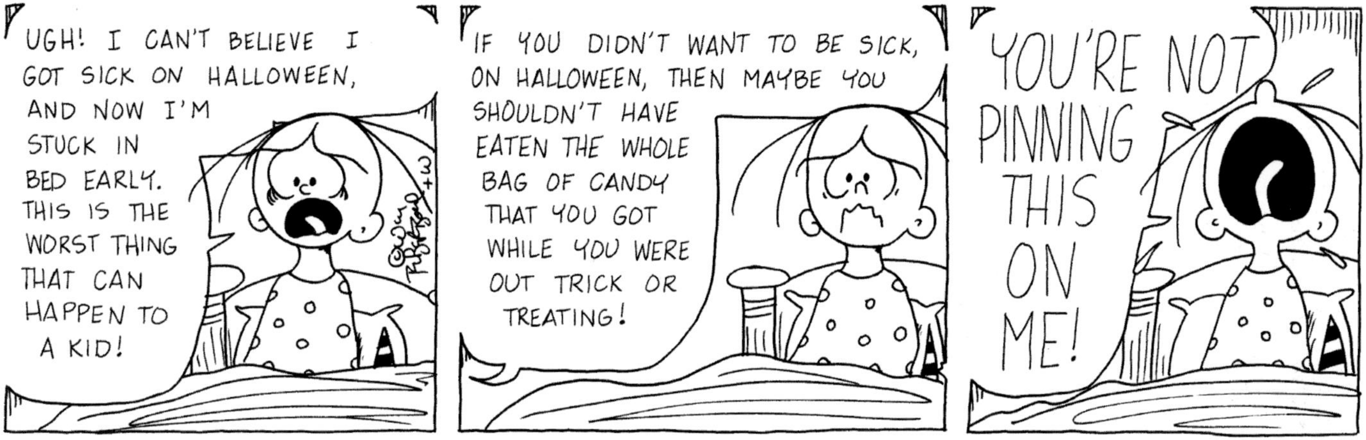
UGH! I CAN'T BELIEVE I GOT SICK ON HALLOWEEN, AND NOW I'M STUCK IN BED EARLY. THIS IS THE WORST THING THAT CAN HAPPEN TO A KID!
IF YOU DIDN'T WANT TO BE SICK, ON HALLOWEEN, THEN MAYBE YOU SHOULDN'T HAVE EATEN THE WHOLE BAG OF CANDY THAT YOU GOT WHILE YOU WERE OUT TRICK OR TREATING!
YOU'RE NOT PINNING THIS ON ME!

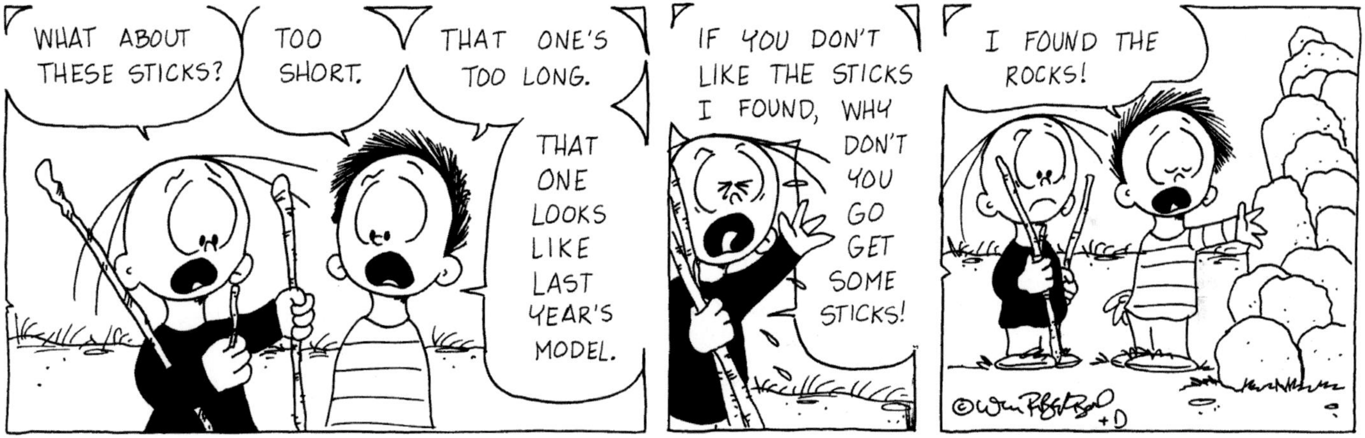
WHAT ABOUT THESE STICKS?
TOO SHORT.
THAT ONE'S TOO LONG.
THAT ONE LOOKS LIKE LAST YEAR'S MODEL.
IF YOU DON'T LIKE THE STICKS I FOUND, WHY DON'T YOU GO GET SOME STICKS!
I FOUND THE ROCKS!

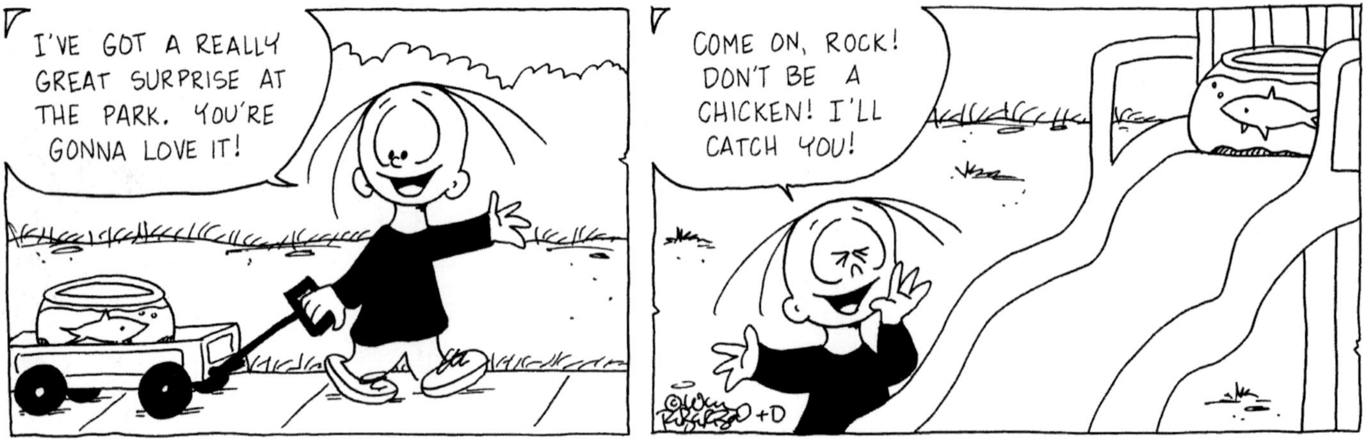
I'VE GOT A REALLY GREAT SURPRISE AT THE PARK. YOU'RE GONNA LOVE IT!
COME ON, ROCK! DON'T BE A CHICKEN! I'LL CATCH YOU!

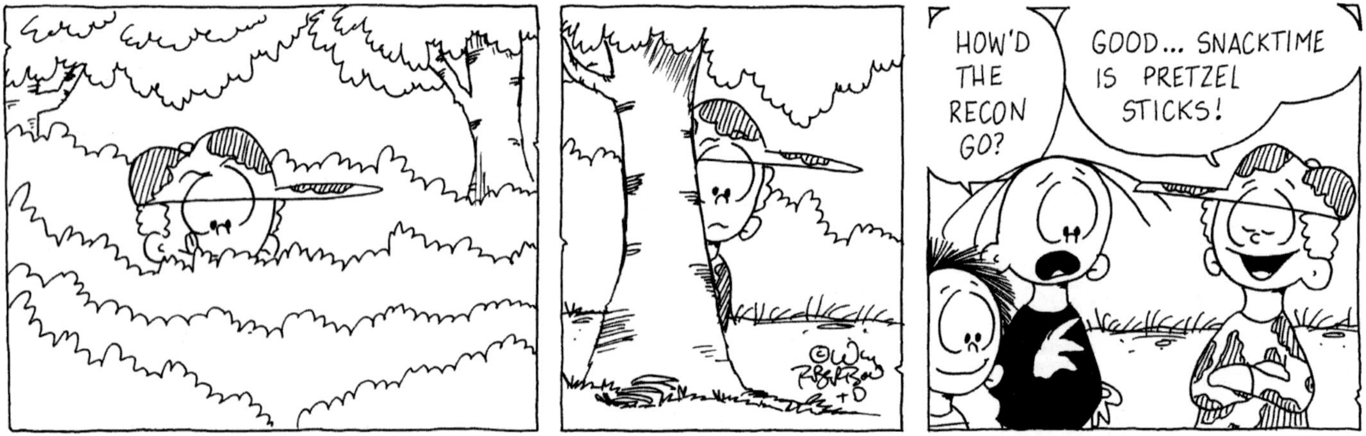
HOW'D THE RECON GO?
GOOD... SNACKTIME IS PRETZEL STICKS!

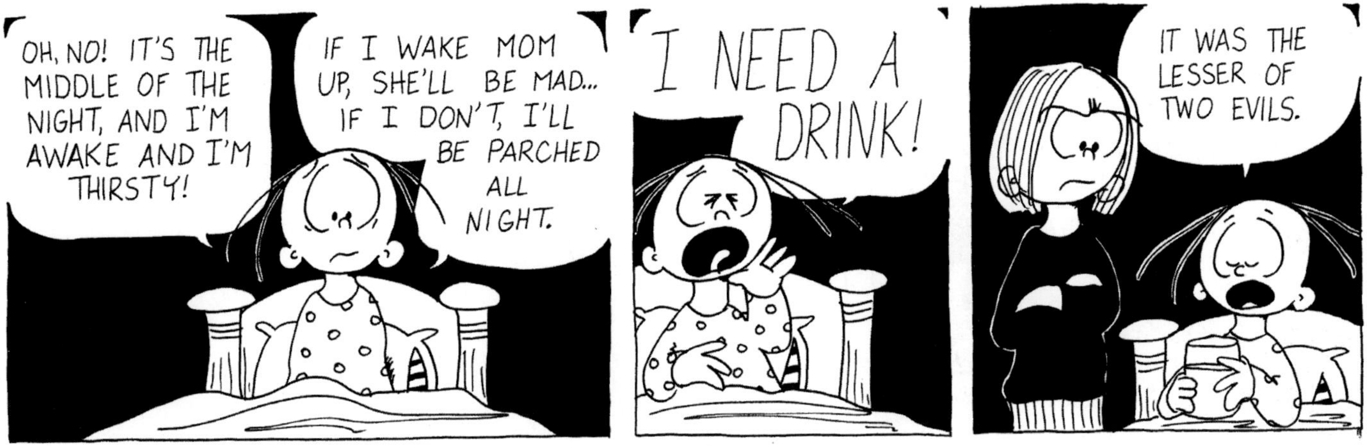
OH, NO! IT'S THE MIDDLE OF THE NIGHT, AND I'M AWAKE AND I'M THIRSTY!
IF I WAKE MOM UP, SHE'LL BE MAD... IF I DON'T, I'LL BE PARCHED ALL NIGHT.
I NEED A DRINK!
IT WAS THE LESSER OF TWO EVILS.

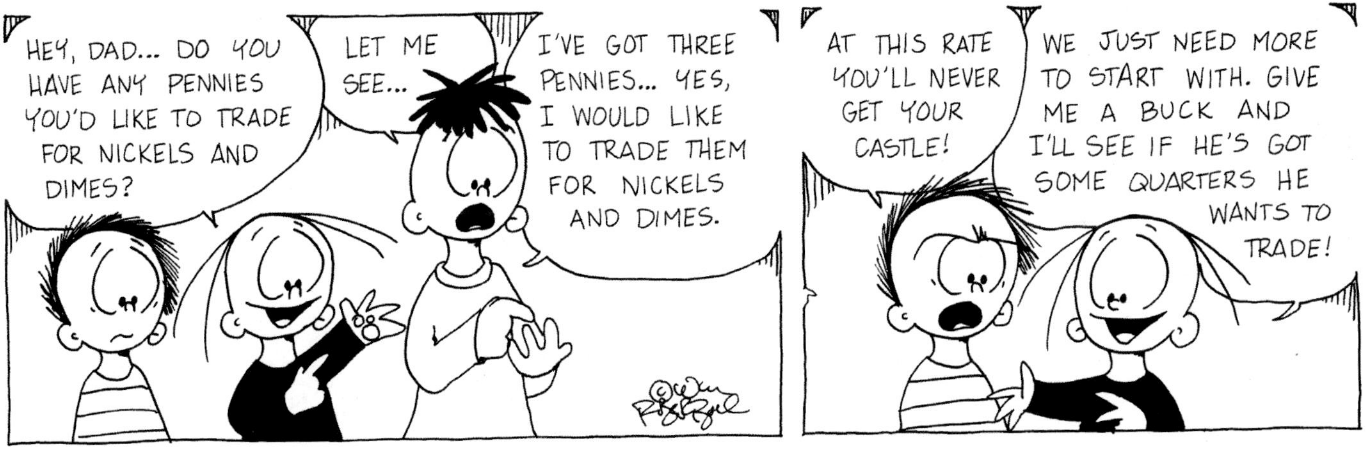
HEY, DAD... DO YOU HAVE ANY PENNIES YOU'D LIKE TO TRADE FOR NICKELS AND DIMES?
LET ME SEE...
I'VE GOT THREE PENNIES... YES, I WOULD LIKE TO TRADE THEM FOR NICKELS AND DIMES.
AT THIS RATE YOU'LL NEVER GET YOUR CASTLE!
WE JUST NEED MORE TO START WITH. GIVE ME A BUCK AND I'LL SEE IF HE'S GOT SOME QUARTERS HE WANTS TO TRADE!

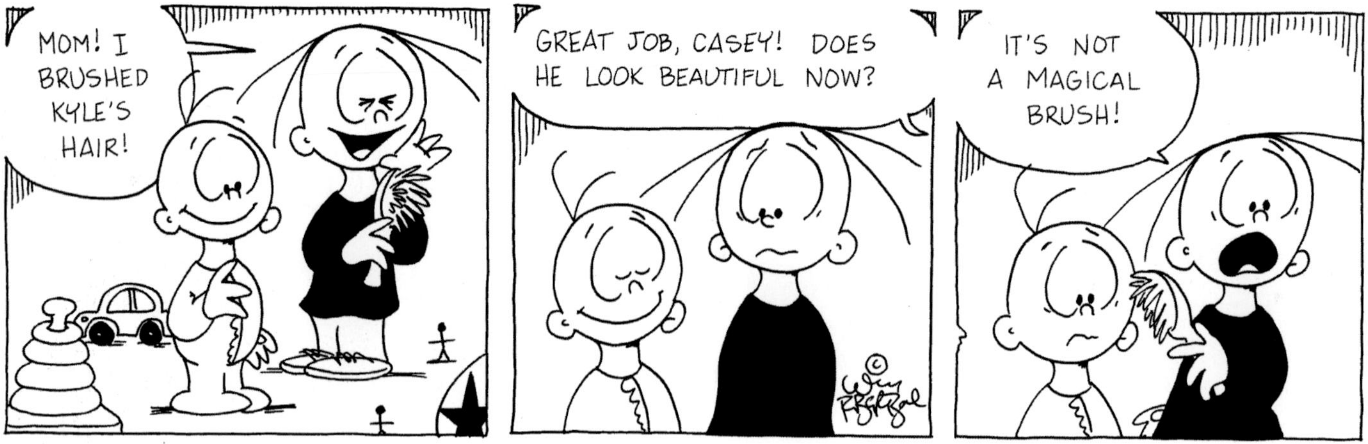
MOM! I BRUSHED KYLE'S HAIR!
GREAT JOB, CASEY! DOES HE LOOK BEAUTIFUL NOW?
IT'S NOT A MAGICAL BRUSH!

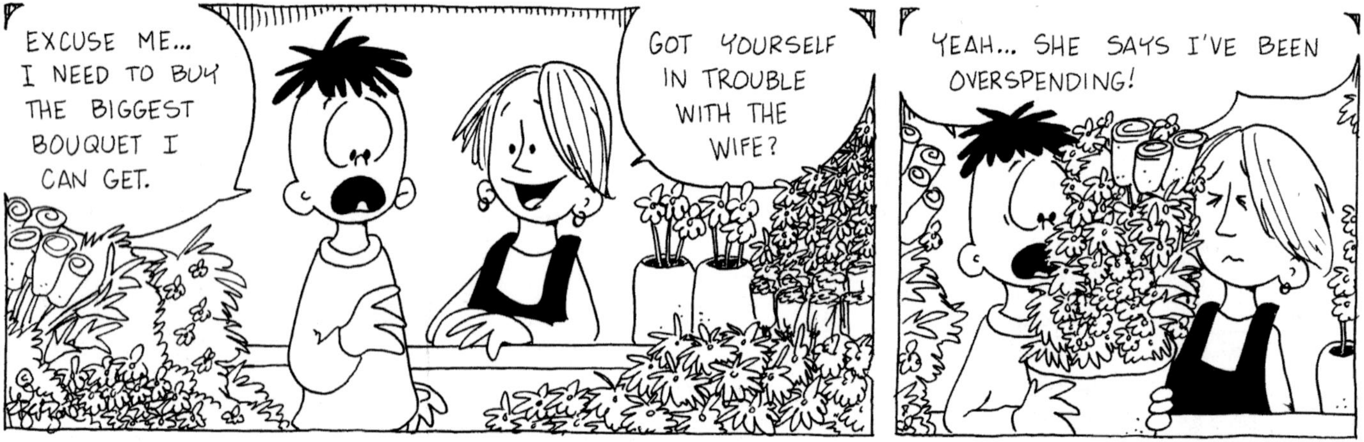
EXCUSE ME... I NEED TO BUY THE BIGGEST BOUQUET I CAN GET.
GOT YOURSELF IN TROUBLE WITH THE WIFE?
YEAH... SHE SAYS I'VE BEEN OVERSPENDING!

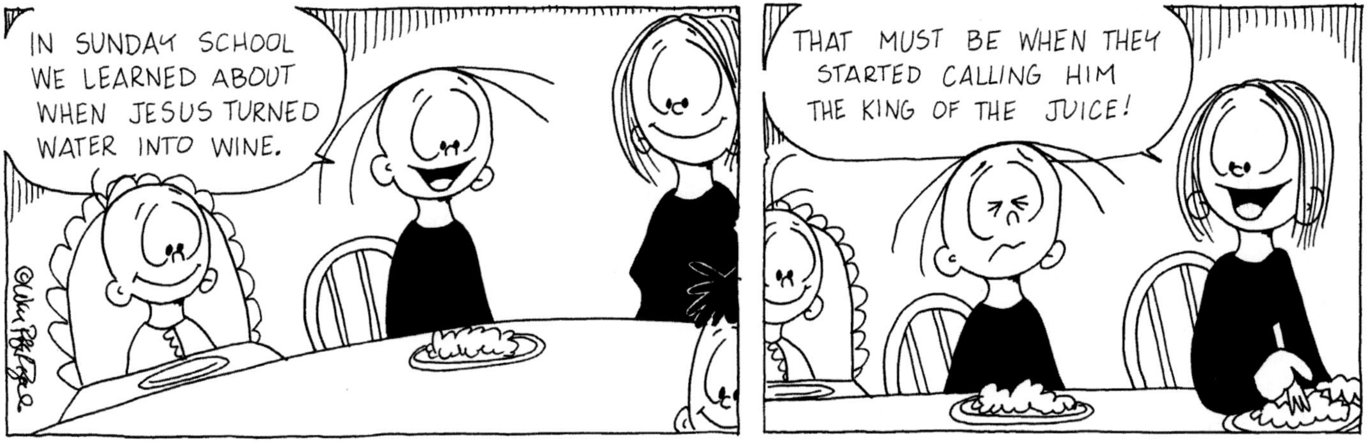
IN SUNDAY SCHOOL WE LEARNED ABOUT WHEN JESUS TURNED WATER INTO WINE.
THAT MUST BE WHEN THEY STARTED CALLING HIM THE KING OF THE JUICE!

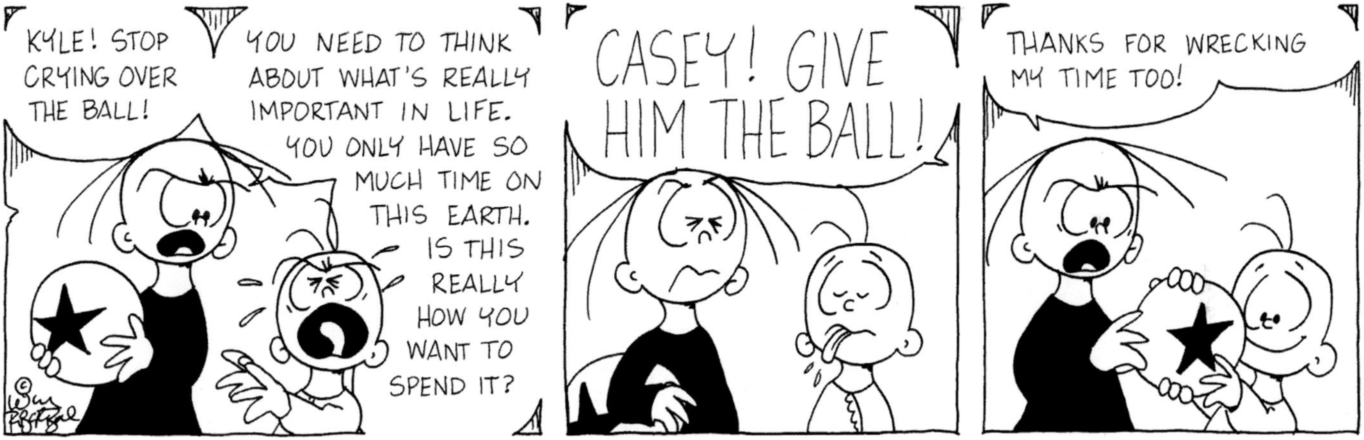
KYLE! STOP CRYING OVER THE BALL!
YOU NEED TO THINK ABOUT WHAT'S REALLY IMPORTANT IN LIFE. YOU ONLY HAVE SO MUCH TIME ON THIS EARTH. IS THIS REALLY HOW YOU WANT TO SPEND IT?
CASEY! GIVE HIM THE BALL!
THANKS FOR WRECKING MY TIME TOO!

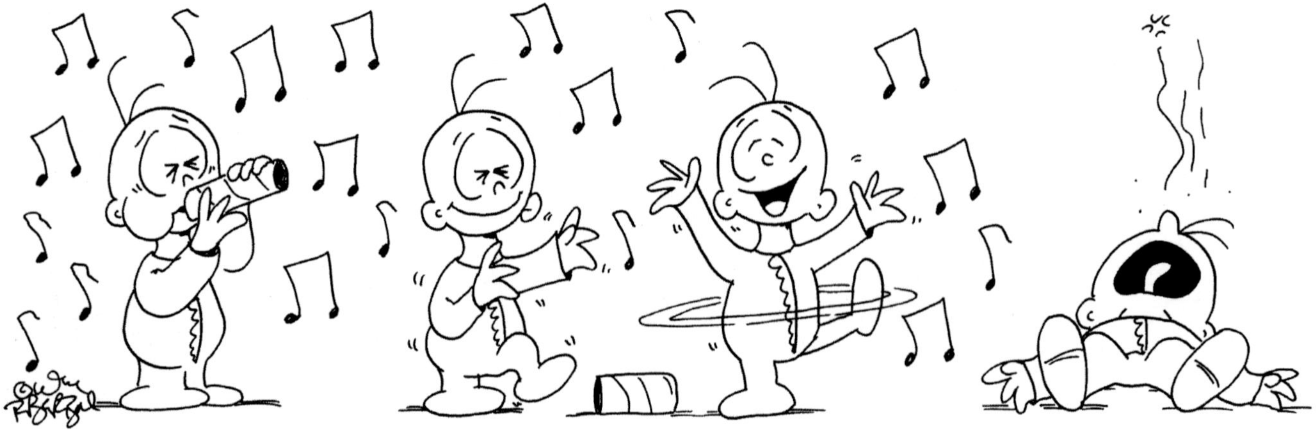

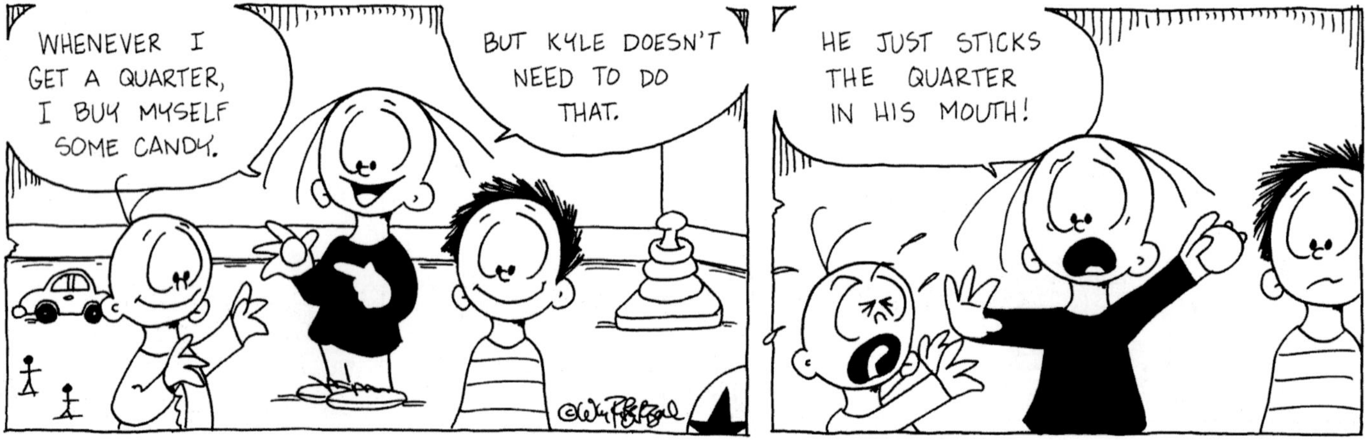
WHENEVER I GET A QUARTER, I BUY MYSELF SOME CANDY.
BUT KYLE DOESN'T NEED TO DO THAT.
HE JUST STICKS THE QUARTER IN HIS MOUTH!

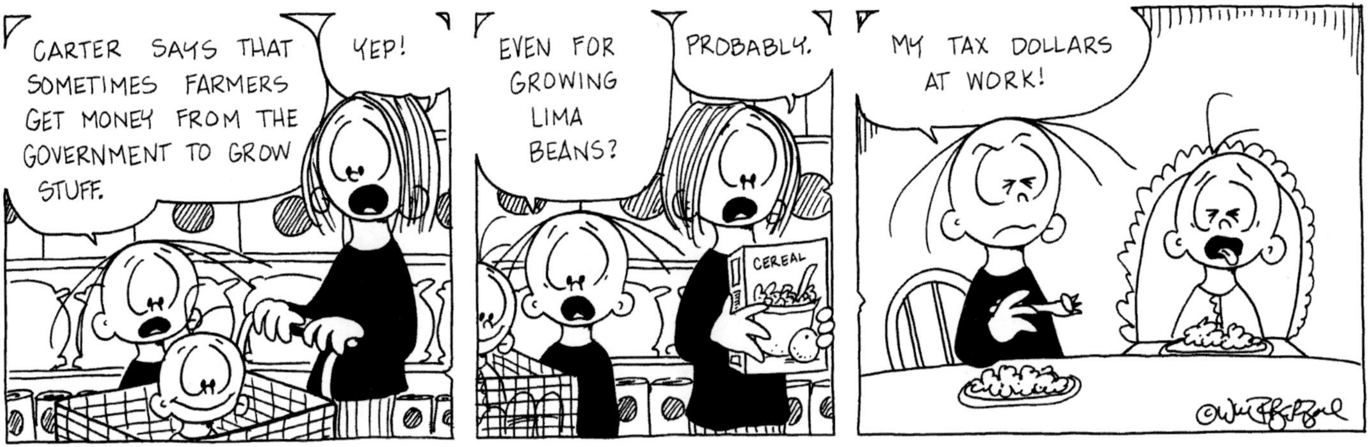
CARTER SAYS THAT SOMETIMES FARMERS GET MONEY FROM THE GOVERNMENT TO GROW STUFF.
YEP!
EVEN FOR GROWING LIMA BEANS?
PROBABLY.
CEREAL
MY TAX DOLLARS AT WORK!

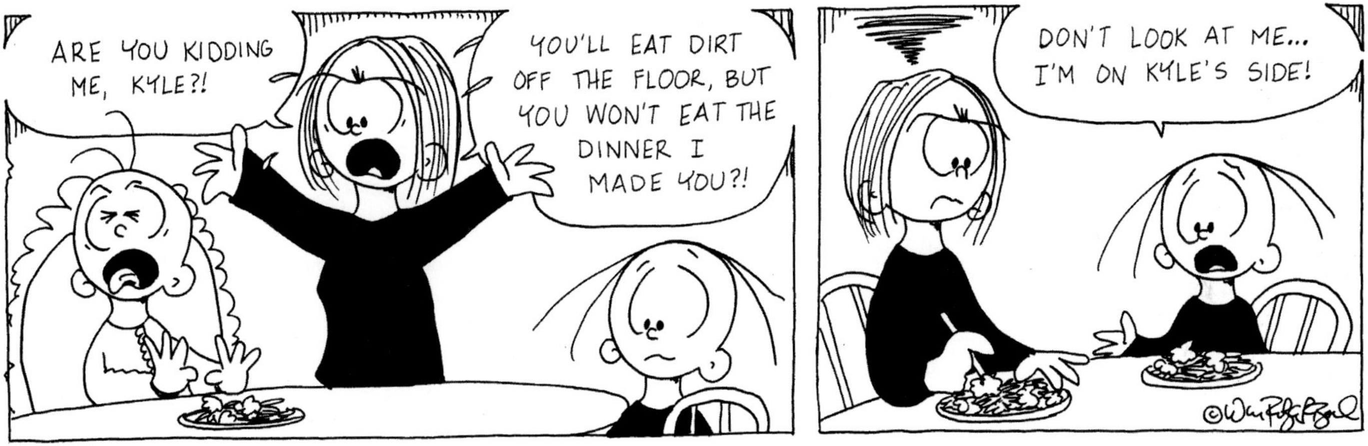
ARE YOU KIDDING ME, KYLE?!
YOU'LL EAT DIRT OFF THE FLOOR, BUT YOU WON'T EAT THE DINNER I MADE YOU?!
DON'T LOOK AT ME... I'M ON KYLE'S SIDE!

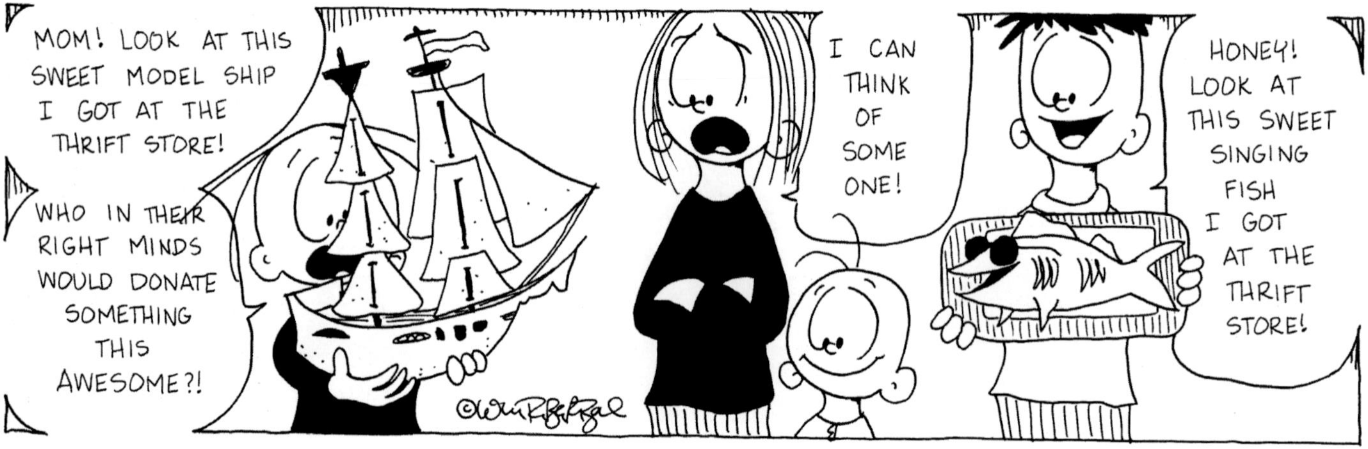
MOM! LOOK AT THIS SWEET MODEL SHIP I GOT AT THE THRIFT STORE!
WHO IN THEIR RIGHT MINDS WOULD DONATE SOMETHING THIS AWESOME?!
I CAN THINK OF SOME ONE!
HONEY! LOOK AT THIS SWEET SINGING FISH I GOT AT THE THRIFT STORE!
©WmRFitzRgal

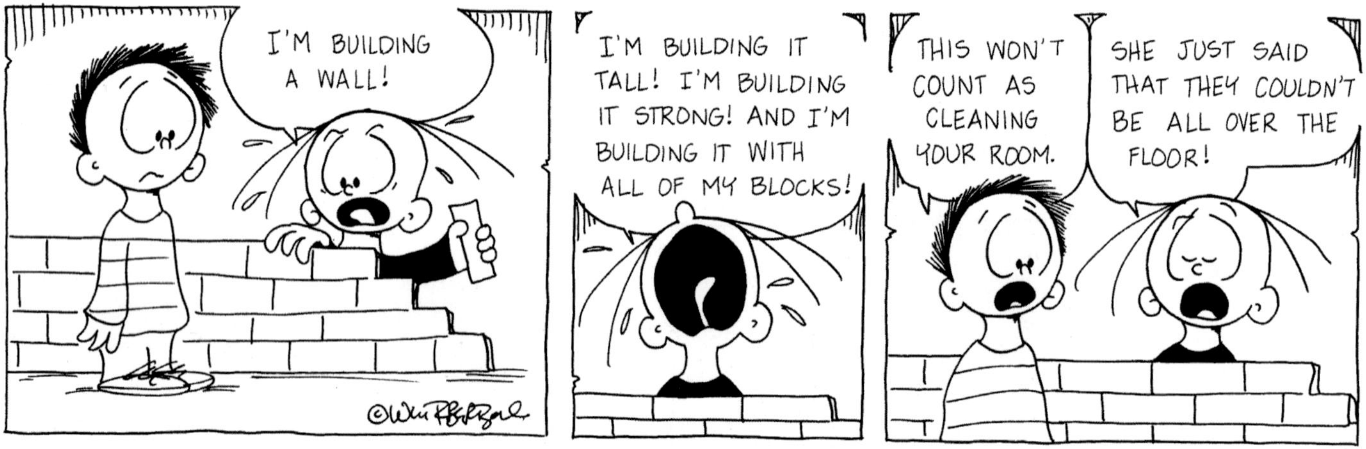
I'M BUILDING A WALL!
I'M BUILDING IT TALL! I'M BUILDING IT STRONG! AND I'M BUILDING IT WITH ALL OF MY BLOCKS!
THIS WON'T COUNT AS CLEANING YOUR ROOM.
SHE JUST SAID THAT THEY COULDN'T BE ALL OVER THE FLOOR!
©WmRFitzRgal

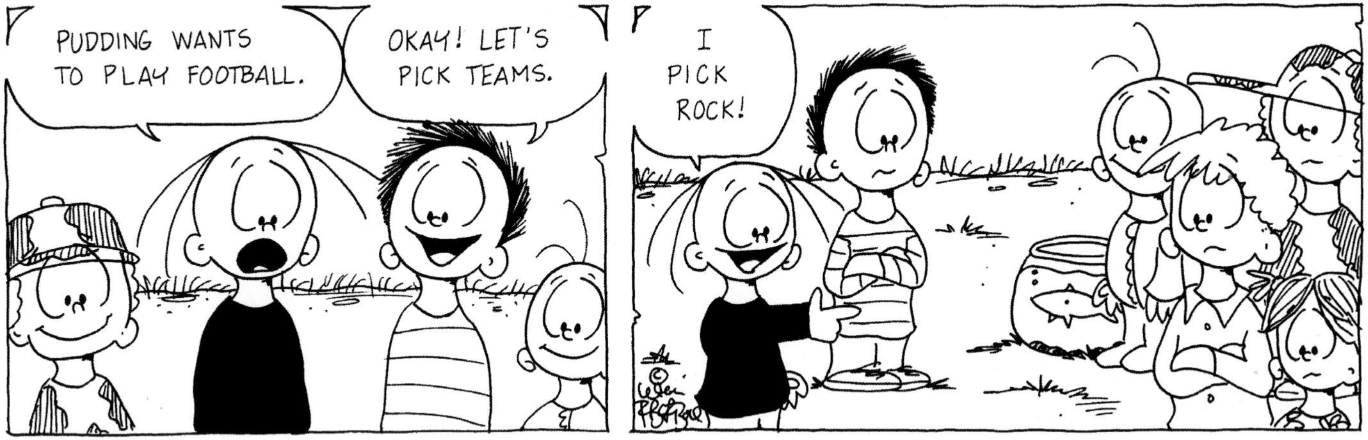
PUDDING WANTS TO PLAY FOOTBALL.
OKAY! LET'S PICK TEAMS.
I PICK ROCK!

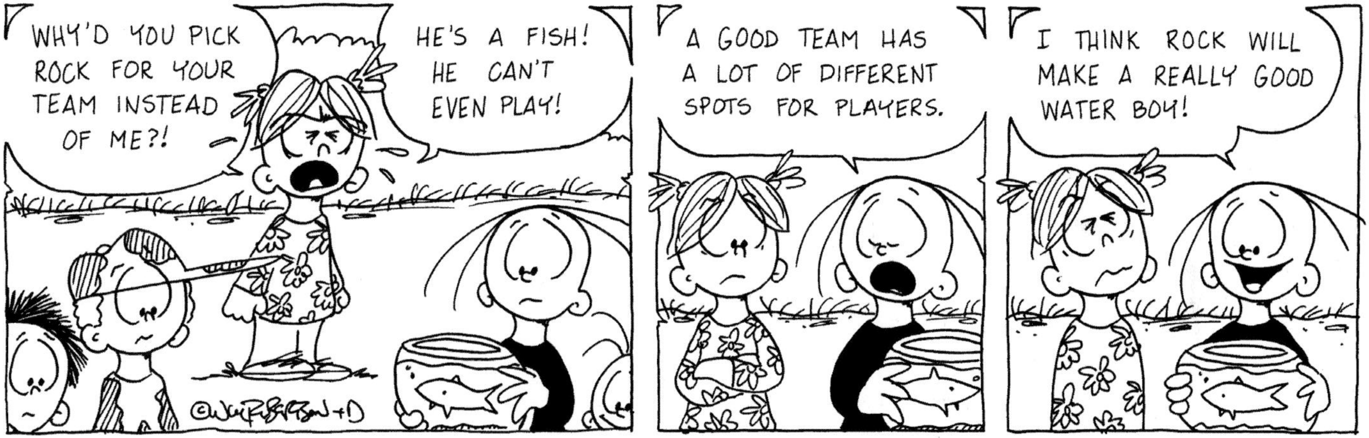
WHY'D YOU PICK ROCK FOR YOUR TEAM INSTEAD OF ME?!
HE'S A FISH! HE CAN'T EVEN PLAY!
A GOOD TEAM HAS A LOT OF DIFFERENT SPOTS FOR PLAYERS.
I THINK ROCK WILL MAKE A REALLY GOOD WATER BOY!

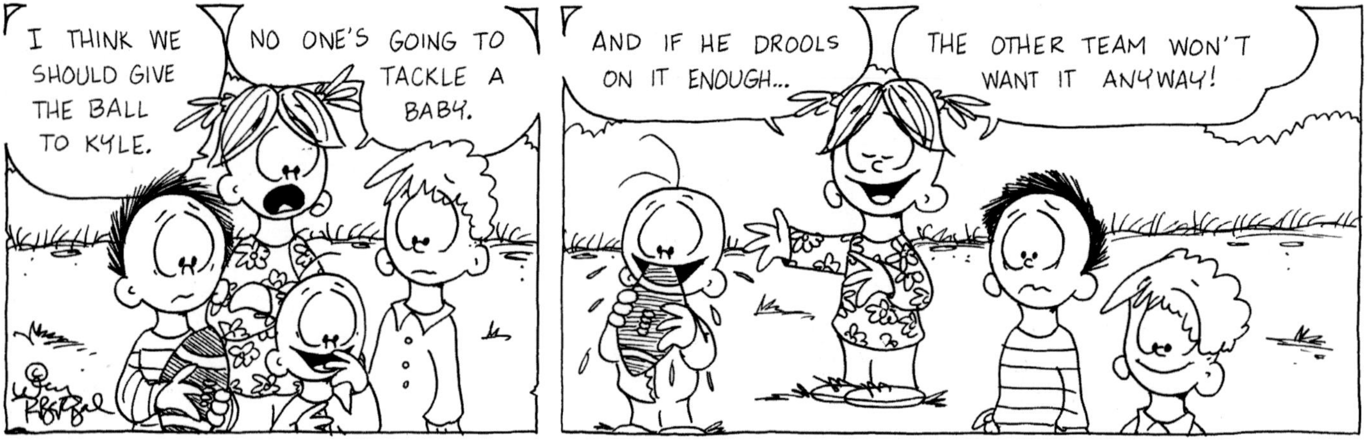
I THINK WE SHOULD GIVE THE BALL TO KYLE.
NO ONE'S GOING TO TACKLE A BABY.
AND IF HE DROOLS ON IT ENOUGH...
THE OTHER TEAM WON'T WANT IT ANYWAY!

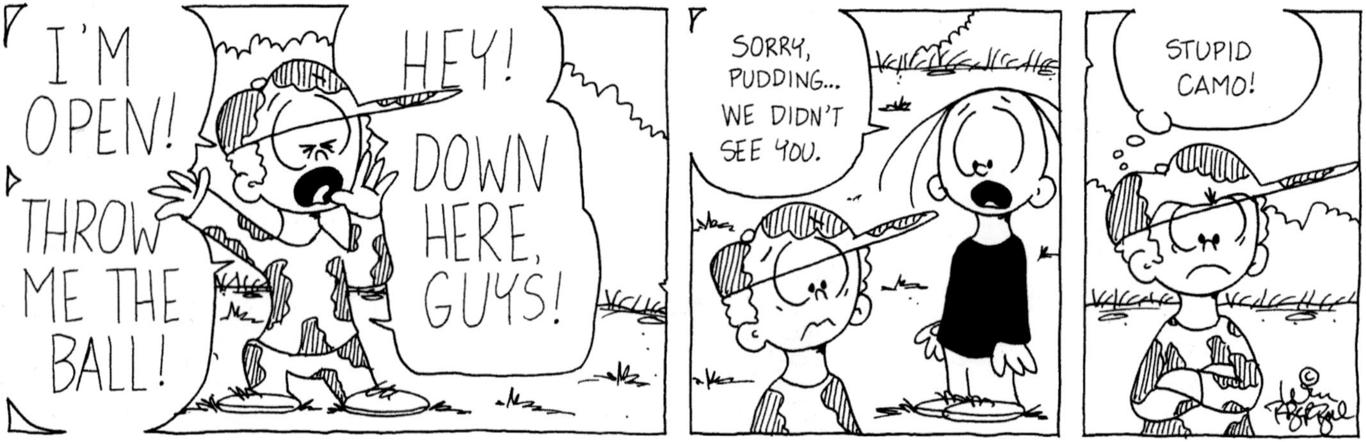
I'M OPEN!
THROW ME THE BALL!
HEY!
DOWN HERE, GUYS!
SORRY, PUDDING... WE DIDN'T SEE YOU.
STUPID CAMO!

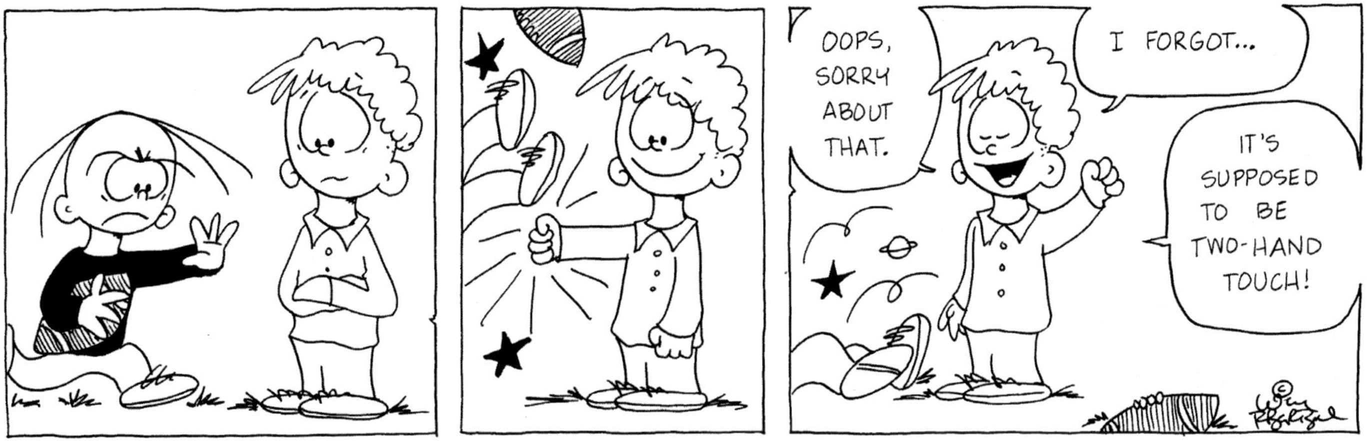
OOPS, SORRY ABOUT THAT.
I FORGOT...
IT'S SUPPOSED TO BE TWO-HAND TOUCH!

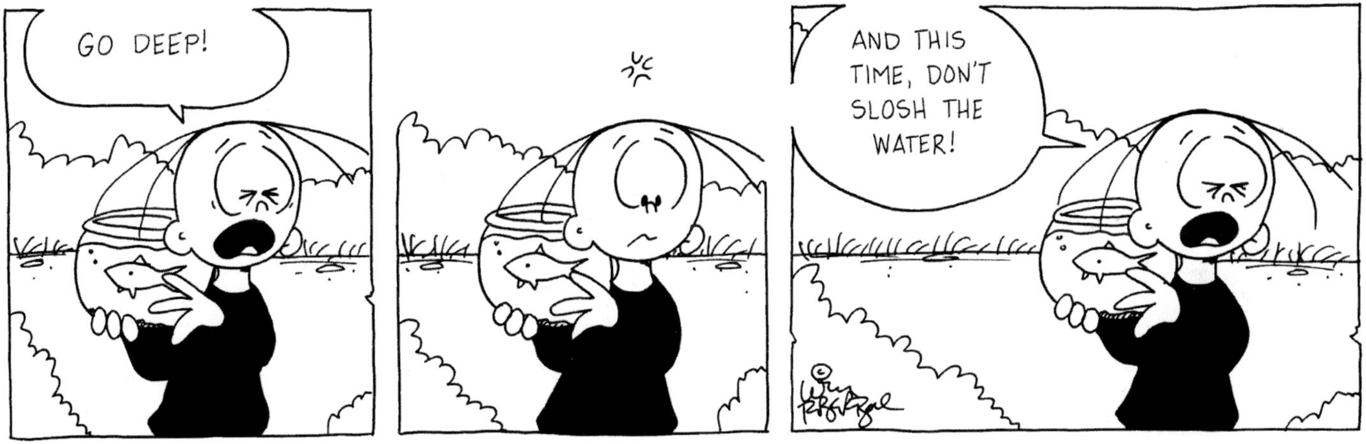
GO DEEP!
AND THIS TIME, DON'T SLOSH THE WATER!

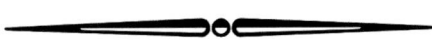

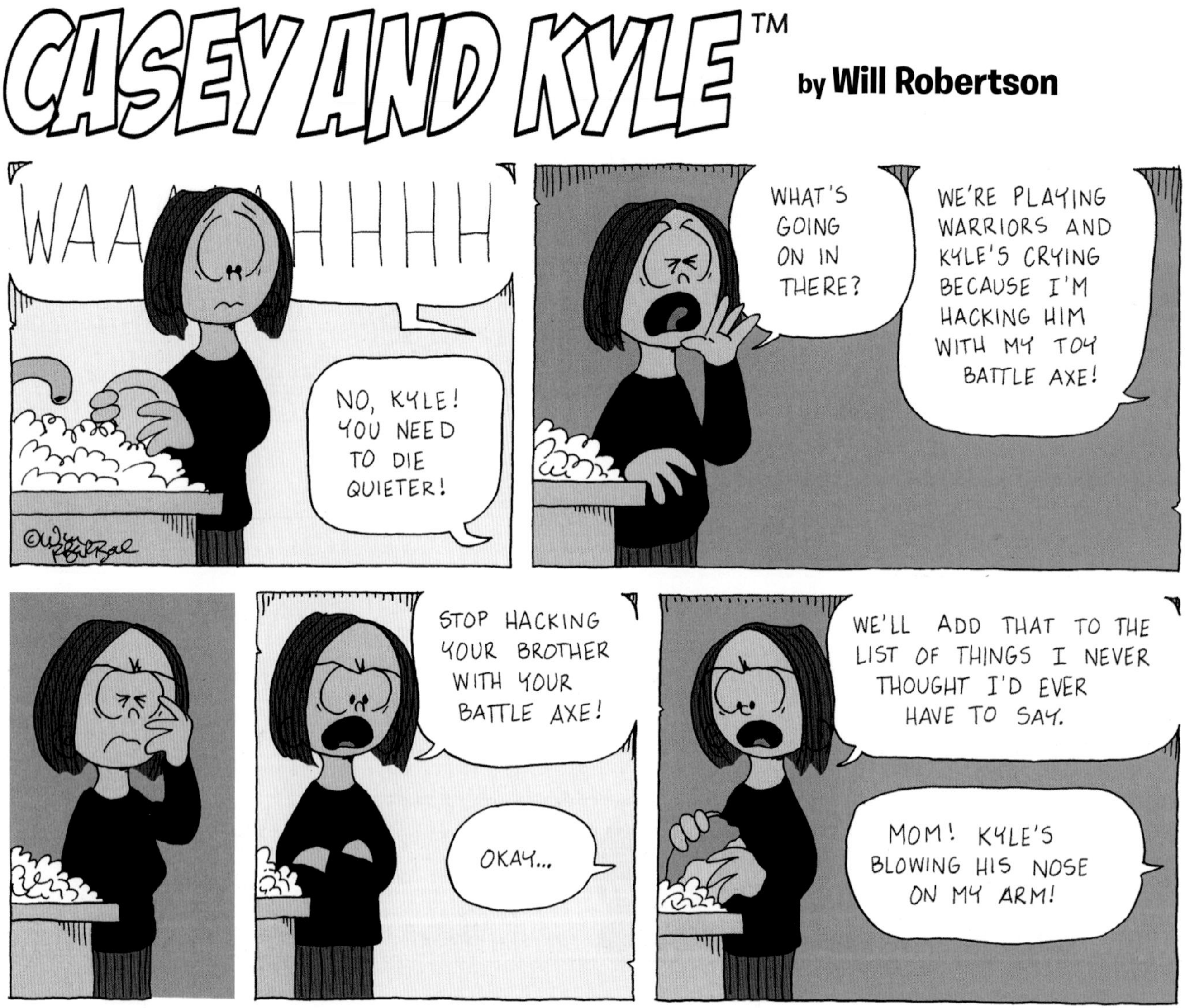
CASEY AND KYLE™
by Will Robertson
WAAAAHHHHH
NO, KYLE! YOU NEED TO DIE QUIETER!
©Will Robertson
WHAT'S GOING ON IN THERE?
WE'RE PLAYING WARRIORS AND KYLE'S CRYING BECAUSE I'M HACKING HIM WITH MY TOY BATTLE AXE!
STOP HACKING YOUR BROTHER WITH YOUR BATTLE AXE!
OKAY...
WE'LL ADD THAT TO THE LIST OF THINGS I NEVER THOUGHT I'D EVER HAVE TO SAY.
MOM! KYLE'S BLOWING HIS NOSE ON MY ARM!

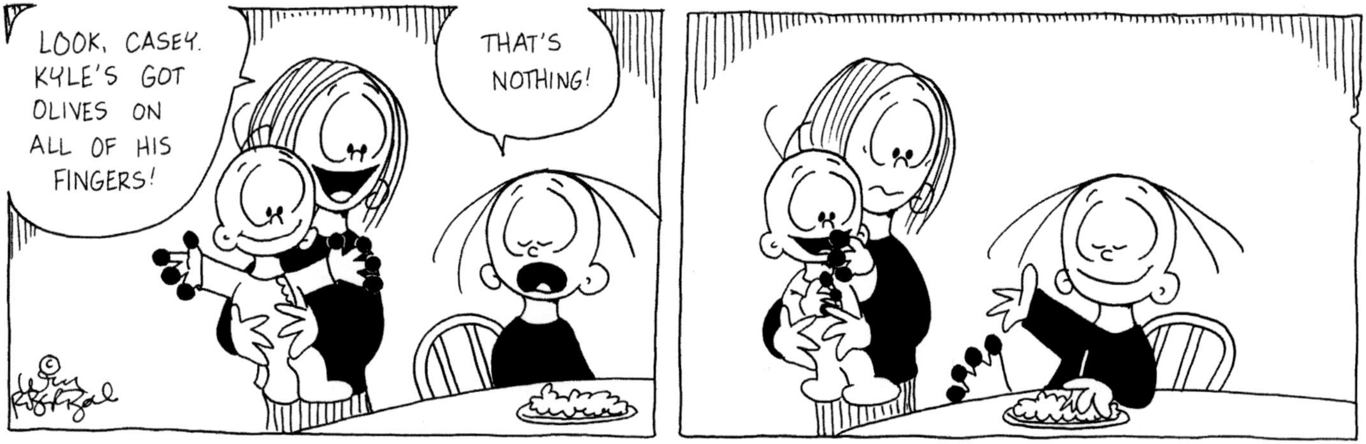
LOOK, CASEY. KYLE'S GOT OLIVES ON ALL OF HIS FINGERS!
THAT'S NOTHING!

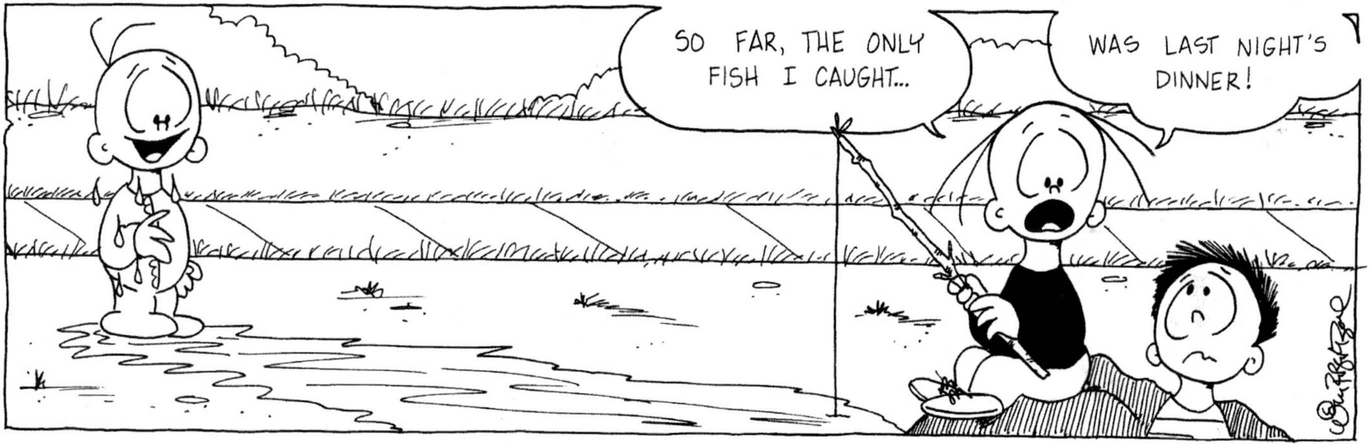
SO FAR, THE ONLY FISH I CAUGHT...
WAS LAST NIGHT'S DINNER!

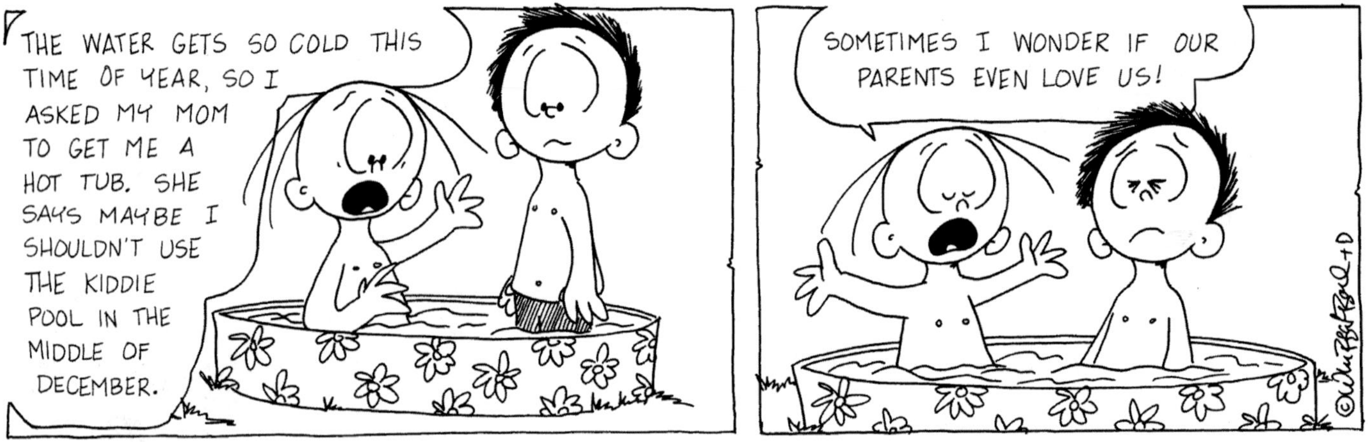
THE WATER GETS SO COLD THIS TIME OF YEAR, SO I ASKED MY MOM TO GET ME A HOT TUB. SHE SAYS MAYBE I SHOULDN'T USE THE KIDDIE POOL IN THE MIDDLE OF DECEMBER.
SOMETIMES I WONDER IF OUR PARENTS EVEN LOVE US!

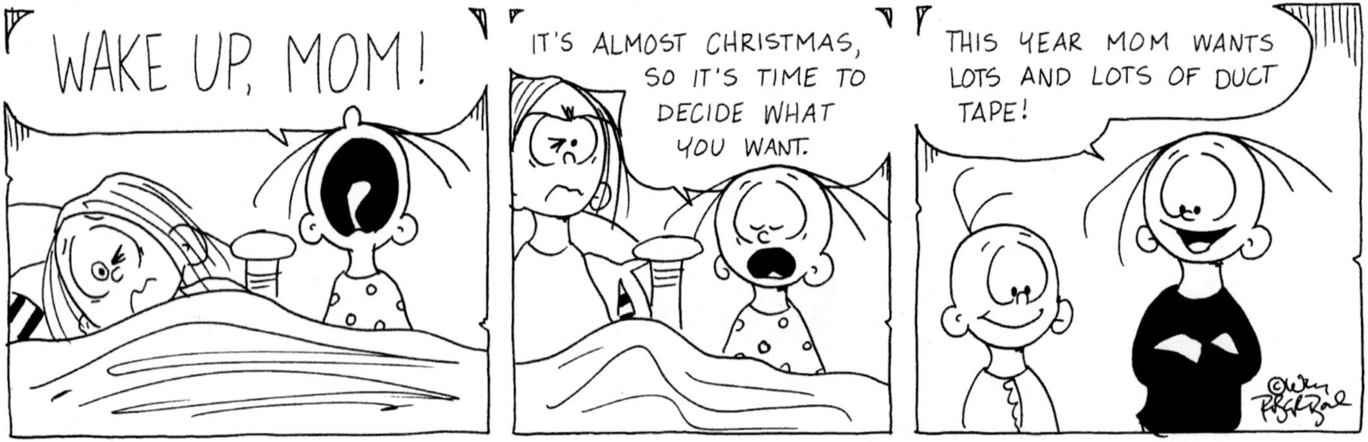
WAKE UP, MOM!
IT'S ALMOST CHRISTMAS, SO IT'S TIME TO DECIDE WHAT YOU WANT.
THIS YEAR MOM WANTS LOTS AND LOTS OF DUCT TAPE!

CASEY AND KYLE™

by **Will Robertson**

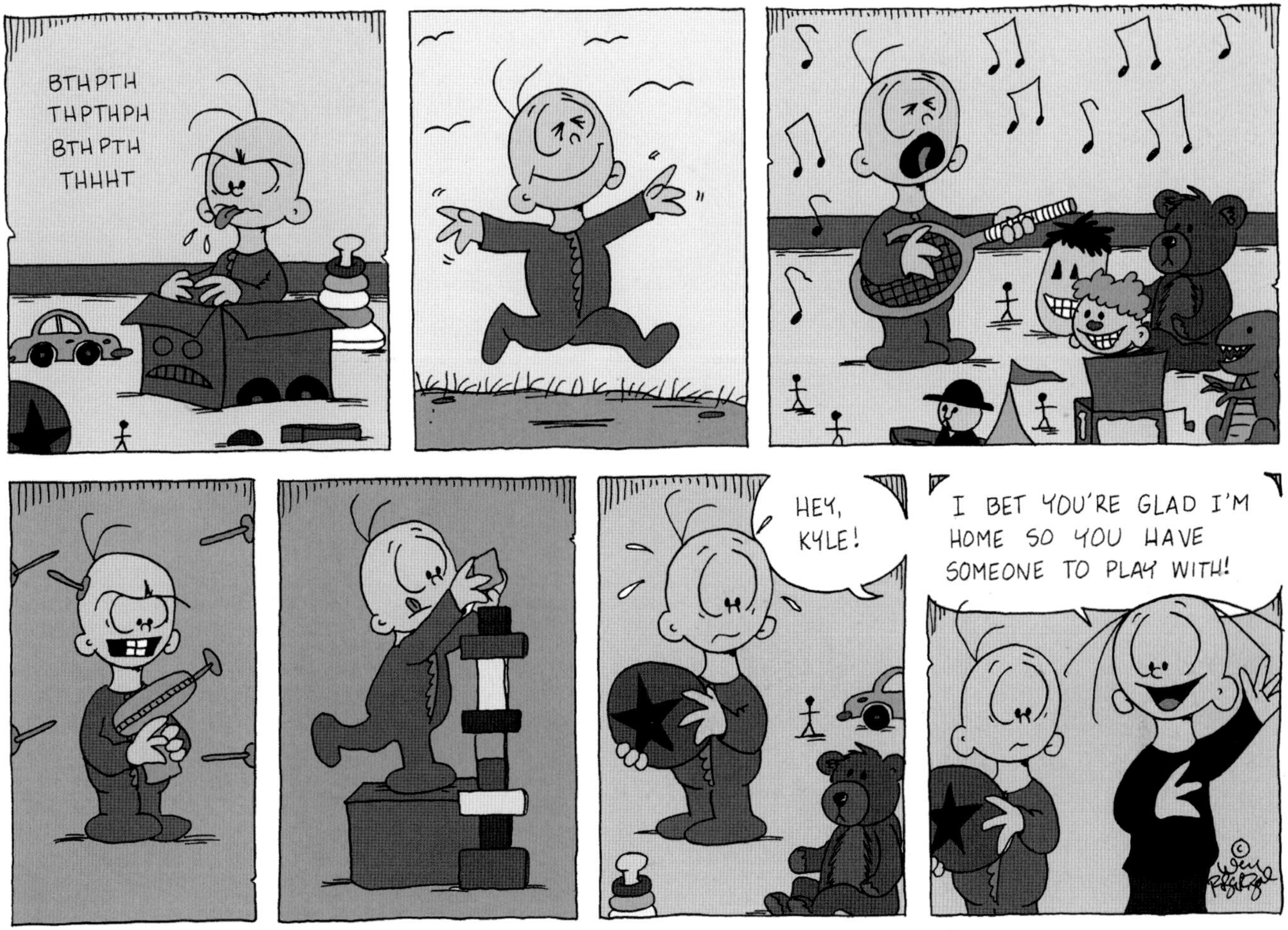

BTHPTH
THPTHPH
BTHPTH
THHHT
HEY, KYLE!
I BET YOU'RE GLAD I'M HOME SO YOU HAVE SOMEONE TO PLAY WITH!

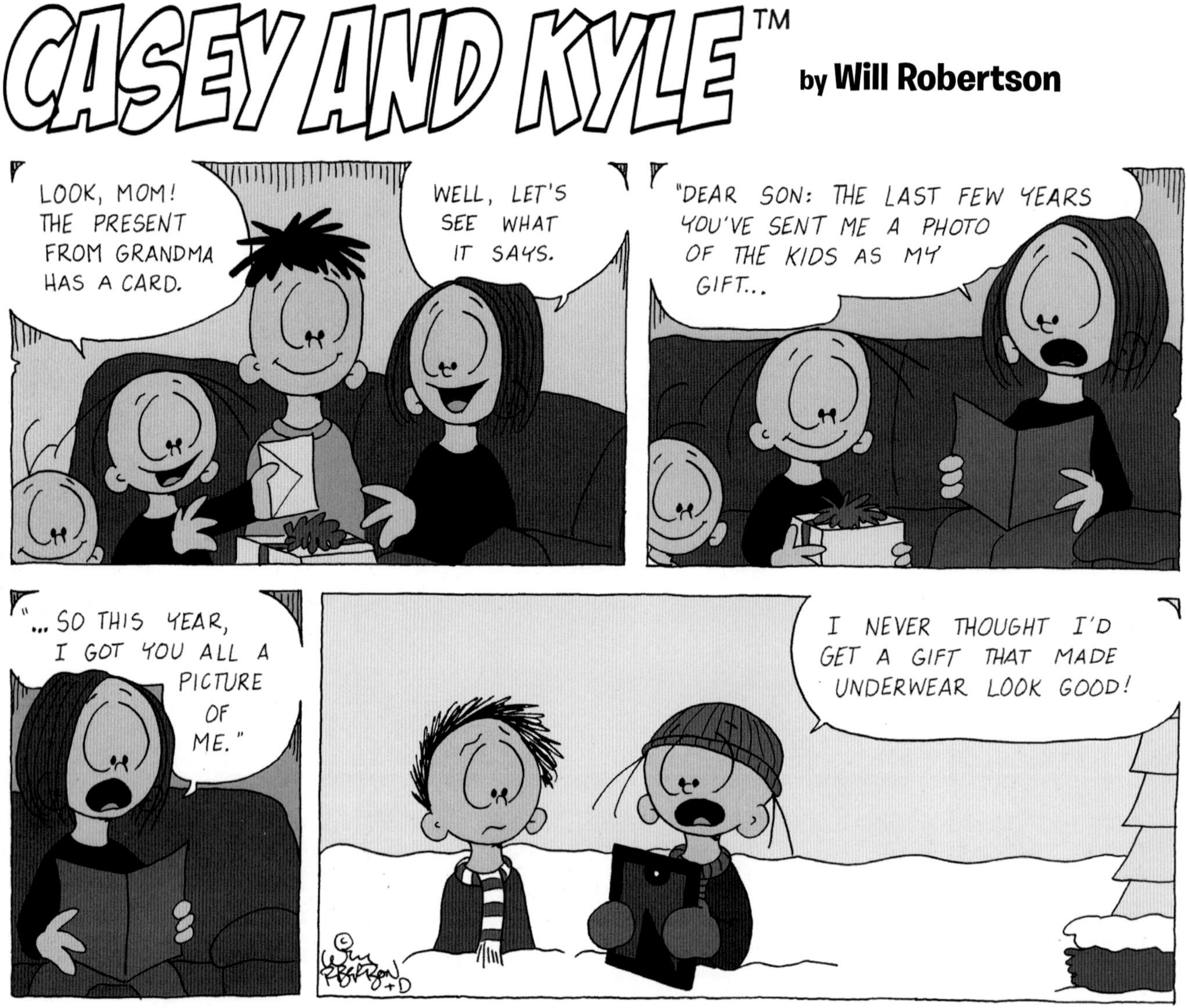
CASEY AND KYLE™
by Will Robertson
LOOK, MOM! THE PRESENT FROM GRANDMA HAS A CARD.
WELL, LET'S SEE WHAT IT SAYS.
"DEAR SON: THE LAST FEW YEARS YOU'VE SENT ME A PHOTO OF THE KIDS AS MY GIFT...
"...SO THIS YEAR, I GOT YOU ALL A PICTURE OF ME."
I NEVER THOUGHT I'D GET A GIFT THAT MADE UNDERWEAR LOOK GOOD!

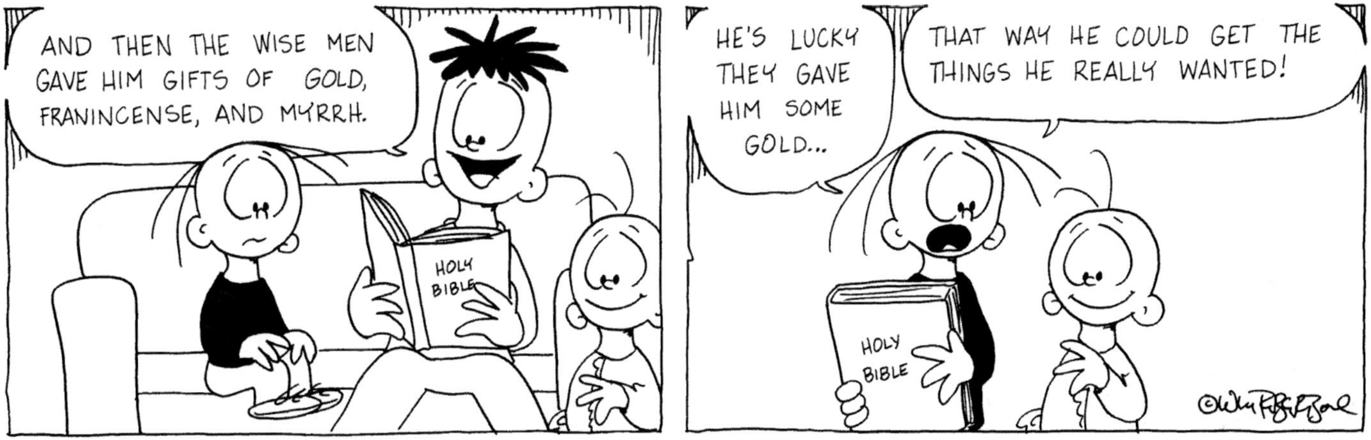
AND THEN THE WISE MEN GAVE HIM GIFTS OF GOLD, FRANINCENSE, AND MYRRH.
HOLY BIBLE
HE'S LUCKY THEY GAVE HIM SOME GOLD...
THAT WAY HE COULD GET THE THINGS HE REALLY WANTED!
HOLY BIBLE

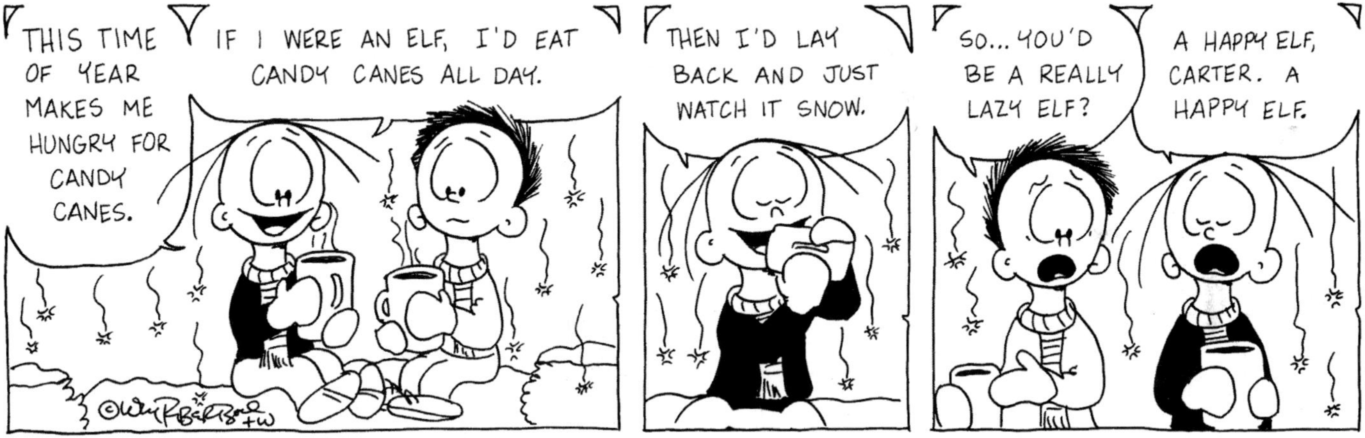
THIS TIME OF YEAR MAKES ME HUNGRY FOR CANDY CANES.
IF I WERE AN ELF, I'D EAT CANDY CANES ALL DAY.
THEN I'D LAY BACK AND JUST WATCH IT SNOW.
SO... YOU'D BE A REALLY LAZY ELF?
A HAPPY ELF, CARTER. A HAPPY ELF.

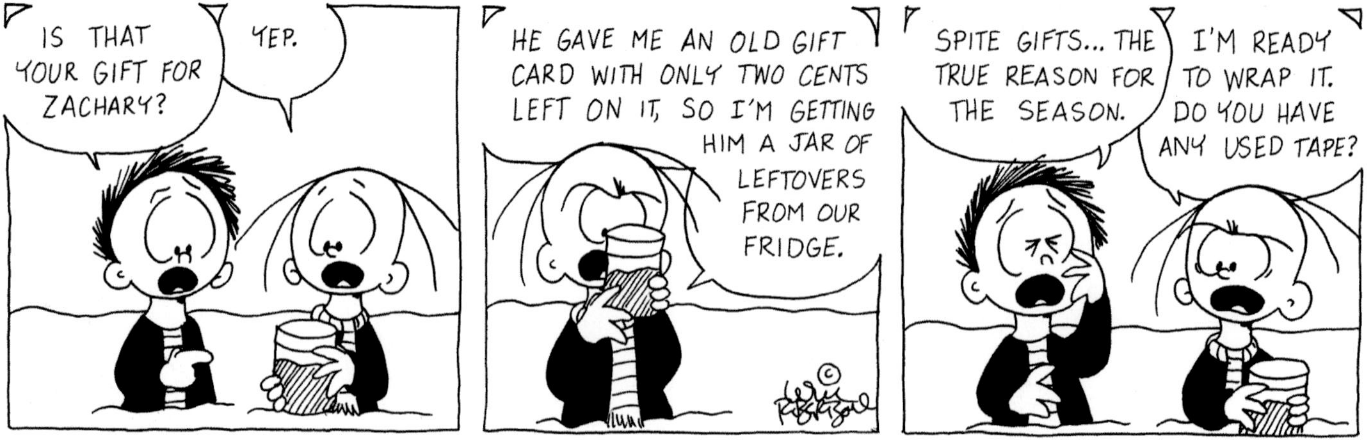
IS THAT YOUR GIFT FOR ZACHARY?
YEP.
HE GAVE ME AN OLD GIFT CARD WITH ONLY TWO CENTS LEFT ON IT, SO I'M GETTING HIM A JAR OF LEFTOVERS FROM OUR FRIDGE.
SPITE GIFTS... THE TRUE REASON FOR THE SEASON.
I'M READY TO WRAP IT. DO YOU HAVE ANY USED TAPE?

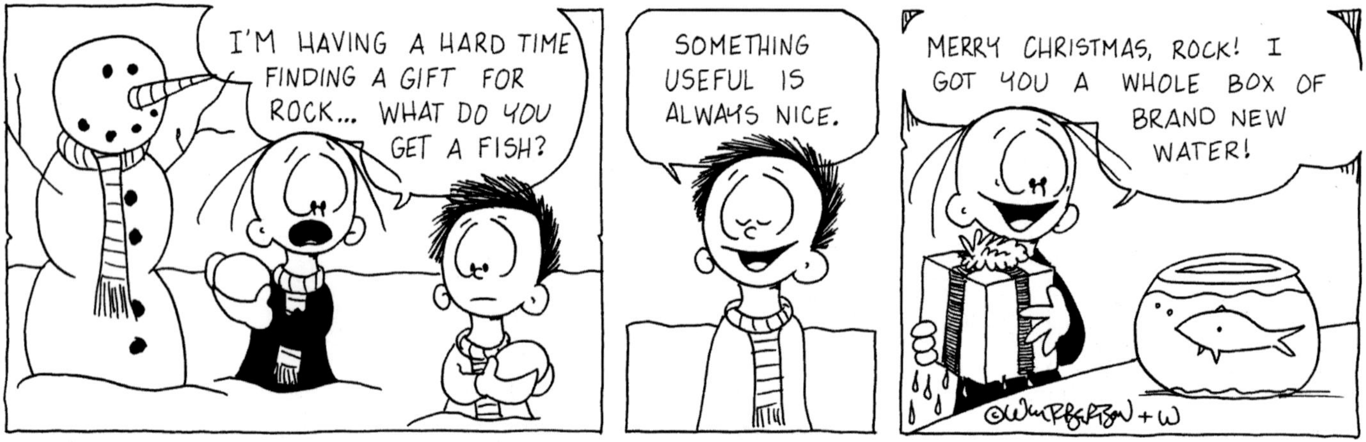
I'M HAVING A HARD TIME FINDING A GIFT FOR ROCK... WHAT DO YOU GET A FISH?
SOMETHING USEFUL IS ALWAYS NICE.
MERRY CHRISTMAS, ROCK! I GOT YOU A WHOLE BOX OF BRAND NEW WATER!

CASEY AND KYLE™

by Will Robertson

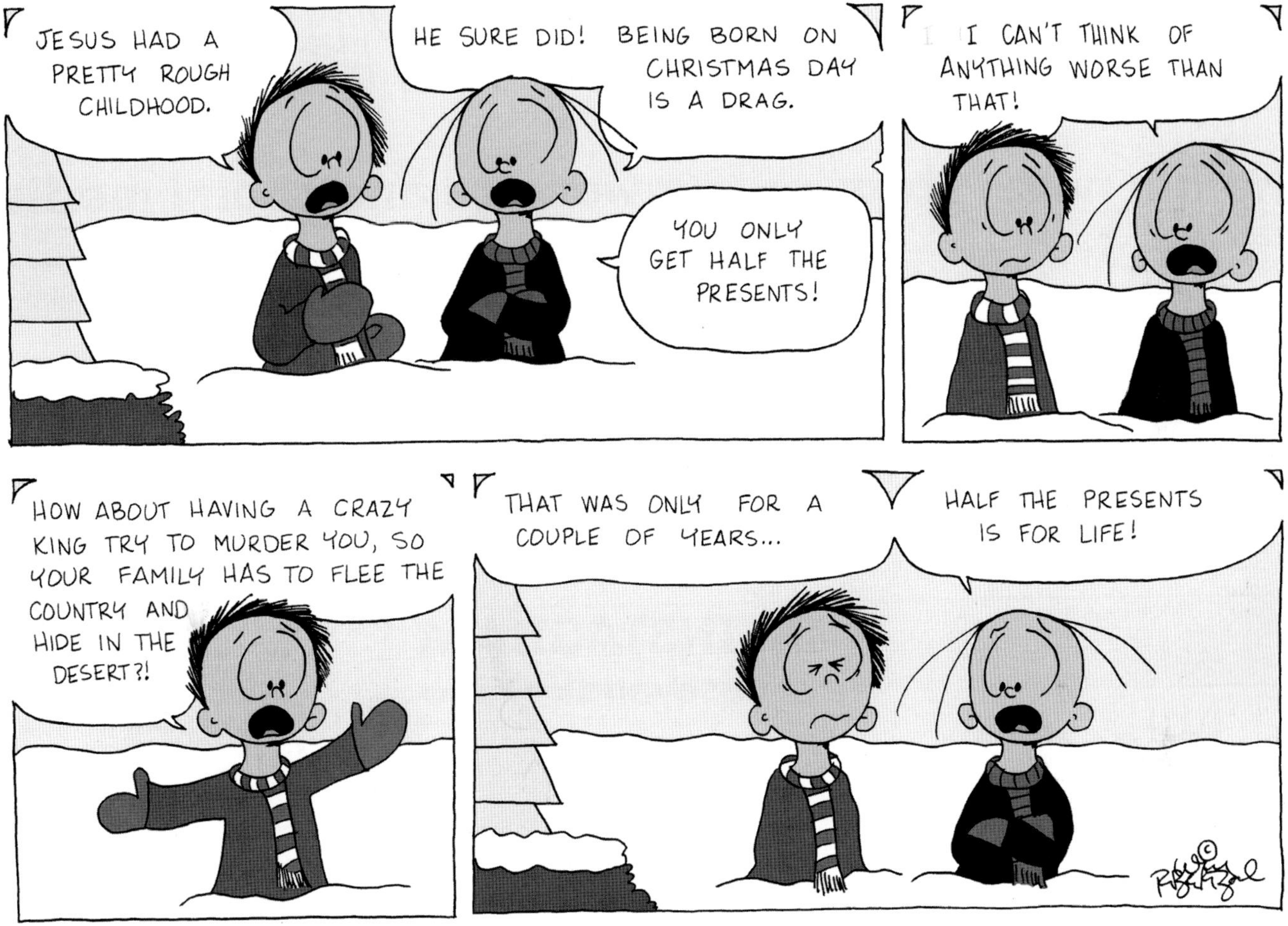
JESUS HAD A PRETTY ROUGH CHILDHOOD.
HE SURE DID! BEING BORN ON CHRISTMAS DAY IS A DRAG.
YOU ONLY GET HALF THE PRESENTS!
I CAN'T THINK OF ANYTHING WORSE THAN THAT!
HOW ABOUT HAVING A CRAZY KING TRY TO MURDER YOU, SO YOUR FAMILY HAS TO FLEE THE COUNTRY AND HIDE IN THE DESERT?!
THAT WAS ONLY FOR A COUPLE OF YEARS...
HALF THE PRESENTS IS FOR LIFE!

Don't miss a single adventure!

CASEY AND KYLE™

The fun never stops on our website and social media!

Visit us online at caseyandkyle.com
or simply scan the QR code to stop by!

On INSTAGRAM
@ caseyandkyleinc

On TWITTER @ caseyandkyleinc

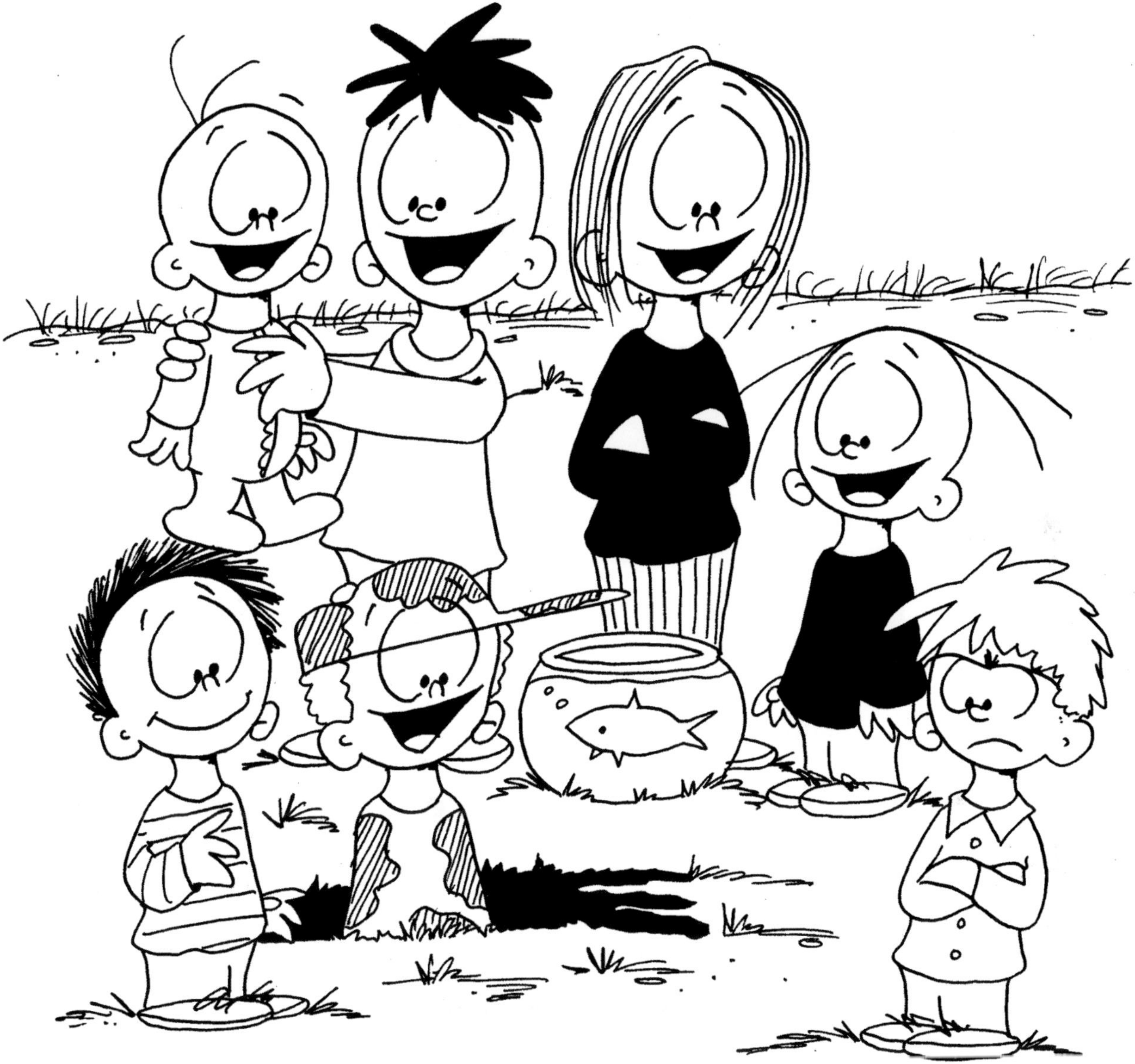